I0612091

SAND'S GAME

SAND'S GAME

Ennis Willie

Introduction by Max Allan Collins

Edited by

Lynn F. Myers, Jr. and Stephen Mertz

RAMBLE HOUSE

Copyright Information

"Methadone Man" the Introduction to this volume ©2010 by Max Allan Collins

"Ennis Willie: Symphony 1911A in .45 Caliber" from the Introduction ©2010 by Lynn F. Myers, Jr.

Death in a Dead Place was originally published as *Passion Has No Rule Book.* ©1964 by Camerarts Publishing. ©2010 by Ennis Willie. Introduction to *Death in a Dead Place* ©2010 by Wayne D. Dundee.

"Con's Wife" originally appeared in the May, 1965 issue of *Rascal* magazine. ©1965 by Camerarts Publishing. ©2010 by Ennis Willie. Introduction to "Con's Wife" ©2010 by Bill Crider

"Flesh House" originally appeared in the August, 1965 issue of *Best For Men* magazine. ©1965 by Camerarts Publishing. ©2010 by Ennis Willie. Introduction to "Flesh House" ©2010 by Bill Pronzini

"The Ugly Redhead" originally appeared in the December 1965 issue of *Best For Men* magazine as "Unsubtle Sensualite" ©1965 by Camerarts Publishing. ©2010 by Ennis Willie. Introduction to "The Ugly Redhead" ©2010 by James Reasoner

Too Late to Pray was originally published as *Game of Passion.* ©1964 by Camerarts Publishing. ©2010 by Ennis Willie. Introduction to *Too Late to Pray* ©2010 by Gary Lovisi

"Ennis Willie Gets the Third Degree" the interview ©2010 by Stephen Mertz

ISBN 13: 978-1-60543-438-4

ISBN 10: 1-60543-438-8

Front Cover Design by Ennis Willie
Back Cover Design by Gavin L. O'Keefe
Preparation by Fender Tucker

A RAMBLE HOUSE Book

TABLE OF CONTENTS

To Max Allan Collins,
Ed Gorman, Stephen Mertz &
Lynn F. Myers, Jr.

–for the long wait.

Ennis Willie

METHADONE MAN

by Max Allan Collins

In 1963, I was a sophomore in high school and at the height of my Mickey Spillane mania. I had started reading Mickey in junior high, having first encountered his Mike Hammer courtesy of the syndicated TV series starring Darren McGavin.

This was all an offshoot of TV's private eye fad initiated by the Spillane-derivative *Peter Gunn* (created by Blake Edwards, who wrote and directed the first Mike Hammer pilot, rejected by networks as too violent) and *77 Sunset Strip* (created by Raymond Chandler imitator Roy Huggins, glorious pappy of Bret and Bart Maverick). The craze was probably sparked by the success of Raymond Burr on *Perry Mason*, where for the first several seasons the scripts were almost all adaptations of his noirish sex-and-money drenched novels.

Before reading Mickey, I started with two of his best imitators, Richard S. Prather and Stephen Marlowe, and I had read all of Dashiell Hammett and most of Chandler before finally daring to purchase a Spillane novel. You must remember that buying a Spillane novel, at age 12 or 13, was a risky venture—the Hammer novels were considered dirty books, and I had read extensively in them at Cohn's Newsland, hiding behind a spinner rack. I knew all about the striptease at the end of *I, the Jury* long before I ever read the first page.

The fever-dream that was Mickey Spillane in those first half dozen Hammer books changed my life. I had wanted to be a cartoonist, and through grade school and early junior high had distributed my own home-made comic books to my peers. But Mickey convinced me that drawing with words

was the way to go—sex, violence, compelling first person—
and I have never looked back (other than in pieces like this
one).

I was delighted that right when I began reading Mickey,
he was breaking his decade-long silence; so I bought his
comeback, *The Deep* (1961) and Mike Hammer's, *The Girl
Hunters* (1962), in hardcover when they came out. Still, it
didn't take long to run out of Spillane novels. Like an alky
with the shakes, I hit the used bookstores and sought out
1950s paperbacks that were blatantly packaged to convince
readers that something akin to Spillane was within those
covers. Rarely was the promise fulfilled.

In my unceasing effort to find methadone to replace the
heroin of Spillane, I found two writers who did the trick. One
was Ian Fleming, whose James Bond was originally sold to
the American public as a British Mike Hammer, and the
comparison was apt; in fact, the first paperback publisher to
successfully do Fleming and Bond was Spillane's—Signet
Books, who used artist Barye Phillips (who had done the
most recent Spillane covers) to further make the sale to
Mickey's audience.

Among the American writers, only one caught Mickey's
magic—only one managed to create a fever-dream world of
sadistic gangsters, willing women and larger-than-life tough
guys. Only one was able to match Mickey's speed, and race
to a shocking conclusion that brought each tale to a quick,
satisfying halt—with nothing of Perry Mason's final-scene
nonsense, explaining to Della why he'd sent Paul Drake out
searching for a buffalo or whatever-the-hell.

No, an Ennis Willie novel—particularly the ones about his
former mobster, Sand—brought you to the finish line and let
you fall breathlessly to the cinders on your own. He didn't
help you recover. He just retreated to smile and laugh to
himself and concoct another outrageous yarn.

Who the hell *was* this Ennis Willie, anyway?

That question was the Rosebud of mystery fiction for
many a year. In 1963, all I knew was I had gambled a whole
sixty cents on a sleazy-looking book called *Scarlet Goddess*.

The cover wasn't even in full color, rather a shades of brown-and-yellow monochrome. The girl was incredibly sexy but (and here's how the publisher got my fifty cents and a dime) was drawn in a cartoony fashion that hit me in my comic-book gonads.

I even thought the artist might be Robert Powell (I don't believe it was) who had done *Sheena* and *The Man In Black* and other cool comics stuff. So the comics look of the cover is how I came in contact with Willie.

I purchased the paperback at a drug store in downtown Indianola, Iowa. I was visiting my grandparents, and I would not have stumbled upon *Scarlet Goddess* otherwise. The publisher was Merit Books, part of Camerarts out of Chicago, who also published the racy Novel Books line. I knew of Novel Books—the most outrageous Mike Hammer imitator of all, Jack Lynn's Tokey Wedge, was the star of the line; these were wild novels that read like satires (and were) about a sex-starved private dick who made Shell Scott look like Philo Vance.

Here's the thing: both Merit and Novel Books were smut. Pornography. Reading these books today, that seems a little odd, although they remain fairly strong medicine . . . but hardly porn, barely softcore. But neither line was one you'd find just anywhere—they tended to turn up in small-town cigar stores and the kind of big-city bookstore that had lots and lots of magazines, including all the girlie ones, and out-of-town newspapers and so on. In my hometown of Muscatine, Iowa, neither Merit nor Novel Books were anywhere to be seen.

Anyway, I downed *Scarlet Goddess* in one gulp, and—with some astonishment—realized I had finally found a worthy imitator of Spillane. What blew me away—I was already trying to be a writer, and thought about such things—was that Willie was not working in Mickey's trademark first-person. Somehow Willie managed a similar magic in the more detached third-person. Looking back, my hunch is that Willie did this to differentiate himself from Spillane—he knew just how much he owed Mickey, and wanted to find his own way into the house.

The anti-hero of *Scarlet Goddess*, the fugitive ex-gangster Sand, was a single-named tough guy very similar to Richard Stark's Parker. Two things should be noted: first, Sand and Parker appeared more or less simultaneously, so neither is an imitation of the other; second, my early series of novels about the mono-named ex-mobster Nolan—which is often (correctly) thought of as a Parker imitation—was influenced at least as much by Sand. (A novel I wrote at age 18, called *Mourn the Living*, is proof of that; the first Nolan, it was published a few years ago by Five Star.)

For the next several years, particularly on family vacations that gave me access to the kind of big-city bookstore that carried sleazy paperbacks, I hunted for Ennis Willie's books. I was in particular after the "Sand" titles, but I got his non-Sand novels, too. When I was unable to find all of them, I ordered the rest directly from the publisher, who—unlike some of the stores I bought the racy paperbacks from—never inquired about my age.

In 1964 I had my parents drive me to Camerarts in Chicago, where I showed up and—I was probably fifteen—submitted a novel called *Kiss Or Kill* at the reception desk. A confused secretary took it from me and delivered it to Tony Licata, the editor there, who did not come out to greet me. I am fairly certain I was the only teenager to show up with a novel submission, in person, anyway.

That began a brief correspondence between Licata and me—he was very impressed with my work, but did not buy the novel or the next novel I sent, nor the couple of short stories I submitted to his magazines. But he was very helpful and I learned a lot from him. The writer he suggested I study was Ennis Willie—of course, I told him I already was studying Ennis Willie . . .

By the end of 1965, after the last couple of Sand novels had been published with weirdly inappropriate covers and titles, Ennis Willie disappeared even from the stands. He had already earned a special place on my bookshelf and in my heart, and over the years, I told a lot of fellow writers about

Willie and turned a number of them onto him. I believe I introduced him to both Steve Mertz and Ed Gorman, although either of these terrific writers were similarly scroungers of hardboiled fare and may have come to Willie on their own. I know I introduced him to co-editor, Lynn Myers.

For many, many years, and in many, many conversations, the topic of "Who was Ennis Willie?" was explored by Mertz, Gorman, Myers and myself, among others. I wrote about Willie a few times, notably in a book edited by Bill Pronzini in which I discussed the wonderful 1964 Sand novel, *And Some Were Evil.*

The common theory was that he was African American; I believe a black poet named Willie Ennis was a prime candidate. A few floated the notion that this had been a deep-cover Spillane himself, publishing under the radar to avoid criticism from his fellow Jehovah's Witnesses.

I never bought the latter, because Willie was one of those rare imitators who was ultimately his own man—his vision was out of not just Spillane but his own vivid imagination, and his third-person approach to this kind of intensely personal narrative was uniquely his.

Now, delightfully, thanks to the Internet, Ennis Willie turns out to be alive and well. Back in '65, he went into another field, most successfully, and his fabulous run of pulp novels lasted less than four years, a creative flame that burned quickly and bright. One hopes he'll get back to the typewriter (or computer keyboard) soon and, if so, one hopes the world will be smart enough to know how lucky it is.

Max Allan Collins
April 27, 2008

ENNIS WILLIE: SYMPHONY 1911A IN .45 CALIBER

by
Lynn F. Myers, Jr.

1960.

The Kennedy-Nixon debate. Richard Nixon, replete with five-o'clock shadow, looked sinister on television. The younger Jack Kennedy looked trusting and sincere.

Ennis Willie was twenty-one.

America's economy slumped. Detroit's car wares were being ignored because of high prices, or ugliness (think Edsel). The companies that had sold quarter paperbacks were failing—forcing the ones that remained to think about raising the price (which they eventually did).

The threat of nuclear war was the headline almost every night. In elementary school, students were subjected to air raid drills where a loud, scary siren would go off over the scratchy P.A. system and kids were told to hide under the desk because you never knew if those slimy Commies were going to press the button and drop the big one!

Nuclear war. Nuclear annihilation. A booth at county fairs showed the latest innovation—a bomb shelter, sometimes luxurious if you wanted to pay for extras, to help your family survive the upcoming and final war—World War III.

You can't pick the time you were born, you just have to play the cards you're dealt. Ennis Willie, a native Georgian, wanted to be a writer. Despite all the global tension, where the world could seemingly end at the touch of a button, life went on; teenage girls and boys thought about what they always thought about. And everybody thought about sex, but talked about it in whispers—or in forbidden books.

Despite the demise of many paperback publishers, Ennis Willie got lucky. There were publishers willing to take him on; 1960 was the golden age of sleaze paperbacks—a perfect training ground for new writers.

American publishing is responsible for many innovations, some of which they are inordinately proud of. Either invented (or perfected) were dime novels, pulp magazines, slick magazines, paperbacks, and comic books. Sleaze paperbacks became the dark side of publishing, hardly discussed today.

The American public has always had a thirst for fiction, and publishers using technology like steam-operated presses, were able to satisfy the demand for low-cost fiction. In America, popular writers, like James Fennimore Cooper and Edgar Allan Poe, became some of the first celebrities. Cooper, who wrote stories about men of the frontier, also invented a basic storytelling formula: action, romance, impossible escapes, and lots of carnage. Meantime, Edgar Allan Poe formulated the first mystery stories. Both basic formulas are still being used today. Other popular genre formulas followed over the years, and all were missing a key ingredient: sex.

Publishers had to tow the line in regards to shows of passion for a couple of reasons. State and local communities had strict laws banning pornography (America, after all, was founded on *puritan* principles). The toughest laws in place were in Boston, where the infamous expression *Banned in Boston* was coined. There was also a government agency that was a watchdog for what Americans could and could not read, and who were also responsible for distribution of magazines—namely, the United States Post Office. The Post Office kept an iron grip on publishers for nearly 80 years.

Then in the 1935, one innovative pulp publisher decided to test the waters and see how much he could get away. Frank Armer, who under several corporate names, published *Spicy Detective*, *Spicy Adventure*, *Spicy Mystery*, and *Spicy Western*. In an era when pulp magazines were selling for a dime to fifteen cents, the Spicy line was a quarter. If readers (mostly young middle-class males) wanted a little sex in their life, they had to pay for it. Armer's noble experiment only lasted a few years. His magazines, which are tame even by yesterday's standards, sometimes came out in both a censored and uncensored version, depending on the region the magazine was selling in. The extra money from the cover price also helped with legal fees. This noble experiment lasted for about seven years before Armer gave up and retitled his company a final time and continued to publish genre pulp magazines until the pulps began to die out in the late 1940's. While he never officially published a sleaze paperback, several things were learned from his experiment: lurid covers sell magazines, formula stories need good plots, have a lawyer ready to fight for First Amendment rights, make a deal with distributors to get the magazine circulated, and—lastly—get as much money as you can from the consumer.

In 1947, there was another significant development in the origin of the sleaze paperback. Mickey Spillane, who had previously worked for a comic book packager (Funnies, Inc.), wrote his debut book entitled *I, the Jury*. With violence culled from the *Black Mask* magazine works of Carroll John Daly (Spillane was a big fan), and the mildly suggestive sex of the *Spicy* line, Spillane created the ultra-tough private detective Mike Hammer. In 1949, Spillane's book was released in paperback and raked up previously unheard of sales in the millions. The success of the paperback edition spawned another market—the paperback original (or PBO) and Gold Medal books (a division of Fawcett who also distributed Spillane's paperback reprints) debuted and with the promise of "an original novel" came up with most of the themes that would launch sleaze paperbacks a few years later. Included as themes in their new line of paperbacks: incest, homosexuality, nymphomania, voyeurism, juvenile delinquency and a host of other previously taboo subjects. Gold Medal had good editors, a pool of good writers (which included the early works of John D. MacDonald), above average cover art, and great distribution. Although pioneering in their choice of subject matter, sometimes the controversial theme in their PBO's was played out in a single scene. Gold Medal's success also opened the floodgates for other PBO publishers as well.

At the time of the upstart Gold Medal line, there was one more significant player in the mix. In Chicago, an enterprising publisher named Hugh Hefner debuted *Playboy* magazine. The magazine endorsed a men's lifestyle from food and drink, entertainment, fashion, to sexually-oriented high quality fiction. The centerpiece to the magazine was a color centerfold of a nearly nude or nude woman—the flavor of the month (which included actress Marilyn Monroe in an early issue). 1950's America was sophisticated enough to handle the text portion of the slick magazine, but the centerfolds created a moral uproar. Hefner had to fight legal wars on several fronts including: his right to publish, his right to have the magazine distributed to retailers, and his right to send his magazine through the mail. It was a tough fight (some legal battles lasted for decades) but Hefner persisted and created an empire.

Hefner's legal victories opened the doors to countless magazine imitators, although Hefner had a lock on quality. By the mid-1950's, newsstands now had a special section for man's magazines and major news distributors who would supply material for this special section. This created a venue for an adult-oriented sleaze paperback market—the bastard son of the mainstream paperback original. And in the mid-1950's they began trickling to the paperback racks

The term "sleaze" is a modern affection term coined by paperback book collectors. When they were debuted, newsstand dealers had other terms for them like "adult books". But sleaze fits better. The mainstream paperback publisher had an editorial director, an art director, a suite of offices, talented writers and artists, typesetters, and access to a commercial printer. Profits on books that sold for a quarter weren't realized until almost the 100,000 copy mark because of overhead. Sleaze publishers didn't need the finer trappings: they had a publisher who sometimes hid behind a post office box, an overworked editor who directed assignments to mediocre cover artists, and hack writers willing to turn out a novel-length manuscripts very quickly and for a few hundred dollars. Typesetting was sometimes done in-house using a Varityper (a primitive typesetting machine that could justify the right margin), and a clandestine printing company willing to take a legal gamble on churning out the finished product, using the cheapest assembly methods known to man: flimsy inferior coated stock for the covers, and an adhesive whose self-destructive ingredients would cause the binding to fail in one reading.

Sleaze paperbacks were distributed by small distributors (also willing to gamble) and newsstands that wanted the product ordered the books in bulk, getting mixed titles from many publishers. Despite the overall cheapness in the quality and content of the books, the titles to these illicit paperbacks were very clever and usually assigned by the publisher or the editor, not the writer. The titles, more than anything, sold the books and make them collectible today; they were clever pastiches of literary masterpieces, motion pictures titles, and in some instances actually zeroed in on the subject matter. I asked current paperback dealers and collectors like Rose Islet, Ron Blum, Lynn Monroe, and for their list of the best sleaze titles. They responded with: *Horizontal Secretary, Killer Dyke, Dammit Don't Touch My Broad!, Great Sexpectations, For Your Sighs Only, Brush The Blood Off My Boobs, He Wore A Yellow Ribbon, For Whom The Belles Toil, Of Vice And Men,* and *The Anatomy And The Ecstasy.*

Despite the racy titles and cover art, the early sleaze publishers played a shell game that ultimately delivered only the tease. There was no explicit sex (only implied sex), only mild cursing, and though many were marked "For Adult Reading" the only thing "adult" about them was the writing formula they were based on—so old the formula was now of voting age.

Camerarts Publishing got into the sleaze market just in time for Ennis Willie, who was looking for writing assignments. Camerarts (who like Playboy was Chicago-based but whose whole operation could have fit into the executive washroom at Hefner's operation) published two pictorial men's magazine—*Best for Men*, and *Rascal*. Camerarts was challenged at least twice (in the late 1950's) by postal inspectors who wanted to take away their second-class mailing privileges for various infractions of postal regulations—including once showing off too much nipple in one of their photo spreads. While Hugh Hefner might have opened the doors to his legion of inferior imitators, he fought back with the best lawyers. After a few years, government watchdogs of decency formulated a plan of their own: prosecute the small publishers individually—a practice that continues to this day.

The small (but mighty) Camerarts valiantly fought back the postal inspectors and somehow managed a victory to protect their own tiny empire. Camerarts had a lot to loose: discounting the hairdo's of nearly fifty years ago and the era where women were more rounded and packed on a few more pounds, some models in Best for Men and Rascal were both tough-looking and a little scary; the publisher's victory against the sinister agents of the post office assured the models temporary but continued employment. Camerarts decided to celebrate their victory by launching two adult paperback lines, both lines to be offered for sale by mail order (with ads in their two men's magazines) and also newsstand sales.

Since Camerarts was still stinging from their brushes with the feds, their new lines of sleaze would take a specific direction: titles for the books would be tame but suggestive and the art would be somewhat tame. Taming the cover art and title was a major step backward as Camerarts would lose two key selling tools. As for the overall Merit cover art, Jim Steranko, a noted paperback cover artist, writes: ". . . they are all third rate, with lackluster photos, fair models, mundane design, and lousy typography. In other words, they look like thousands of similar offerings and are impossible to tell apart." That left the story to sell the book, which was a chancy decision. The stories would have to have some spice, but also a cohesive plot and would mirror elements of the legitimate paperback original. To accomplish this task, they would need good writers. They got Ennis Willie. Willie had already written *Vice Town* for Vega Books, and knew exactly what Camerarts wanted. He gave readers swift action, suggestive sex, and stories good enough for repeat sales under his byline.

Willie incorporated a lot of early Mickey Spillane in his books, but was never a clone. Willie strictly used third-person, introduced a supernatural element in some of his stories, and created a durable hero in Sand, star of about a third of his Merit titles. While Spillane's Mike Hammer was a vigilante private detective, Willie's hero was a big-time criminal who left the mob because he was fed up with "the life". Mike Hammer had to answer to a licensing board; Sand answered to no one except the reader. When Sand was introduced, Spillane was coming out of a long hiatus and his style had changed with his new books. The new Mike Hammer was less instinctive and more calculating; an undercurrent of menace replaced the savage action of the earlier books (at least until the explosive ending). Willie wisely kept several key ingredients from the earlier Spillane: the noirish big city backdrop where the seedier side of town became a living, breathing secondary character, the baser character elements of the protagonist, and the explosive ending. Willie's Sand character also got laid more than the early Mike Hammer.

Willie became the star player for Merit. Tombstone ads appeared in Best for Men heralding the backlist of the "Uncensurable Ennis Willie". He continued to dish out the product for nearly five years. Willie wrote quickly (about four 35,000 to 40,000 word novels a year), and made his self-imposed formula work. Hunched over a manual typewriter, chain smoking, Willie would tap the keyboard and improvise his own fictional jazz—punctuating his prose with the short staccato bursts from Sand's 1911A Colt .45 caliber automatic.

Readers bought and loved the books—the raw first-draft writing which had the same potent effect as drinking fresh moonshine, and Willie became one of the most dependable writers of the entire paperback line. The editor, except for assigning the provocative title, left Willie pretty much alone. But after four years and close to two dozen books, Willie began to experience the warning signs of burnout. His last book got hung up and it took him nearly five months to finish. His sleaze days were numbered. Sleaze itself was on the way out as well. Legal battles were won in the late 1960's and eventually sleaze evolved into smut. However, remnants of the sleaze formula live on today, in—of all places—romance novels for women, where sex is meted out in various strengths (depending on the edition)—from simmer to broil.

In 1964, Willie walked away from writing on the eve of a contract that would have paid five thousand dollars a book advance against royalties from a mainstream paperback publisher. Willie became a rich and successful businessman in the graphics and printing business. Walking away so suddenly and completely left him to become a legend in the sleaze paperback business. His old books were championed by outspoken writers like Max Collins and Ed Gorman, and his books became prized collectibles from paperback dealers and on eBay.

Ennis Willie stepped out of the shadows in 2004 in Ed Gorman's blog, unashamedly admitting his culpability in corrupting a legion of aging baby boomers. If we were corrupted, it was lovingly and willfully so. As young men we were lured to read Willie's books by the promise of forbidden pleasures, however, we came away still ignorant of sex but with memories that his terse, ultra hard-boiled stories were hugely entertaining. Today's sleaze paperbacks are collected for almost everything but the story. Willie remains one of the few sleaze writers to be scrutinized for his story-telling abilities.

I could make a pronouncement that Ennis Willie is "The King of Sleaze", but foisting such a title has obvious drawbacks. Despite the fact that sleaze paperbacks now have a cult following, they are only now becoming seriously studied and embraced as being part of America's past pulp culture.

But there is still a stigma attached to sleaze that makes it somewhat less than wholesome; for example: many of the people I contacted to do this introduction were happy to supply bits of history, but didn't want their names attached to it. Some famous writers who got their feet wet in the sleaze era still refuse to acknowledge their own contributions. Lest everybody forgets: the words and themes of today's mainstream novels were fought and won years ago by publishers (including sleaze publishers) fighting First Amendment legal battles, not for art's sake, but for money's sake. That's the American way, and today's writers have profited from it whether they want to admit or not.

This volume was assembled with the cooperation of Ennis Willie. He gave the editors access to copies of his rare paperbacks (some sell for more than fifty dollars each!) for us to select from. We chose two Sand stories—about a Cold War end-of-America plot which smacks of the era it was written. America lived through the Cold War unscathed, it took another enemy in another generation to wreck havoc, that makes this nightmarish Sand story stand out even more. A second Sand novel with Sand very much on the offensive is included as well as three excellent Sand short stories from Best For Men. These well-crafted short stories also illustrate the best of Ennis Willie the writer. All of the stories in this collection carry Ennis Willie's original title (not the ones created by the original editor).

The stories in the volume can be read for either their historical value or for their excellent entertainment value. Think diamonds in the rough.

We leave you with alternative reading instructions: read the stories at night in bed with a flashlight—millions of ex-teenage male Baby Boomers can't all be wrong.

Lights out! Pleasant reading!

Lynn Myers,
Carlisle, Pa

DEATH IN A DEAD PLACE

When my buddy Lynn Myers first made me aware of Ennis Willie's Sand series a year or so ago, I was surprised and a little dismayed that I had never discovered them for myself. I mean, how could I—unlike the editors and most of the other contributors to this collection—not have run across these terrific books back in the sixties when they were originally being published? As a prowler of every spin rack in a considerable radius, I certainly was no stranger to the Novel or Merit line of paperbacks. And while I wasn't above plunking down a few quarters once in a while for an "adult novel" simply because its racy cover featured some scantily-clad babe I found particularly appealing, what I sought most fervently were the tough-guy tales by writers like Spillane (of course), Brett Halliday, Richard S. Prather, Mike Avallone, and so on. (With covers, incidentally, usually featuring babes who weren't hard to look at, either.)

So how the hell did I miss Ennis Willie and Sand back then?

I don't know. The thing I do know, however, is that I now have been introduced to them and the pleasure is all mine.

The stories are hard, fast-paced, and exciting. The writing is as lean and spare as any to be found, and is pitch-perfect for Sand's world. With only a few masterful word strokes Willie can set a scene, a mood, or a characterization as clear and sharp as the flash of a knife blade.

From DEATH IN A DEAD PLACE: "The medical examiner's name was Hendrix. He looked like an average, likable Joe until he smiled, and then you knew he was a pompous son of a bitch. He smiled like he had just had his teeth cleaned . . ." Absolutely nothing more needs to be said. We know all we need to know about Hendrix because we all know somebody exactly like him, right?

Willie knows when to be explicit in his descriptions and when to say just enough to tap into the reader's imagination and let the mind do the rest. Another example from DEATH IN A DEAD PLACE: *"He nearly gagged. He knew it was Sticky because he recognized the clothes he had been wearing. Only, at the same time, it wasn't Sticky. It was bigger than Sticky,* much *bigger. With the overpowering smell of sweet rot.* And it bore no resemblance to a human being!"

When it came to describing the luscious women Sand frequently encountered, however, Willie became somewhat more detailed: "White-blonde hair that would fall down past her shoulders when the pins were out, and breasts that pushed against the dress she wore without any encouragement. Tall, self-possessed, and beautiful . . . "

So, all tallied, in the Sand books and stories you have what could be called the Total Package—above average writing; a protagonist who is tough as nails yet capable of compassion and possessing an unwavering sense of loyalty to those who are loyal to him; lots of sexy, drop-dead gorgeous dames; and plenty of action in the form of fist-fights, shoot-outs, and encounters with the aforementioned dames. What more can you ask for?

All of these elements are on fine display in DEATH IN A DEAD PLACE. *Here Sand encounters a cell of imbedded terrorists who are on the brink of releasing a biological horror intended to bring the free world to its knees. With his fists, his .45, and his brains, Sand races to find a way to stop them . . . Oh yeah, and he must do it while carrying around a couple bullet holes and dodging the trio of syndicate hit men who put them there in the first place and are hell bent on finishing the job.*

Tough odds? You bet. But we're talking about Sand here. If you've been paying attention, you ought to know better than to bet against him.

Wayne D. Dundee

ONE

E WOKE UP with the old derelict shoving a wine bottle at him and the smell of something foul in his nostrils.

"Go on," the old man was saying, "—got another when this one is busted."

And somewhere close a disharmonized gathering was singing hymns. . . .

His name was Sand, a tall man with dark hair just beginning to gray and eyes that held no expression. There was a growth of beard on his face and a pain in his middle. He shook his head to clear some of the fuzziness away and tried to figure out where he was and what he was doing here.

It was an alley, long and narrow, with a light fog hugging its floor and barrels overflowing with bottles and trash. He was stretched out with a brick wall to his back. The singing was coming from a Mission behind the wall. The sour smell belonged to uncollected garbage and the many unwashed bodies of drunks and derelicts that had occupied this space before him. Everything, all of it, held down close to the ground by the oppressive pressure of the night.

He knew where he was, not the number of the building or the name of the street, but the place where the low and forgotten gather. Skid Row.

The old bum gulped from his bottle and offered it again. "You look like you need it, mister, you really do. Muscatel. Ain't got no wallop like hard booze, but it kinda saturates."

Sand took it, more to keep him quiet for a few minutes than anything else. The sweet wine made him gag, and the pain in his gut flared with the effort. Cold sweat peppered his forehead.

The old man's eyes showed genuine concern. "You don't look so good, mister, you sure don't. I was fixing to slip in the side and join the congregation. After the singing and preaching they serve soup and maybe sandwiches. Could be what you need is something in your stomach."

What he needed was time to think. But the soup might not be a bad idea. He climbed to his feet and the pain hit him again.

Leaning against the wall, he pushed his hand inside his shirt and found the bandage. Not a professional patch job. He had probably done it himself. He also felt for the gun he knew instinctively should be under his arm. It wasn't. No wallet either. No nothing.

"What's your name?" Sand asked the old man.

"They call me Sticky—on account of I got sticky fingers. Whatever you're missing though I didn't take. I wouldn't of hung around if I did. Besides, I already made one good score today. I ain't greedy."

"They got a place to wash up inside the Mission?"

"Sure. Ain't you never been in there before?"

"I don't think so. Lead the way."

That was when the two men stepped into the mouth of the alley. Sticky recognized them and stiffened. One of them was wearing several layers of clothing without regard to the temperature. Down here, whatever you owned you kept close to you.

"We been looking for you, Sticky," Layers said. "We heard you made it big today, real big."

"Yeah." The other one. His voice sounded like it crawled over jagged glass to get out his thick throat. "We hear you walked off with a whole suitcase just packed full of fancy stuff to hock. Maybe even some cash, uh, Sticky?"

The little guy was scared. He had suddenly developed a bad case of shakes. "It . . . it wasn't like that, Crow. It wasn't even a suitcase, just a satchel sort of, and it didn't have nothing in it but some little bottles. The stuff wasn't even hooch. I tasted one of them and it wasn't nothing. The only thing worth pawning was the case and Gruber didn't give me but five bucks for it."

Crow looked at the one in the jacket. "We gonna believe that shit?"

The other one shook his head. "Hell no, we ain't gonna believe that shit—not till we turn him upside down and shake him a little. Whatever we find, I guess that's what Sticky has been saving for our cut. We know he wouldn't want us to believe he ain't willing to share the wealth."

From the darkness the tall man named Sand spoke softly. "Believe it. Save yourself some grief."

Maybe they hadn't noticed him before. Or maybe they simply hadn't expected interference. They were used to people minding their own business. Now they noticed him. They didn't scare. He was big, but so were they and they had him outnumbered.

Crow said, "Butt out, mister," his voice crawling over that jagged glass again.

"I'm in."

It was their move then and they made it. They moved in fast, going after Sticky. Whatever money he had would be on him and they wanted it.

Sticky scrambled back with a little yell and Sand cut the first one down like a tree, his fist connecting with a jawbone hard enough to tear it loose. But it also brought his own pain back in a major surge. He forgot it and concentrated on Crow.

As Layers hit the concrete Crow forgot about the little man and took a swing at Sand. The huge fist sailed through the air like a shot put, then staggered to a halt as the tall man's foot lifted, hard. A scream tore out Crow's throat as he tried to double over.

"Mother, *mother . . .*" he cried.

Sand held one arm tight around his own middle to hold back the pain and kicked out again. The kick caught him in the chest. The force of the kick set the bum's butt down hard on the concrete like he was sitting in a very low chair. His eyes were open but staring at nothing. After a second or two his upper body just leaned backward and made a thump on the floor of the alley. His eyes stayed open and now looked up at the sky.

Layers looked up soon enough to see his buddy take his

final fall. He jumped up and scrambled down the alley, stumbling and falling every few steps until he reached the street and disappeared around a corner. He never looked back. There was nothing behind him he wanted to see.

Then nothing. Just Sticky's heavy breathing.

And the burning pain in his gut.

"Son of a bitch," the little man said, awed. "Slap, bam, boom! Mister, you're *mean*."

"Yeah," Sand said. "Let's go find that can."

On the other side of the door were a dozen paint-cracked pews half-filled with unwashed derelicts, here and there a woman thrown in. They were singing for their supper the way they did every night of the week. Some of them were putting everything they had into it; maybe they were really seeking salvation. Most of them just dragged along a word or two behind because it was the way to the soup. Like the old man who called himself Sticky, they needed the free eats so any money they had panhandled or pinched during the day could be used for cheap wine to fill the void of the night.

"That's Reverend Garfield," Sticky whispered, pointing his nose at a dumpy white-haired man leading the singing from the pulpit in a hoarse but vigorous baritone. "He watches the front door pretty close to see who comes in late. That's why I had to come in the side. That's the door to the can over on the other side. We can sort of ease our way over without disturbing anybody."

When they got to the end of the row Sticky hung back and Sand went on alone.

The place could have been cleaner, but at least it was empty. Except for a gallon jug sitting on the flush tank that had once held some kind of liquid detergent.

Above the lavatory there was a mirror. He looked into it. The man who looked back belonged here, in the can of a charity mission for drunks and deadbeats who had only their souls left to bargain with. He had a week-old stubble of black beard and a thin streak of long-dried blood close to his hairline. His clothes had been expensive, but that was before they had been ripped and dragged and rolled and slept in.

Now they looked like the clothes any bum would wear, stuff bought for nickels at some second or third hand store or pulled from a dumpster when he happened to be at the right place at the right time. He looked lousy.

He unbuttoned his shirt to get at the makeshift bandage underneath and lifted it. He found what he knew he would. The ugly pucker of a bullet wound.

He was remembering it all now. For at least a week and maybe even longer he hadn't been remembering anything. He touched the dried blood from the slug that had glazed his head. He must have been walking around in a daze.

He took another long look at himself in the mirror.

Sand. The great Sand. Hard. Tough. The fair-haired boy of the underworld elite until the day you decided you'd had enough, that you couldn't stand the stink of corruption any longer. So you decided to get out. They said you would never make it, that nobody gets out of the organization alive, not even you with your reputation of being too damn tough to kill. They said a lot of things, but you quit anyway. Sure they came after you. You knew they would. In Frisco they planted a bomb and the next day the guy who planted it was floating face down in the bay. In Detroit they made their play with a machine gun in a speeding car and ended up roasting inside a mass of flames while blood ran out of the flames into the street. That was when you started becoming a legend, the man the organization couldn't kill. But it was a lie. You know it and the organization knows it. One day they'll catch you off guard, or you'll be too slow. The bullet hole in your gut shows it can happen.

The syndicate sniper had been laying for him on the roof of a building across the street from his apartment hotel. There was the sudden pain of the slug biting at the side of his head and the *spat* it made flattening against the stone building; then he was reaching automatically for the gun riding in a shoulder holster under his arm. The second slug hit him with the force of a sledgehammer. Then nothing. Nothing until waking up in the alley outside with his wallet and gun gone and an old man pushing a bottle at him.

He splashed cold water on his face.

By now the organization would be sure of two things. One, that he was still alive. Two, that he had at least one hole in him. They would have their boys scouring the town for him. Their sniper missed, but he had given them an opportunity they had been after for years. They had him on the run—limping.

The face in the mirror told him why they hadn't found him yet. They were looking for the legendary Sand, not some bum in the gutter. The beard and the street had been his camouflage.

The words of a hymn came through the door to him.

He checked the wound again, thoroughly this time. It was bad enough, but it was clean. The high-powered slug had ripped its way all the way through. By some freak chance it hadn't gotten infected, and as long as it didn't it was just a matter of time before it would heal. He was a man who knew bullet wounds.

He buttoned the shirt back, opened the door and stepped outside.

He nearly collided with a woman as beautiful as they come.

TWO

WHITE-BLONDE HAIR that would fall down past her shoulders when the pins were out, and breasts that pushed against the dress she wore without any encouragement. Tall, self-possessed, and beautiful. The eyes were blue, and as they looked up into Sand's there was a moment, after the first startled expression, when she seemed to look past the beard and find the man.

"Excuse me," he said.

She smiled, showing him even teeth. "Of course."

Then she was walking on toward the front and disappearing into a small room behind the pulpit. In her hand she carried a black leather bag.

"That's Dr. Street," Sticky told him. "A couple of times I heard Reverend Garfield call her Marilyn."

"A lady doc? For this crowd?"

"Yeah, and a lot of all right. She comes down here once, twice a week to hand out medical advice where it's needed and give shots for this and that. Never charges a cent. Don't make no fuss about it neither like those phony humanitarians that show up down here all the time." The old man looked almost wistfully at the door where she had disappeared. "Reminds me almost of an angel. You know what I mean?"

Sand knew what he meant. Not because she reminded him of an angel but because she reminded him he was a man.

The singing had stopped. The dumpy preacher said a few words about food for men's souls and then got around to the more pressing problem of food for their bellies. Soup was on.

With the derelicts in the Mission it was an old story and an orderly procedure. A line was formed past the pulpit and into the room where the beautiful lady doctor had disappeared. On the other side was soup and sandwiches without much conversation or etiquette.

Sand had never had any burning desire to taste Mission soup; now he discovered he hadn't been missing anything. It was mostly water. But it felt good in his stomach. What it was joining down there he didn't know, probably nothing.

The lady M.D., looking more like Venus with arms than Dr. Kildare, was setting up her operation in one corner of the room, complete with draw curtain and consultation chair. A couple of times he caught her watching him, but he didn't think it had anything to do with recognition, not of him. Maybe she recognized the expensive suit beneath the dirt, or maybe it showed that he wasn't used to taking handouts. Could even be she was on the make, but that didn't stand up. She was probably all fire in the bedroom, but she wouldn't do her picking in the gutter. All she was spreading around down here was a little charity.

"Could be you oughta let her take a look at you," Sticky suggested. "I mean, I seen in the alley how you was favoring your middle. Put that with how you was missing something when you come around—I figure must be somebody knifed you and took your stake."

"It doesn't need a doctor," Sand said.

"You need something," the old man insisted. "You handled those two in the alley, but right now you don't look too good. Sort of white, like you been losing blood or something. I know a good place where you can hole up for a little while, better than any flophouse."

The doctor was watching him again. Maybe, like Sticky, she could see that he was nearly out on his feet, that blood and energy had been draining out of him for a week while he walked around without putting any food in his belly.

He said, "You don't owe me any favors, Sticky."

"Sure I do. Hell, you saved me from a beating. Those two don't joke. They're bad news to every bum on the street. They been going around saying how from now on they get a cut of everything heisted or begged or they start spreading broken bones around. A couple of guys they busted up already. I was going to be next. I owe you favors plenty."

Chow time was over and the derelicts were beginning to disappear, except for those who had formed a line to see Dr. Street.

"Ain't far," Sticky said. "I don't never stay there myself, except for once in a while when I figure I ain't got no drinking to do."

Sand gave it some thought and decided he had nothing to lose. Right now he was as safe from the mob gunnies here as anywhere. Sooner or later he would have to make a move, but trying it with a bullet hole in him would be playing right into their hands.

He said, "Okay, Sticky—let's go."

They went. Like the other bums, they disappeared into the night. The only one to see them go was the lady doctor who sometimes got herself called Marilyn. Her eyes followed them out of the room through the chapel.

Outside, the fog roamed along the decaying streets like a vapory tiger on the prowl, crowding into dirty corners and stalking the occasional streetlight.

"It's this way," the old man said.

In the summer a vacant doorway is as handy as a dirty cot in a flophouse. It saves a few nickels and the wine the nickels buy softens the concrete. As Sand and the old man walked down the street he saw that the derelict's problem in summer was finding an unoccupied doorway.

From the bowels of skid row to the outer fringe, a six-story tenement with cracked steps and dark stairs. The room was on the third floor halfway down a hall filled with the smell of cooked cabbage. It was locked.

"I got a key," Sticky said. He rummaged through his clothes until he found it and stuck it in the lock. "For emergencies like this."

One room with a bath attached to it. Double bed, dresser, chest of drawers, and an unfolded couch under the window leading to the fire escape. It was clean.

Sticky was proud. "Nice, huh? You can take the couch. It'll be all right." He was already backing out the door.

By the time Sand turned around the little man was gone. He gave the situation some thought, shrugged and stretched out on the couch. He wished to hell he had managed to hold on to the gun. It was like waking up without his arm. It was a part of him. They had been together a long time.

Fatigue pulled his eyelids closed and he was out.

~ ~ ~ ~ ~

He woke up with her staring down at him, a naked rage in her eyes, while behind her the light bulb hanging by a cord from the ceiling swished back and forth from the violent tug she had given it.

"Get out!" she demanded. The rage was also in her voice. "Get out before I call the police."

She had crossed twenty-five, but not too far. Hair black and short, lips full and red, a face that wouldn't be half bad when she stopped twisting it up, and breasts that didn't like being harnessed.

The only things that had moved were his eyes. He said, "What's your trouble, sister?"

She nearly strangled on whatever it was that tried to get out of her throat. "Out!" she said again. "Get out!"

He sat up. He didn't know how long he had been asleep. Not long. His head hurt.

"I heard that part," he said.

Surprise played around the edges of her face.

He ran his fingers through his hair. It didn't help the banging inside his head. "Suppose we start with you telling me what you're doing here," he suggested.

"I pay the rent. My name is Beverly Farmer and this is my room."

"You know an old guy named Sticky?"

That surprise again, along with a glimmer of understanding. "Uncle Sticky?"

Sand shrugged. "Maybe he's your uncle. Doesn't figure he's your boyfriend. He suggested it might be a good place to rest up. I haven't been well."

At mention of her uncle the rage had settled down to a steady anger. She looked better. In fact, she looked fine.

"Uncle Sticky acts foolishly sometimes," she said. "I let him stay here when he has no place else to go, but that doesn't mean I intend to take in his friends."

If he had known there was a dame involved he wouldn't have come here to start with, but now his head hurt and he was remembering a missing wallet and a missing .45 and a bunch of syndicate hoods out there somewhere combing the town for him. He lay back on the couch and closed his eyes again.

"Now what are you doing?" Her face was probably screwing up again.

"I'm getting some sleep. In the morning I'll clear out. Until then just make like I'm not here"

After stumbling over a few words, she managed, "You're getting out now!"

He opened his eyes again. "Sister, I walked a lot of blocks to get here. I don't feel like walking back. If it's your virtue you're worried about, cease to fear. At the moment you appeal to me about as much as raw liver." It wasn't exactly true, but it was psychology of sorts. Nothing throws a good-looking dame off balance more than to tell her she doesn't jiggle your hormones.

Pause.

For a moment he was almost convinced she was going to act like a broad with sense, but it didn't last.

She stamped her foot on the floor. "Either you get out of here right now or I call the police."

She had already turned and started for the door when he straightened up and caught her hand. He didn't intend to have a bunch of cops piling in here.

She was game, this girl. Instead of trying to break loose she spun around and came flying at him with nails flashing. He caught her wrists and pushed them up behind her back, but she was a lot of female. She intended to fight him. Then suddenly something changed in her face and she stopped struggling.

He didn't need a crystal ball to tell him what had happened. His gun was gone, but the empty holster was still strapped under his coat. She had found it.

She was looking hard into his eyes, recognizing for the first time the hardness. Not the glassy look of a wine-soaked bum at all, but the coldness of a man who could kill.

"You're no friend of my uncle's," she said. "He's a little man. He has little friends."

"Well now he has me. You going to behave if I let you go?"

She wouldn't promise, but he let her go anyway and she continued to stand there watching him.

"Who are you, mister?"

"The name is Sand."

"That all?"

"It's enough."

She thought about it. "Normally I fix some coffee when I come in. You want a cup?"

She still wasn't exactly happy, but at least she was being sociable. He said, "Sure."

She plugged in a hot plate that sat on one corner of the dresser. The place had no facilities for whipping up a meal. Then she got a boiler from somewhere and filled it with water from the lavatory. When it was boiling she poured it into cups with instant coffee.

"I don't keep anything stronger around," she said when she handed him one of the cups. "Uncle Sticky would find it and drink it if I did." She realized that sounded like an apology and immediately regretted saying it. Nothing had changed. She still intended to get him out of here. Before, he had been one of her uncle's drunken cronies flopping in her pad. Now he was something a lot different and that didn't change things any for the better.

Sand let her think about it while he put the coffee down there with the soup and sandwiches. Then he handed her the empty cup and stretched out on the couch again.

"You still have to go," she insisted.

He didn't bother to reply. He thought of his own apartment, with its soft bed and air conditioning and well-stocked bar—and then he thought of the syndicate assassins who would be waiting around outside, and suddenly it wasn't a pretty picture.

"I thought we had that settled. I'll leave in the morning. Until then you be a good girl."

"I can still call the police," she said. "You're probably wanted for something. There might even be a reward."

She started for the door so he grabbed her again, this time intending to tell her okay, she could have the damn place to herself. But this time when she struggled her breasts were against his chest and her hips twisted, shifting . . . and the empty days without a woman rolled across his nerve ends.

He turned her loose, but she didn't go. It was a two-way thing. Maybe her days had been empty too. Maybe a dozen things. It can happen sometime—the right time, the right people. Something had clicked, and they both knew it.

His lips reached for hers. Or it could have been the other way around. There was no sense to any of it.

Her teeth bit him as her arms went tight around his chest. Her breasts throbbed against him and a moan escaped her throat as a fire swept through both of them.

"This is crazy," she said, "crazy, crazy, crazy . . ." But she didn't try to stop it.

It was already past stopping. You don't stop the eruption of a volcano or the fury of a hurricane. You ride it. You let it carry you. You don't ask what caused it or where it's going.

They rode it, all the way. He forgot the banging in his head and the hurt in his middle. They didn't exist. There was only now and the urgency.

There was nothing nice about it, nothing refined. Passion has no rule book, and this was passion at its wildest. The couch found its way under them, and if it hadn't been there the floor would have done just as well.

They didn't worry about clothes. He snatched and something gave and the brown nipple of one full breast jutted up for the feel of his hand. She moaned again, something completely indefinable. His mouth covered hers and the sound stopped.

Later there were other sounds, but they didn't hear them. They were riding the hurricane, and it was moving too fast for anything else to catch up.

THREE

THREE DAYS. On the third day he even grinned at himself in the mirror. He hadn't done that in a long time. He grinned because he had been on the bottom and now he was on the way up. The organization had him set up for an easy kill, but they hadn't been able to find him. Now he had teeth again.

He checked the loads in the .45, jacked a shell into the chamber and picked up a pair of spare clips. The weight of the gun felt damn good in his hand. It was a backup he had kept tucked away in his apartment. Bev had paid the place a discreet visit and returned with the goodies he needed. She hadn't spotted anything that she thought looked suspicious, but he hadn't expected her to. If they still had the place staked out they would be well hidden.

He shoved the gun into the holster inside his coat and looked out the window over the couch. A lousy day. The sun hadn't been able to get out for the clouds overhead.

"Aren't you going to put on the clothes I brought?" the girl had asked him before she left for work.

He had shaken his head. The clothes could wait a while. The bullet wound in his gut was healing okay, but he didn't want to rush it. The ruined suit and beard had camouflaged him so far. It wouldn't hurt to let them go on doing it a little longer. Step outside in a fresh suit and a clean shave and he would be a freak. He wouldn't belong to the neighborhood any longer. In two hours the word would be out and the syndicate boys would have it. They would come. Not as fast as they would have a week ago, but they would come. Cautiously. Because, crippled or not, he was still Sand, the one the stories were about, the one they called indestructible. *Very cautiously.* Because he was Sand and tough and the ones who came before had returned in pieces.

He looked out at the gray day again and thought about
Sticky. The old man who had got him a place to hole up
when he needed it bad had said he would be around but in
three days he hadn't shown up. Bev said it didn't mean anything, but there was the possibility the two bums from the
alley outside the Mission had made another try.

Sand left the apartment and went looking for the little guy.

At the Mission he found a couple of bums hanging around
working on a half pint. Neither of them had seen Sticky
lately, but he usually spent a lot of time in the park at Cooper.

He went to Cooper. No Sticky. Just an ancient derelict
with one big yellow tooth in the front of his head who knew
Sticky hadn't been in the park for the last couple of nights
because he wasn't feeling well. Probably he was holed up in
a flop, probably Ralph's, over close to 49th.

Ralph's was a foyer too small to squat down in and a long,
narrow room with forty or fifty surplus Army cots crowded
into it side by side. It was also Ralph. Ralph had two teeth
and a bad breath. Sticky had been here a couple of nights
ago, but the others had started complaining because he was
looking green. They were afraid they might catch something.
To keep the peace, Ralph had refunded the rent paid for the
cot and kicked him out. He had also reminded him there was
a place down the street where he could get a room to himself
for an extra buck.

"Sure I rented him the room," the woman said. She was
obese and untidy and, like Ralph, she had bad breath. "I already told the other fellow a while ago. He gave me enough
rent for three days. I ain't seen him since. I got other tenants.
Long as he don't set fire to the place I got no more dealings
with him till his time is up."

"Which room is it?"

"Top floor, end of the hall. It ain't got no number on it."

Sand climbed the stairs, spotting the broken one in time to
step over it. The building had three floors and the staircase
got worse all the way up. Everything got worse but the smell.

Somebody had left a skylight open.

Then he was nearing the room he wanted, and the smell was back. No. *A different smell.* Like the stink of rotting meat, but with a sickening sweetness hovering over it. It was a smell he had never encountered before. And it was getting stronger.

He knocked on the door. "Sticky, you in there?"

If he was, he wasn't answering his door.

Sand knocked again. "Sticky?"

The odor at this end of the hall had climbed up his nose and was threatening to gag him. It almost seemed to be coming from . . .

He grabbed the doorknob, twisted, and shoved it open. The smell nearly knocked him down.

And so did the man who came charging out!

The sudden plunge knocked Sand off balance, but he got a good look at the guy as he went past, tall and lean with the smooth good looks of a gigolo and something frantic in the eyes. He sprinted down the hall and was nearly to the stairs when suddenly he spun around, a strange look of concentration on his face. He lifted a pistol and pulled the trigger.

The first shot missed, but the second wouldn't have. He should have kept on running. He would have lived longer. But he didn't know that. He wasn't expecting the unshaven derelict to be packing a rod. Probably he never saw it; that was how fast it got into the act.

Sand palmed the .45 and fired in one greased motion, a practiced speed that comes with years of experience and the knowledge that one time slow is a long time dead. Two slugs from the .45 caught the guy high in the chest and tossed him down the stairs like a disjointed puppet.

Three shots fired in a narrow hallway make a lot of noise. Down below some dame started screaming.

Sand kept the gun in his hand as he moved toward the stairs. Blood was spurting out of the twin holes in the guy's chest. He had rolled halfway down the stairs. His gun had made it all the way. His eyes were open wide, like a man looking for the bony fellow with the scythe.

Sand bent over him. "Why, buddy?"

He coughed and a trickle of blood ran out the corner of his mouth and down his chin. "You'll know . . . soon . . . you'll know. Didn't fail . . . already started." He coughed again and his eyes rolled. He was dead.

Downstairs the dame was still screaming.

Sand went through the dead man's pockets hurriedly. A European passport for J. Fachman, a wallet with enough dough to keep him from going hungry and an address scratched in pencil on a piece of note paper stuffed in one of the wallet's leather pockets. That was all, except for some small change and a room key to an uptown hotel.

Sand stuffed everything back and climbed the stairs again, three at a time now. Fachman wasn't one of the organization's boys. They don't import gunnies from outside the country. That left only one reason for him making the play with the gun—he knew Sand had gotten a good look at his face as he ran past.

The door was still open and the smell was crawling out in nauseating waves. No happiness was going to be found at the end of this hall. Inside the room nothing moved. The shades were drawn, but there was enough light for him to see the thing on the bed.

He nearly gagged!

It was Sticky. He knew it was Sticky because he recognized the clothes he had been wearing. Only, at the same time, it wasn't Sticky.

It was bigger than Sticky, *much* bigger.

With the overpowering smell of sweet rot.

And it bore no resemblance to a human being!

FOUR

I F DR. MARILYN STREET wasn't the angel Sticky had called her, she must have at least had wings. She beat the cops getting there. She came hurrying up the stairs, her bag in her hand, and dressed in what was probably the latest style for lady doctors during office hours. Her blonde hair was piled on her head the way she had worn it at the Mission.

He had called her while everybody else was calling the cops.

She reached the body on the stairs, felt of him a couple of times to see if he was through breathing, then stepped over him and kept coming.

"Down at the end of the hall," Sand told her. "And hold on to your stomach."

Her stomach didn't give, but one look at the thing on the bed and the color washed out of her face. Give her credit for guts—she walked right in there and went to work like the thing was still a man.

Her voice was shaky when she said, "He's dead."

Sand was glad. It was better that way.

"What are you doing now?" he asked her. She had taken a syringe from her bag and was loading it.

"Sometimes a shot of adrenalin—"

With a lot of noise, the police had arrived. A brusque voice was telling the people to keep down the stairs and away from the body. There were other voices too, and one of them was that of Captain Max Mohannah of homicide.

Sand stepped out of the room and the sloppy fat landlady shot a dimpled arm out at him and screamed, "That's him! He's the one! He did it!"

A young cop in plainclothes got carried away and went

hunting for his gun. Mohannah slapped it down and growled something curt at his subordinate.

Sand said, "Hello, Max."

The homicide captain wasn't glad to see him. He took in the ruined suit and beard with distaste. "What the hell happened to you?"

"Vacation."

Max grunted, a heavy man beneath his suit. He glanced down at the body. "Looks like it's over."

"Yeah, and it was just getting good."

Another plainclothes cop came up the stairs and handed Fachman's rod to Max. "Here's the gun, captain."

Mohannah took the .38 revolver, swung the cylinder out and checked the loads. "One fired."

"You'll find it stuck in the wall close to where my head was at the time. He cut down on me."

"Self-defense and all that," he said sarcastically.

"And all that," Sand admitted.

They had hustled the fat landlady back downstairs with the rest of the crowd and now they were going through the dead man's pockets. They found the passport and money. The hotel key and the note with the scribbled address were no longer there. After seeing the thing in the room, Sand had decided to hold onto them a while.

Mohannah looked at the passport, mildly surprised. He would know that the organization was after Sand again even if the sniper with the silenced rifle incident hadn't drawn the fuzz. He had figured Fachman for a hood. Now he knew better. Now explanations were called for.

Sand gave it to him straight, the way it had happened. Then he took him down to see the thing in the room. Marilyn Street had come outside and was standing in the hall. The color hadn't come back to her face, and she was visibly shaken.

Max took one look and turned a pale green himself. "Riley!" he yelled over his shoulder, "Get on the box and find out what the hell's holding up the M.E. and his crew!"

He pulled the door closed tight and they all moved down

the hall far enough to be away from the stink. "What the hell happened to him?" he wanted to know.

"I'm not sure," the blonde said. "He seems to have started growing."

"*Growing?* He did more than grow. He looks like some kind of giant fungus-saturated cantaloupe."

"An uncontrolled growth—in all directions. Like a mass tumor, but on a vastly accelerated scale."

"What could have caused it?"

She shook her head. "I don't know. I've never seen or heard of anything like it."

The medical examiner arrived. For the next thirty minutes there was plenty of activity. Word leaked out about Sticky and the size of the crowd doubled, then tripled. Both bodies were loaded into the meat wagon and carried away with screaming sirens.

The blonde doctor and the M.E. had a serious conference full of puzzled expressions and head shaking before they left.

The place started to get deserted.

Mohannah said, "Okay, Sand, let's go down to the station. You've got a lot more talking to do."

"I'm surprised I'm not in handcuffs."

"You would be, except one of the tenants happened to be looking up the stairs when the guy took a shot at you. Let's get the hell out of here."

They got the hell out.

It was a silent trip, broken only by the noises that came out of the squawk box. Sand thought about Bev and wondered how she was going to take her uncle's death, and he thought about the words Fachman had said before he died. What he was thinking wasn't pretty, but it added up right when you put all the pieces together.

At the station Sand made his statement, waited for it to be typed, and signed it.

Then he said, "Now, off the record, you want to know how I read it, Max?"

Mohannah had been chewing on a cigar, his face and the cigar suddenly bearing a strange resemblance to each other.

"I'm listening."

"I think a few days ago Sticky made a big mistake. He stole something that belonged to this guy Fachman, probably an attache case, thinking he was getting away with something big. But when he opened it all he found was bottles. He tasted the contents of one of them to make sure it wasn't booze, then got rid of them and pawned the case."

"Nice friends you got. You've been coming up in the world."

"That's not the point."

"You think the stuff in the bottle did that to him?"

"I think there's a possibility. After all, Fachman came after him with a gun he had acquired since entering the country—which, according to his passport, was the same day Sticky made the snatch. He must have wanted the stuff back pretty bad."

The cop thought about it, slowly shook his head, "No. No, it doesn't hold water."

"He was there. Add that to what he said when he knew he was dying and take my word for it he would have been a lot sorrier about dying if he hadn't just seen what was in that room."

"You talking about some kind of biological weapon thing? That what you're talking about?" His voice was more than just a little incredulous.

"I'm talking about a little old man who three days ago was as normal as the two of us, a kind soul just drifting along where life took him."

Mohannah shook his head again, more slowly this time. "I don't believe it. It doesn't make a lot of sense, and it's all assumption." But he picked up the telephone and said to somebody, "Get hold of the medical examiner and tell him I want to talk with him when he has any kind of report on the body in autopsy."

FIVE

T HE MEDICAL EXAMINER'S NAME was Hendrix. He looked like an average, likable Joe until he smiled, and then you knew he was a pompous son of a bitch. He smiled like he had just had his teeth cleaned, a smile of slightly pleased pity for those less brilliant than himself.

"Some kind of *biological weapon!*" He had that *'how stupid can you get?'* look on his face. "Nonsense. Possibly, of course, triggered by a reaction to something taken internally. Interesting. I will need to explore it in the text of my article. I have already been in contact with several major medical journals, and they are quite interested. But the other thing—nothing like that."

His vision drifted off into space. "Perhaps even a book . . ."

The bastard was practically stroking his own fur.

"In other words, just a freak anomaly for the medical world to chew on?" Max asked around the cigar.

"Precisely. Strange though it may be, to put some nefarious connotation on it would be ridiculous."

"You're sure?" Max was pushing it all the way.

"Positive." He gave them that superior grin again. "Now, if you gentlemen will excuse me, there is still much work to do. It is unfortunate that Dr. Street in her haste to try to revive the patient administered formaldehyde rather than adrenalin. An understandable mistake under the circumstances, I suppose. The site was certainly enough to rattle anyone but, still, it will hinder the final results of the autopsy. He had already been dead for hours anyway."

When he was gone Max looked across the desk at Sand. "You heard it. Eases my mind, too. You were beginning to get through to me with that damn scare story."

"You're going to let it go at that?"

"He's the doctor. He writes articles. You heard him. Perhaps even a book. He's a doctor's doctor."

Sand stood up and stubbed out a cigarette. "I'll see you around, Max."

The homicide captain remained seated. "I don't want you to see me. I've told you before, I don't like hoods—or exhoods. And if you're thinking of trying to chase down this half-baked idea of yours on your own, take my advice and forget it. The word's around that mob exterminators are on your tail. Just staying alive you've got enough trouble."

He stopped at the door. "Something to think about, Max. If Hendrix is wrong and it is contagious . . . in a few days I could look like the thing we found in that room.

~ ~ ~ ~ ~

He flagged down a cab outside the police station and gave him Bev's address. The beard and clothes nearly made the cabbie ask to see his money, but the eyes changed his mind. When they stopped Sand tossed a bill into the front seat and climbed out.

He hadn't expected the girl to be home, but she was, stretched out face down across the bed, her make-up tear-streaked from crying. Well, it saved him from having to break the news to her.

He said, "I'm sorry, kid." There should have been more. After all, they had spent three days and nights together. They had given something to each other, had gotten to know each other. There should have been more, but there wasn't. He stroked her head gently and went into the bathroom and started running water.

He was nearly through with the job of scraping the brush off his face when the bed squeaked and she came to stand in the open doorway.

"I . . . I thought you weren't going to do that."

"Things have changed. This morning was a big fuss. They know where I am now." He splashed water on his face. "But they also know I'm on my feet, so the time for the mad rush is past. The small-time boys who would have been glad to join the hunt when they figured I was holed up somewhere more dead than alive will back off fast now. They would like to make a name for themselves, but they don't want it to be on a tombstone."

"But the others . . ."

"Are pros," he finished for her. "And their edge is gone. They had their chance and they muffed it. Only one miss to a customer. If they try again and miss there won't be enough left of them to send home in a box. They know that. They know me. I'm a pro, and I'm alive while a lot of men who thought they could take me have died because I was a little bit faster, a little bit tougher, maybe a little bit luckier. I take a lot of killing."

"Maybe they'll go away."

"Maybe." He said it but he knew better. Usually the pattern is to hit and run, but they had broken the pattern when they reported to the top that they had him on the run with a couple of slugs in him. Now he was back and walking around without even a limp and somebody might start thinking they had lied. They would try again.

He went into the other room and pulled on the clothes she had brought him. She watched silently until he was nearly done.

She said, "You won't be coming back, will you, Sand?"

"When a few things are settled. You're a nice kid. I wouldn't want you to get caught in the middle."

"Suppose I told you that since that first night I think I've been in love with you? What would you say?"

He reached out for her and pulled her against him. "I would say you aren't as smart as I gave you credit for."

She gave him a short laugh, but there was no humor in it. It wasn't a funny day. "I guess you're right. I guess I don't have much sense." She reached up and kissed him. "I'll let you go, but if you don't come back soon I'll have to come looking for you. There are better things than being smart."

"Don't start thinking of me as something I'm not, kitten.

Don't let the clothes fool you. You wanted to run me out when I was a bum with a case of the shakes. Maybe you should have. When the real Sand stands up he makes that bum look like a Boy Scout."

"I'm a girl who takes life as it comes," she said. "And you came to me, remember?"

He left her standing there and went downstairs.

The sun still hadn't managed to break through the clouds. Everything was gray, the sky, the street. Gray and bleak.

A bum came up and asked him for a handout. He was no longer a member of the clan. He was Sand again, and he had a lot to do.

He grabbed a cab and gave him an address uptown. On the way, he lined it up in his head.

Mob hitters.

Rotting death in a dark room.

A dying man saying, "*It has already started!*"

And some little bottles that weren't even hooch.

From the front seat the cabbie said, "Clouds are getting darker. Looks like it might turn into a rough day."

"Yeah," Sand said. "It looks that way."

SIX

T HE SPARTAN'S PLAYROOM was sandwiched between a hot dog stand and a pawnshop with one of its balls missing. It had an open front like a garage. Inside, game machines rang and banged and flashed, and guns went pop and monsters dropped, and multi-colored lights danced in the dark as scores were tallied. The place was crawling with Spartans, every one with a pocketful of quarters.

A kid in need of a better pimple cream was holding down the cash register. The noise didn't bother him. Nothing bothered him but the pimples and the latest hole in his nose beginning to resemble a serious error in judgment.

Sand handed him a bill to break. "Paddy in?"

"Who?" He tried to look stupid but the effort ruined it.

"Paddy Clay. Your boss. The guy with the horse parlor in back."

"Yeah, yeah . . . he's in."

Sand took his change and walked over to an upright booth guaranteed to give him passport photos for a buck. He pulled the curtain closed and walked through the door on the other side that slid open as the kid behind the cash register pushed a button under the counter.

The big board wasn't getting much action right now, but the floor was covered with wadded paper to prove it hadn't been cool long. Half a dozen men were scattered around the room.

A guy with a thin mustache and suede brogans was lounging close to the door. He looked up and suddenly his backbone turned to stone. He almost went for his rod, but couldn't quite make up his mind. Indecision trampled all over his face.

Sand reached out and stuck an index finger against the tip

of his nose and flicked it. The snap of cartilage was followed by a bellow of pain. He got his hands up there in time to catch the first gush of blood, but some of it spilled down on his suede shoes anyway.

"The game is called Freeze," Sand told the others before they had a chance to figure out what was going on. "You play it by standing very still. The first one who moves— becomes a stiff." He grinned to show them how glad he would be to blast them all to hell.

Then he walked across the room and knocked down the door of Paddy Clay's private office.

The girl was naked from the waist up. From the waist down she still wore garter belt and stockings. Some things never really go out of style. She was in the process of lying down on the couch. The door ripping loose from its hinges startled her a little, but she looked up without much concern, figured it as one more for the money and went on about her business, unfazed.

Paddy *was* fazed. He hadn't been expecting company. He was standing back of his desk in Jockey shorts and under-shirt with his gun ten feet away hanging on a coat tree. He started for it. He wasn't as young as the one outside. He made decisions faster.

"Three steps and you're out, Paddy. I'm going to give it to you high, about the third vertebra below the neck. I want to see if I can plug the hole with a half dollar."

The gang boss changed his mind. He turned around and smiled big like for the birdie. "Oh, it's you, Sand. Been a long time. You shouldn't ought of come slamming in here like that. For all I know, it could of been anybody."

"Like you said, Paddy, it has been a long time. I must have gotten in too much of a hurry. Old friends should see each other more often, don't you think?"

Sweat trickled down his face and ran down under his jaw-bone. One of his eyelids started jerking. "Yeah. Sure. Sure."

Paddy Clay was a rat. He handled the horses for the or-ganization, put in the fixes and made the payoffs. Right now he was scared spitless. Paddy always grinned when he was scared, and he was grinning plenty. They had started out in the rackets together, Sand going further and faster because he was smarter and tougher and in those days had a driving ambition to climb the pile. Paddy had seen him in action and knew how close a man could stand to death.

The broad on the couch spread her legs and looked at Paddy, but it was a wasted effort.

The door stayed open and outside in the big room everybody was still playing the game. Everybody but the one with the crooked nose. He was moaning softly, either about his nose or his suede shoes. They were both a mess.

Sand said, "A little conversation, Paddy."

His head bobbed up and down. "Sure. Sure. Only I don't . . ."

"About names."

"Names?"

"Names, Paddy. Too new in town to be in the phone book. One of them has a fondness for rifles and rooftops."

The scared grin got bigger and the sweat poured faster. His bony legs began to buck just a little and his complexion was turning a funny color.

"I . . . I don't know nothing about that, Sand. Honest, I . . ." He stopped because Sand's face had changed a little and it wasn't nice to see. It called him a liar and put flakes of ice in his blood. It reminded him of death.

"You know, Paddy. You make it a point to know. That's why I came straight to you."

The gang boss looked nervously out the open door at his men, his twitching eyelid going wild. "Maybe . . . maybe you can shut the door," he suggested. "More private. We can sit down and have a drink? For old times?"

Sand didn't move.

"Okay," he said. "Okay. Maybe I heard a word going around. Maybe the word said three guns from the West Coast, that somebody at the top remembers he don't like you and feels like attending a funeral."

"How did the word pronounce the names of this *bon voyage* crew?"

Paddy looked nervously out the door again. He was losing a lot of face. He didn't like to lose face. But he liked the thought of having it ripped off even less. "Rawlins is one, baldheaded, but wears a toupee that don't fit so good most of the time. One of the organization's top guns since Tracetta got it down in Mexico. The other two I don't know. Honest. All I know is it's Rawlins and two others."

"Where are they? I owe them a visit."

He shook his head hard. "I don't know. They could be a million places, but I don't know. Maybe they ain't even in town no more. It was last week that the word was going around."

Again Sand just stood and waited for the answer to come, letting him figure out who he was most afraid of, him or the Rawlins crowd.

It came.

"A beer joint called the Blue Grotto over on the west side somewhere." He realized his words were gushing and forced his voice back to normal. "Not much of a place. They got a couple of strippers that work out back of the bar. One of my boys spotted them in there a few nights ago. Maybe it's a regular hangout for them while they're in town or maybe it was a one-time deal, I don't know."

"Fine, Paddy. You're a real pal. Now I'll be going so you can get back to work."

The gang boss glanced over at the broad on the couch. He had forgotten about her. The spark was no longer there. Hell, his guts were tied in knots. It was all he could do just to stand up.

Sand walked out of the private office and across the room with the big board. Everybody was still playing the game. If anybody was itching to go for his rod, he was making a huge effort not to let it show. Busted nose had passed out. Real tough they were making them these days. Couldn't stand the sight of his own blood.

He hit a button beside the sliding door with the heel of his hand and the good-time sounds from the Playroom came rushing at him through the curtain. A girl squealed. She had either won something or been pinched. The Spartans hadn't run out of quarters. He pushed the curtain back and walked through to the other side.

Behind him Paddy Clay dropped limply in the chair behind his desk and stuck his head down between his skinny knees. His gut felt funny as hell and he thought he was going to throw up. In the room outside one hood squeezed a loud breath out between his lips and the others realized they had been sweating under their clothes. They felt very lucky to still be breathing. It didn't occur to any of them that he hadn't even pulled a gun, that all he had done was flick one finger. Except to the broad on the couch. She was wondering why everybody was so scared of the tall, handsome guy. But there was something she didn't quite understand.

The man was Sand.

SEVEN

T HE BARTENDER AT THE BLUE GROTTO drank too much of the stuff he pushed across the bar. He looked puffy. The stuff he pushed across the bar was mostly beer and you got it in a bottle because bottles don't have to be washed. A sign back of the bar gave notice the price went up two bits after dark because of the floorshow.

"We got a couple of beauties doing the show," the bartender confided. "One of 'em got tired of traveling the county fair circuit. The other is the kid sister of the boss's wife. Real talent. She wanted to be in show biz."

Sand slugged down part of a cold beer and asked him if his buddy Rawlins had been in today.

"Rawlins?"

"Yeah. They've been in town about a week from the coast. They told me they've been stopping in here for a few beers. Him and a couple of other guys."

The bartender thought about it, shook his head. "Can't place 'em."

"Wears a toupee. Has trouble sometime keeping the damn thing straight."

"Oh, that bunch. I don't remember if I ever heard his name or not. They don't ever come in this early, though. Always it's after dark. The little guy likes to watch the pieces peel."

"Don't suppose you know where they're staying. They told me, but it slips my mind."

"Nope. They don't talk much?"

Sand finished the beer. "Well, maybe I'll stop by a little later and catch them."

"Sure. You want me to tell 'em you was in?"

"No need. I'll catch up with them all right."

On the street Sand checked the tag of the key he had taken out of Fachman's pocket and caught a cab. "Northcrest hotel."

The Northcrest wasn't one of the giants you read about in the tourist literature, but it was big enough and luxurious enough. You got deep carpets and clean sheets with a rooftop pool and putting green in season.

Sand took the elevator up to the sixth floor and walked down the hall until he found the door marked 608. He stuck the key in the lock and twisted it open.

The redhead was a surprise. If he was right about Fachman, it didn't stand to reason he would be carrying that kind of baggage. She was watching television, stretched out on the carpet with pillows propping her up. She giggled as Yogi Bear told her how he was smarter than the average bear and it was a wonder the fuzzy fellow didn't faint.

Because when she giggled she rippled, and there was a lot of her to ripple—none of it covered. It was his day to find naked dames lying around.

She craned her neck around when she heard the door open and started to call, "I thought you would never get back—" Then she got surprised but not embarrassed. "Who are you?"

"I'm the manager. Somebody complained a guy had a movie star in his room up here."

She sat up and giggled again. Ripe breasts jiggled and flat tummy rippled and the TV set went on the blink. "*Darn!* It keeps doing that." She smiled for him. "I can't imagine why anyone would complain or anything. Besides, I'm not really a movie star. Are you putting me on?"

"Just a little. Fachman not back yet?"

She shook her head and cascading red hair played with the tops of creamy breasts. "No. He's been gone since early this morning. Maybe he ate himself. The way he's been growling and carrying on, it wouldn't surprise me none. You a friend of his?"

"We've met."

"I guess that's a pretty stupid question, especially since he gave you his key."

"Yeah. I was supposed to pick up something. My name is Sand."

"I'm Bonnie. He didn't say anything about anybody coming by."

"Probably he forgot."

"Yeah. The way he's been raving ever since I got here, you would think he doesn't appreciate me. Most men appreciate me."

"He was probably pretty shook up over the stuff that was stolen," Sand said.

"Yeah, that's what he was carrying on about. And when he was on his way to make the delivery, too. If it was so important why didn't he call the police, I asked him—but he just got madder and said he would find it himself."

He had found Sticky, only Sticky hadn't been the same.

Sand went past her into the bedroom. Everything was unpacked like Fachman hadn't expected to be leaving in a hurry. The redhead had gotten to her feet and followed him as far as the doorway. She didn't put on any clothes and he didn't see any for her to put on. Maybe Fachman had believed in keeping them penned up that way.

"You been friends with him long?" he asked her as he started pulling open the drawers of a dresser.

"He's no friend of mine. Snakes don't have friends. I'm in business. I got a bank account. Cash on the line."

"Fachman put the cash on the line?"

"Whew! He didn't even use the merchandise. He's got some kind of gripe against the world, that guy. You should hear him carry on. That's all he's interested in. A little cripple guy paid me for a whole week in advance and sent me up here. As a present, sort of, you know. He sure wasted his money. What are you doing, anyway?"

What he was doing was searching the place. He didn't know what he expected to find.

"I'm looking for the thing I'm supposed to pick up," he said.

"Seems like he would have told you where it was.

He kept searching. It wasn't a big job. Fachman had arrived with two suitcases plus the one Sticky had snatched, probably a lot smaller, like an attaché case. The two big ones were in the closet empty, the contents scattered around in various drawers. In the bathroom was the regular equipment and in the living room nothing that didn't belong to the hotel.

Except Bonnie. She was back watching the tail end of Yogi Bear. The only feminine apparel he had found in the place was a mink coat with matching handbag hanging in the closet. Except for her physical attributes, she was a girl who traveled light.

He was about to leave when the phone started to ring.

Sand and the girl looked at the jangling instrument like they had never seen one before.

"Who does he talk to on the phone?" Sand asked her.

She shook her head. "Nobody. This is the first time it's rung since I been here."

Sand picked it up. "Yes?"

The voice on the other end was small and nervous. "Mr. Fachman?"

"Yes?"

"My . . . my name is Steigman. George Steigman. I know, of course, that we were not to contact you, but . . ."

Sand's voice was stern. The man at the other end didn't expect him to be pleased with the call. "If you know, why are you doing it?"

"It's just that I—that is, all of us . . . we've been so upset. First the delivery not going off as arranged. And now—" The voice was scared. "Now we understand that it has already begun. We were wondering, all of us, when you are going to meet with the group."

Sand got the impression that if he said he was not going to meet with the group the voice would die of heart failure.

"Of course, it is your decision to make," the voice continued quickly. "But I'm sure you can understand our anxiety."

"I'm sure I do," Sand told him, "I've been busy. There were complications, as you know."

"Yes, yes. We were wondering if tonight—"

"Tonight will be fine. Pick me up here at my hotel."

"But I thought, the risk—"

"The risk is nil," he said harshly. "You people, let anything not go off exactly as mapped out and you all come to pieces at the seams. You will pick me up here at eight-thirty."

"Yes, yes, I will be there, of course."

Sand hung up the phone.

The red-headed Bonnie was looking at him with a funny look on her face. "What in the world was that all about?"

"I'm still trying to figure it out myself," he told her. But it didn't really take a lot of brainwork. If Fachman had brought the ingredients for some kind of biological attack into the country, he had to be bringing it to someone. Steigman and his group was a good bet. Only the delivery had never been made because Fachman was still searching for it when he was killed. Steigman and his friends knew they didn't have the stuff, and today they discover it has already been turned loose. Yeah, they were scared.

He lit a cigarette and stood there trying to put the pieces together. They fit, but they didn't form the whole picture. There were too many pieces missing.

Bonnie wasn't quite as dumb as she was naked. She said, "I think something strange is going on around here."

"The guy who brought you here, what was his name?"

"He didn't give me his name. Names are for checks, and a girl in business will never see a check that don't bounce. He was a little old man and cripple, like I told you. He wore some kind of gadget on his leg, but he still had a lot of trouble walking."

"Did he see Fachman?"

"No. I don't think he wanted to see him. As a matter of fact, he didn't actually bring me here. He just told me where to come."

Sand nodded. "Well, you can consider your tour of duty up. Fachman won't be coming home."

"Is that what the man on the phone said?"

"No. That's what the coroner said when they pronounced him dead on arrival at the morgue this morning."

"Are you sure?" She sounded hopeful.

"I put the bullets in him myself."

She said, "Oh, well," with a shrug and her breasts jiggled the way they were prone to do. She went into the bedroom and came back a moment later in her mink coat and carrying her matching handbag. On the way to the door she stopped and gave him a look that would make statues come alive in the park. "I've been paid for another couple of days," she mentioned, "and if you're going to be here . . ."

"Thanks, but I'm going to be pretty busy."

"Another woman?" She let the mink fall open to discourage the idea.

"With something that escaped from a nightmare."

She couldn't understand it, but she accepted it with a philosophical shrug and left.

For a long time after she was gone, Sand didn't move. He was still shuffling the pieces of information he had. Significant, Steigman knew about Sticky's death but not about Fachman. And if he didn't find out before tonight, he was going to be showing up at the hotel at eight-thirty.

Before then, there was a hell of a lot to do.

EIGHT

HE SAT IN A CAB parked across the street from his apartment hotel for thirty minutes before he climbed out and handed the puzzled driver enough cash for his trouble. There was no stake-out covering the building.

He crossed the street and picked up a paper in the lobby. Then he rode the elevator to the sixth floor and walked down two. The apartment hadn't changed any, except for showing the signs of Bev's visit.

He dropped the paper on the bar and poured himself a drink. He kicked it off quick and had another. Then he started scanning headlines. Sticky's unusual death was interesting, but it had been pushed into a small column in the bottom corner of the front page by a big day in international news. The world was a mess. Fachman's death wasn't mentioned at all. He started flipping pages and found it buried in the back. Flophouse killings don't usually hit the sheets at all, so the papers don't go rushing their reporters down there when it happens. The information was strictly off the police report. Victim, J. Fachman shot and killed, investigation ongoing. They even misspelled his name. Steigman had no reason to tie a shooting in a flophouse with either Fachman or the thing they had found in a dark room with the smell of rot.

He folded the paper and finished off the second drink.

The phone started to ring and he answered it, hoping it was Mohannah calling to tell him all was well and he could stop checking for swelling. No such luck, but it could have been worse.

The voice was female and carried sex around in a very businesslike manner. She said, "Mr. Sand?" and he saw blonde hair and the lush anatomy of a soft and warm Venus.

"You must have the largest clientele in the country, Dr.

Street."

"I'm afraid I don't understand."

"It's just as well."

"Captain Mohannah of the police told me where I might be able to reach you," she said. "He told me everything. As terrible as it seems, I . . . I think you could be right. I would like to help if I could."

"Convince the medical authorities," he suggested.

She laughed shortly on the other end, but without humor. "I'm afraid I'm not even able to convince myself. But I would like to talk with you about it."

"Where are you now?"

"My apartment." She gave him the address. "I'll be here the rest of the afternoon. Tonight is my night to go down to the Mission. If I knew what to ask I might be able to get some information. The men will talk to me where they wouldn't to the police."

She was right about that. Sticky had called her an angel. She was something special to the bums down there.

"Don't go away," he said. "I'll be there before you leave for the Mission. And something to think about. I was in pretty close contact with Sticky not long after he drank the stuff. For that matter, so were you and everyone who was in the Mission that night."

It was a chilling thought. "I'll be waiting for you," she said.

After he hung up, he went down to the parking lot and got his car. Then he went looking for a pawnbroker named Gruber.

~ ~ ~ ~ ~

The place was in the belly of skid row. Painted on the plate glass window was the legend *Gruber's Place*. And below: *Buy, Sell, Trade—Anything!* At night iron bars were placed across the windows.

Inside he did a big business in used clothes. One entire wall was covered with shelves loaded with shoes. Scattered over the rest of the place was practically everything imaginable, cameras, musical instruments and anything electric, all of it dusty.

Gruber himself looked a little dusty, like he stood still a lot. He wore the same stuff he sold and his glasses had been repaired with Scotch tape. He looked at the tall man with the strange face and saw money. He licked his thick lips and waited.

Sand took a look around the place. There were valises in all sizes and colors, but he didn't see one that fit his idea of what he was looking for. Behind the counter where the proprietor was standing were more filled shelves, most of the items with pawn tags on them.

"I've got this quirk," Sand told him.

"Yeah?" He had trouble adjusting to that. Somehow it didn't fit into anything.

"Yeah," Sand said. "When anybody tries to bullshit me I break things. Sometimes I break people."

"Yeah?" again. It still didn't make any sense, but already he could feel his day going downhill.

Sand nodded seriously, almost gravely. "For instance, if I were to go into a pawnshop and ask about a certain object brought in by a certain bum and I wasn't happy with what I heard—well, in a case like that, things could get pretty messy."

Gruber tried to swallow a lump in his throat—his Adam's apple. It bobbed, but it didn't go down.

"We understand each other?" Sand asked him.

"Yeah. Yeah." He got the message. He licked his lips again, this time not greedily.

"The bum's name was Sticky. And the item is a case of some kind. I want to see it."

Gruber didn't spend any time arguing. He got it. He tore the claim tag off and threw it on the floor as he brought it out of the back nervously and laid it on the counter. It was a leather attache case that matched the luggage he had found in Fachman's room.

Sand snapped it open.

Empty.

Clamps were built into the case to hold twelve small bottles securely, but the bottles were gone.

Was it empty when he brought it in?" Sand asked him.

He didn't want to answer that one.

"I'm no cop."

That made it different. "Was some bottles in it. Mouthwash, I think it was. Two rows of 'em, half with red labels and half with blue. Sticky has been working again, I figure. Must be he met up with a mouthwash salesman. Two-thirds of the stuff I take in is heisted, but how am I supposed to know that? I tell Sticky I can't take no case with mouthwash—somebody might ask didn't I know he wasn't no mouthwash salesman."

"So what did he do?"

"He stuck the bottles in a paper sack and gave me just the case."

"What happened to the bottles?"

"I don't know."

Sand handed him a ten. "Okay, I'll take the case."

Sight of the money made him greedy again. "It's worth twenty, maybe more."

"Remember my quirk, friend."

He grabbed the ten and buttoned his lip.

Sand took the case with him, wondering if Sticky had dumped the bag of bottles in one of the trash cans scattered up and down the street.

NINE

THE TAIL WAS WITH HIM when he left the pawnshop, a shiny new Buick. The car stood out like a new nickel in a smudge pot. The bums down here didn't ride around in new buggies.

It must have been behind him since he left his apartment. Which meant it must have been staked out after all. He checked the rearview mirror. One man.

Mob shooter after Sand?

Or one of the Steigman group thinking he was following Fachman?

Sand led the Buick around for fifteen minutes until he spotted an auto junkyard, half a block of banged-up rust buckets waiting to be stripped and crushed. At the next corner he made a quick turn and then another, speeding up to convince the tail he was trying to get away.

A couple more sharp turns and they were headed back toward the auto graveyard. The tires of the Buick squealed behind him. The guy back there hadn't had time to think about it yet, but he was no longer a tail. When the quarry runs, it comes natural to give chase.

Sand skidded the car in next to the curb on the wrong side of the street and jumped out, giving his best impression of a man running scared. He ran into the junkyard, the weeds pulling at the legs of his pants, stepping over shattered windshields and broken axles, skirting rumpled fenders and dead transmissions.

Behind him he heard the tortured tires of the Buick squealing to a stop and the door slamming.

The guy back there had taken the bait. He was in hot pursuit. He was about to make a name for himself. The man who got Sand.

Sand weaved in and out of the wrecked auto skeletons until he was too deep in the jumble to be seen from the street. Then he stopped and waited. He slipped the .45 out of his holster and kicked off the safety.

It didn't take long. The guy came in puffing like a steam engine. Hell, he didn't even have a rod in his hand.

Sand stuck a foot out at him and he went sailing through the air with the greatest of ease. He didn't land so easy, though. He did a belly flop on the ground and the wind swooshed out of him on the heels of a loud grunt.

He was a game boy. The realization hit him that he had been sucked in; it showed in his face, in his eyes. He got a knee under him and charged. Either he didn't see the .45 in Sand's hand or at the moment he just didn't give a damn. Sand stepped aside quick—too quick according to the pain that came up from the wound in his gut—and laid the .45 against the side of his head. The scalp split and red started to flow.

This time he didn't get up so fast.

If he was one of the West Coast boys, he wasn't Rawlins because his hair was real. The bartender at the Blue Grotto said one of them was a little guy. He wasn't that either. This one was big, and he looked mean and ready, even with the dirt and blood on his face.

Sand showed him the nose of the .45 and said, "Shuck your rod, friend."

He tried to shake his brain back into place. "I don't think I can move. I think maybe I'm paralyzed."

Sand thumbed back the hammer. "Do the best you can."

He stared at the automatic leveled between his eyes and found a way. He lifted a gun out of his belt with the tips of his fingers and dropped it on the ground. He was smart. He had fallen for a sucker play and got himself snarled up in an ambush, but now his thinking machine was working. The gun he had gotten rid of was Sand's .45. This one must have picked it up after the attack. With a little luck it might have worked, but Sand knew the gun too well, had lived with it too long.

Sand let it go, let the hood think he had pulled it off. He still had his rod. When he figured the time was right he would make a go for it. While he was waiting for his chance he might be inclined to talk.

"We'll start with your name," Sand told him.

"Hayes. Richie Hayes."

"You drive a fancy car, Richie."

"I like cars. Some guys, they like broads. Me, I like cars."

"You leave the broads to the little guy."

He got surprised, but he tried to keep it to himself, "I take 'em or leave 'em."

"And what about Rawlins? Which does he go for?

"I don't know no Rawlins."

"Big fellow with a toupee. Lousy shot with a rifle."

"He ain't so—" He nearly bit his tongue off.

"I'll tell him you thought he was a swell guy. When I see him. He'll probably wish you were still alive so he could thank you."

"You wouldn't shoot me down in cold blood!"

Sand laughed at him. It was a fitting sound in this dead place.

"There's no hurry," Sand said. "We've got time for you to tell me where your buddies hide out when they're not shooting at me."

"Not a chance."

No, probably not. The organization doesn't send out softies on the kind of mission Hayes had drawn. He could have been made to talk, but it would take time and Sand didn't have time. Besides, he knew where they would be sometime tonight.

"You ain't really going to blast me, are you?"

"This is no kid's game, pal. The stakes are high. You played and you lost. Think what you would do."

The hood thought—then he made a wild grab for the rod inside his coat.

In Sand's hand the .45 bucked and roared. The slug caught the hood in the middle of the chest and kicked him backward through the empty doorframe of a squatting wreck.

Sand stepped over and looked down at him. He wasn't going to get any deader.

He reached down, recovered his lost gun from the dirt and left the junkyard. Behind the wheel of his car, he took a slip of paper out of his pocket and studied the address on it. Then he tucked it back in his pocket and drove away.

The address fooled him. He didn't know what to expect, but he didn't expect what he got. It looked a good bit like a red barn, but a sign out front proclaimed it *The Drama Playhouse*. It was closed up tight at the moment but it appeared to be one of the many small theater groups that could be found scattered all over town, made up of amateur and semi-pro talent.

Nothing unusual.

Except that the address had been stuffed down in Fachman's wallet.

The rain that had been threatening all day began to fall. It beat at his windshield as he drove across town to Marilyn Street's apartment.

It was beginning to get dark. The panel clock told him he had a couple of hours before his meeting with Steigman.

He switched on the radio and listened to the news. Nothing about either Sticky or Fachman. He switched it off.

For a gal who spent her nights in a skid row mission, the blonde lady doc lived in pretty high style the rest of the time. A uniformed doorman took his car and saved him from getting wet and inside a smartly tailored desk clerk called upstairs to inform Dr. Street that she had a guest.

The guest was welcome.

He went up.

She opened the door with music playing softly behind her, adding an enchantment to the flowing white river of her hair, the smile that was more illusion than fact, the exquisite symmetry of her body beneath the pale negligee she wore.

Their eyes locked, the way they had in the Mission that first time. He had been a bum that night, but she had looked past the beard and seen the man. Now the look was the same and she saw the same man. She saw the toughness and the old hates, and she didn't dislike what she saw.

"I've been waiting," she said and led him into the room. It was big with a real fireplace for those chilly winter nights when the central heat went on the blink and a gleaming mahogany bar for any time.

"I was about to have a drink," she said. "Join me?"

"Make it something straight and tall."

The way she moved to the bar and behind it did something to him. Standing still she did something to him. Maybe it was the smile, or the thrusting breasts, or the way creamy flesh had a tendency to show through that pale wisp of smoke she was wearing. Or maybe it was just her.

She glided back to him and handed him his drink. Another look into those eyes and he knew he didn't have to tell her she did things to him. She knew. It was a two-way street.

They sipped.

"Captain Mohannah told me some interesting things about you today," she said. "I think he was trying to shock me. I haven't quite been able to figure out whether he is your best friend or your worst enemy."

Sand laughed at that. "Neither has he."

They sipped some more, their eyes playing more games that they both knew would lead somewhere if they let it. But first there was the unpleasant, the necessary. They held it off a little while because they both knew it was going to be all questions and no answers.

Finally, though, it had to come.

"Dr. Hendrix is right about it being some form of cancer," she said, "apparently affecting every organ of the body, external and internal. And he should be right about it not being contagious. But with something so radical . . . every possibility should be allowed for."

Sand told her what he had so far, which really boiled down to the missing bottles. Where were they? Did Sticky dump them in the trash or were they still around somewhere?

"Twelve bottles labeled or resembling mouthwash—half the labels red and half blue. Suggest anything?"

She nodded. "If someone were planning a biological attack there would have to be some way to be sure their own people weren't affected. There would have to be some kind of antidote."

"And the labels would distinguish the two," he finished.

"It becomes more plausible by the minute," she admitted.

They had another drink and kicked it around some more but it always came to a dead end.

Then the words ran out and the game with the eyes started again. He sat his glass down on the bar and took her into his arms.

Her lips were soft and warm and responsive under his.

TEN

"I KNEW THIS WAS GOING TO HAPPEN," she said. Her voice had a husky quality about it now. "It had to."

Her large breasts were cushions and her hips were a bed of hot coals that gradually began to move gently.

They let it grow.

Slowly.

Like flickering flames from the bed of coals.

She did something to the negligee and it slid gracefully to the floor, a slithering invitation all the way down. Underneath, there was only the creamy, vibrant flesh of the most beautiful creature in the universe.

Her breasts were high and full, the nipples pink and erect, tiny temples of desire reaching out for the feel of his hands. He touched each of them and then let his finger glide down across the soft firmness of her belly. Under the roving of his hand her flesh quivered slightly, as though there was too much electricity in the air.

"Are you going to be rough, Sand?" There was a jerk in her voice that came from the pulling of something inside her. "Do you take your women the way you live?"

He didn't answer. She didn't expect an answer.

He pulled her against him and tasted the hot moistness of her mouth, the hunger. The fire raged out of control. They were two animals caught up in an insane passion, each wanting to devour the other. Her lips parted and the flaming lance of her tongue searched for his soul.

A moan grew in her body and spilled out her throat. "Ohhh . . ." Then, "I don't care, Sand! I don't care if you take me rough! Take me any way! Just take—"

He carried her into the bedroom and watched the sharp contrast between the flowing milk of her body and the dark spread as she waited for him, her eyes urging him on now, faster, faster. Her lips liked the taste of his, every part of her craving the exploration of his hands.

"Ohhhh . . ."

The fire consumed them. There was no reason left. Reason would have told them this wasn't possible, that it was too much, but reason was lost in the heat of passion. They fond a peak and rode it.

"Sand! Sand! Oh, my God! I'm coming to pieces!!!"

They reached for that elusive something.

And together they found it.

It was a long time later that either of them spoke, and then only very softly, for no real reason at all. They smoked and breathed, and they were close. They'd had it and now they were holding onto it for as long as possible.

Finally, though, it had to end. All good things end.

She said, "You have to go, don't you?"

He glanced at his watch. "Soon." He didn't tell her where he was going. Probably he wasn't going anywhere. Probably Steigman had found out about Fachman by now and wouldn't even show up.

"You'll stop by the Mission later?" Her hair rested like silk against his shoulder and her breath touched his neck.

He blew smoke at the ceiling and thought of what he had to do. He said, "If I can."

~ ~ ~ ~ ~

On his way back to the Northcrest hotel to play Fachman he bought the latest edition of the paper and learned nothing had changed.

At the hotel he rode the elevator up and used his key. This time he used the button beside the door first. There was the possibility the police had already gotten here, in which case the whole action with Steigman would be shot.

No answer.

He used the key.

The place was empty and he could see Fachman's suitcases still in the bedroom where they had been earlier.

He looked at the blank television and the pillows still on the floor and missed the redhead. Yogi Bear was never going to be the same again.

Fachman hadn't kept any booze in his room. And he hadn't taken advantage of bountiful Bonnie. Maybe killing people in brand new ways was his only pleasure.

Sand smoked a cigarette and when it was finished he smoked another one. At eight-thirty on the nose the phone rang. Steigman was in the lobby.

He pulled the .45 from under his arm, checked it for action and slipped it back. He had no way of knowing what he was walking into. Then he picked up the attaché case he had brought up with him from the car. A final touch to put him in the role of Fachman. Inside, fitted into the clamps, was the spare automatic to give it weight.

As he stepped out of the elevator he spotted Steigman from Bonnie's description; a little guy with a sad face and a crooked leg supported by a brace.

The little man looked up and Sand saw funny things happen to his eyes. For a minute he figured it wasn't going to work, that Steigman either knew Fachman or had seen his picture, but then he realized what the little man's eyes were glued on was the case. The thing held a fierce fascination for him.

"Mr. Fachman?"

"Of course."

"I . . . I have my car outside."

Sand nodded and let him lead the way. He had a hard time walking with his cripple leg. Even more than usual because he kept trying to look back over his shoulder as though he thought the case might disappear if he took his eyes off it.

He was scared of Fachman, the way the insecure often are of a superior. That much was certain. But he was in love with the leather case. Maybe, like the real Fachman, his one thrill was the idea of spreading misery. Or the fear of getting caught in the middle of it.

"This is it," he said, pointing out his car parked by the

curb.

It was an old Dodge van with lettering on the side that read *Steigman's Tailor Shop*.

Sand kept his face blank and crawled in. Even though nobody seemed to know much about Fachman except his name, Fachman likely was supposed to know a good deal about Steigman and the others. That meant one slip of the tongue could give him away, or one question asked to which the real Fachman would have known the answer.

The rain had settled to a fine drizzle that kept the windshield messed up and defied the wipers. Steigman drove slowly and carefully, like a man who would never get a ticket. It was hard to imagine what a crippled tailor was doing mixed up in a thing like this.

"We are all very excited," the little man said nervously. "Of course—you can understand our anxiety."

"I can?"

"I mean, after days of waiting . . . Of course, we never doubted . . ." He couldn't seem to talk in sentences.

"I understand," Sand said, his tone implying what he understood about Steigman and his group wasn't entirely pleasant.

The little man swallowed something loudly. Then, after a few minutes of silence, he rounded up as much of his spine as he could and tried to say, "We're loyal, every one of us. We deserve . . ."

"And what do you deserve? I'm listening."

Now Steigman was really nervous. "I . . . I'm sorry. Please excuse me. It's just that we've been under such a strain. You understand, I hope." He wiped a shaky hand across his forehead. "A week in incubation, we were told— no longer. Less, even, if there is an abnormal amount of fatty tissue."

"I fail to see why you were worried," Sand said.

"Not worried," the little man lied quickly. "No . . . not worried . . . concerned. Yes, concerned. We are dedicated, but . . . concerned. Yes—we were concerned . . . that's all."

Sand made no reply. The silence could have meant anything.

The little man shriveled up a little. He didn't look like a man bent on taking over the world. He looked like what he was, a frightened little tailor with a bum leg. He said nothing else the rest of the way.

Sand lit a cigarette and looked out at the night through the greasy film of rain on the windshield.

ELEVEN

H E WASN'T REALLY SURPRISED when they stopped in front of a building that looked somewhat like a red barn with a sign out front reading *The Drama Playhouse*.

A nice cover for a terror cell. Nobody would question the frequent meetings. Maybe once in a while they even put on a play to make it look good.

Clever.

It explained the address being in Fachman's wallet.

It didn't explain why he was where he must have been when Sticky snatched the case. This place was a long way from skid row. According to Bonnie, he had said he was on his way to make the delivery when it happened.

The two men climbed out of the Dodge and Steigman hobbled up to the door and tapped out a signal.

A woman with a square body and sour face opened the door. Her eyes touched Sand's face briefly, then shifted to the case in his hand. Like Steigman, it fascinated her.

"Everyone is here?" Steigman asked.

"Yes."

There were eight or ten people in the large room, men and women, all of them straining to look at ease. Folding chairs were stacked against the walls and at the end of the room was a bare stage. A table had been set up and there was a punch bowl and sandwiches. A regular social gathering.

Steigman introduced the sour face, but Sand didn't catch the name. He made a sound that could have meant anything.

She said, "You don't know how happy we are . . ." and it trailed off. "Is something wrong, Mr. Fachman?"

He shook his head. "No," he said. "I just thought there would be more of you." But there was something wrong.

Fachman had the look of a hardcore pro. This bunch was clueless. They were copies of Steigman, little people with flawed bodies or flawed lives looking to take it out on the world. They were sheep. They were the herd.

"There should be more," the sour face was saying. "But recruiting was always difficult because of the discretion necessary." Suddenly her smile was one of pure evil. "Now, of course, things will change."

Sand let her take him around and introduce him to the others. Like a rather boring party, except that these people weren't bored. They were trying very hard to be nonchalant, but their eyes kept following the attaché case.

"Some date nut bread?" a mousy spinster introduced as Flora Roberts asked. He had already accepted a cup of punch as he made the rounds.

He shook off the date nut bread and had a cigarette instead. They kept up a string of meaningless small talk, the kind of things strangers say around a punch bowl. Nobody mentioned the case he carried, the one they were pretending not to stare at.

There was a guy named Hyde or Clyde with a big nose and a bad lisp when he tried to talk.

A middle-aged couple nursing a perpetual peeve at something, maybe everything.

Not much of a cell. Wimps. Joiners. Anything wannabes.

No posters on the wall proclaiming world domination. No photographs of a Glorious Leader. They would be somewhere but he didn't see them.

Butcher.

Baker.

Candy maker.

Followers all. Significance none.

The odd guy from next door or down the block, the one who reminds you of a whipped dog with his tail between his legs. At least he's got something going for him. Couple of times you've seen him going in that Drama Playhouse, place that looks like a barn. Little bastard's liable to have a couple of starlets tugging his line down there. Those types, you never can tell.

The mousy spinster, Miss Roberts, who teaches piano to your kids and seems like such a sweet person, but so withdrawn. What she needs is an outside interest. The Drama Playhouse? Really? How nice.

He had it tagged now. No hardcore terrorists here, no muscle boys or trained specialists. This was the herd, the flock of misfits and discontents that can be rallied to any cause, no matter how far out. These were the eyes and ears and scapegoats, not the hands or brains.

He drank his punch and watched them watching him and he knew something was cockeyed.

He had cornered a lamb and not a wolf.

"You sure everybody is here?" Sand asked Steigman.

"Of course. No one would dare be absent tonight . . . not *tonight.*"

A thought had begun to creep into his brain, a thought that made sense and also explained what Fachman was doing so far away from this place when he was supposed to be on his way to make his delivery.

Two deliveries!

This group would never be trusted with an important job. But they *would* have to be protected. No wonder they were so damn jumpy. It wasn't the weapon they were expecting— it was the *antidote*, the stuff that would keep the horror from engulfing them along with everybody else.

That was what they thought he had in the case!

He said, "Very good punch, Miss Roberts. You make it yourself?"

"Yes. Yes, I did. Thank you, Mr. Fachman." She tried to smile, but it didn't quite come off.

To the woman who had met them at the door: "This is a nice place. How many plays do you perform each year?"

Her sour face couldn't help wondering what he was doing talking about such things instead of the important thing, the thing they were all waiting for. "One usually. Always at least one. Nobody comes, but that's just as well, I guess."

"Nonsense." He gave her a small grin. "I'm sure the group

does a good job."

But nobody was really interested in his faith in their act-
ing talents. In fact, the more punch he sipped and the longer
it took him to get around to doing anything with the case in
his hand the more nervous the group got. He kept it up, the
guest of honor bearing up under a listless gathering. He
started looking down at his watch as though it would soon be
time for him to leave.

The third time he glanced down at his watch the atmosphere snapped under the strain. Somebody was bound to
crack. The room was filled with mental instability.

The mousy Miss Roberts was the weakest link. Suddenly
her face started breaking up and with a wild frail of her arm
she knocked a dozen cups off the table.

Everything froze.

Shock.

All eyes were on the spinster.

"Can't you see?" she screamed. "*Any of you?* Are you all
too stupid to see? He doesn't intend to give it to us! Why
didn't he come when he was supposed to? Why is he taunt-
ing us now? He isn't going to give it to us. We're all going to
die!" She fell to the floor, hysterical, *"We're all going to
die."*

For a long moment her whimpering was the only sound in
the room.

Sand was every bit a disgusted Fachman. "She is right,"
he told them curtly. "First there had to be the test. Weakness
will not be tolerated. It cannot be tolerated. This case is
empty."

Steigman nearly strangled. "You . . . you mean—"

"I mean that this one failed the test." He pointed a stiff
finger at the woman on the floor. "She has disgraced herself." Then he shifted gears and added a small smile. "I am
pleased to see that the rest of you have conducted yourselves
well. Miss Roberts' place in our group will need to be discussed at a later date. Perhaps under the circumstances al-
lowances can be made."

"But . . . but the—" Steigman tried to say.

"Delivery will be made tomorrow night," he told them. "Everyone will be here. Same time. There will be no refreshments. We have better things to do than conduct tea parties. Now you will drive me back to my hotel."

He turned and walked out. After a few steps he heard Steigman shuffling along behind him as fast as he could with his bum leg. A light murmur moved through the crowd, a mixture of disappointment and hope.

On the trip back to the hotel the little tailor was so nervous he missed three lights. He assured Sand of his loyalty over and over again. Like the scared little man he was, he pleaded nobody's case but his own.

At the hotel Sand climbed out and watched the van drive off before he entered lobby. Instead of going upstairs he climbed into a phone booth and put in a call to police headquarters. It didn't take him long to get Max Mohannah on the line.

"Sand! Where the holy hell have you been?"

"You're bellowing, Max."

"I've been trying to get in touch with you."

"Been on the move. A busy day. You can call your buddy Hendrix some dirty names for me. While the cops have been sitting on their cans I've been out turning over stones, and Hendrix is full of—"

"He knows what he's full of. We've got another case."

"The landlady at the building where Sticky was found," Sand guessed.

Max must have been smoking his cigar. He nearly swallowed it. "We just found her a hour ago. How did you—"

"She was fat. That speeds it up."

"Sounds weird to me, but the feds are flying in from all over to get a handle on this thing. One of the things they're going to want is you. You found the first body."

"And while they're trying to figure out what it is a lot of people are going to be dying, including me. There's an antidote, Max. Sticky had his own cure, but he didn't know it. If I'm lucky I just might find it in time."

"Officially, I'm telling you to stay put and get lots of

rest," the cop said, "That's what you tell sick people."

"Yeah, Max, that's what you tell them. Now I'll tell you where you can find a nice little cell of terrorists who will talk enough without much squeezing to maybe convince your authorities what they're up against. . . ."

TWELVE

SHE WALKED WITH A STRUT, a very sexy strut, with thrusting hips and thrusting breasts and long legs with heels so high it was a wonder she didn't topple over on her face. She bumped, she ground, and there wasn't much doubt there was a lot of female beneath the pile of veils she wore. To eliminate all doubt, she began slowly to peel them off.

The three-piece band played, the drums beating out the tempo.

One veil.

Two.

Bump!

Grind!

A drunk at the end of the bar yelled, "Take it off, baby. Let your old sugar daddy see."

She strutted toward the end of the bar. She was a girl who liked encouragement. She waved a veil in his face and gave him a bump that nearly dumped him off the stool.

The bartender had been right. She was a girl with talent.

The Blue Grotto was crowded with men and smoke and the steady noise of conversation being batted around. Except for the drunk at the end of the bar and a few others, nobody was paying a lot of attention to the stripper behind the bar right now. When the tempo of the drums got faster and the veils got fewer would be soon enough for them to perk up. The management liked it that way. They were selling booze, not tickets.

Sand found a warm stool at the bar and the same bartender who had been back there earlier pushed a bottle of beer at him.

"My pal Rawlins been in yet?" Sand asked him. "I don't

see him."

The bartender shook his head. "Nope. I ain't seen him to-night. The little guy was around though." He stood up on tip-toe and craned his neck. "Yeah, there he is—over there at the table in the corner."

"Sure is," Sand said. "Didn't recognize him sitting over there."

"Yeah," the bartender laughed. "When the girls are on you can't see nothing but his eyes."

Sand took his beer with him and walked over to the table. The hood didn't see him coming. All his attention was focused on the girl under the thinning veils. The bartender was right about his eyes.

Sand pulled out a chair and sat down. "Mind?"

His eyes didn't leave the gyrating girl. "Free country."

"You got a name?"

"Spivey. Joe Spivey. Only I don't see why—"

"Mine is Sand."

At first he didn't want to believe it. Then his head came around and he saw and he looked like he wanted to cry.

"Surprise." Sand grinned at him mirthlessly.

Spivey's hand reached for his coat.

Sand tapped the nose of the .45 against the bottom of the table.

The hand froze. Everything about the little hood froze. Even the stripper had lost her appeal.

"Lay your hands palms down on the table," Sand told him.

"You wouldn't blast me in here, all these people."

"It's your gamble."

He laid his hands on the table; slowly, but they got there.

"Smart."

"Now what?"

"Now we talk, Spivey."

"About what?"

"Your friend Rawlins."

He shook his head. "I got no friend with any name like that."

"That was what Richie said."

His eyelids barely twitched. "Richie who?"

"Your other pal from the coast."

He shook his head again. "I don't know a Richie either."

"You'll know him next time you see him. He's got a hole where his chest used to be."

"Richie's dead?"

"Died of exposure—all that air going through. Let's get back to Rawlins."

"Rawlins ain't going to like Richie getting it."

"That's only one of his problems. Come on."

Spivey didn't like the idea. He knew he wasn't going to get any safer than here. "Where we going?"

Sand said, "Your choice, friend. We're going to start walking. If we don't find your pal in fifteen minutes that last minute is going to be your last minute. Move."

The little hood got up like a man walking in his sleep. He moved through the crowd like a last stroll down death row, the nose of the .45 in Sand's hand following the curve of his spine.

Back of them the drums were going wild and the drunk at the end of the bar was beating his foot against the floor.

"Go, baby, go!"

Tough. Spivey was missing the finale.

Outside, the misting rain crawled over their faces and tried to get under their collars. The little hood turned to the right and started walking. Sand followed. With the hoods showing up at the Blue Grotto every night they were probably staying some place close by.

At the first alley they passed, Sand lifted Spivey's rod and stuck it in his left-hand pocket. A .357 Magnum. The little guy liked big holes.

The name of the hotel was The Clarkmore, a neon sign hanging on six or eight stories of pigeon spotted stone.

Like a good boy, Spivey led him inside and past the desk clerk. In fact, the little hood was being too good about it. He still had ten of his fifteen minutes to go. He was heading now for the elevator.

"Not that way," Sand told him. "The stairs."

"Why you want to do a thing like that? It's four floors up."

"I need the exercise."

Spivey said, "I always tried to figure out why you cut out on the organization and all that dough. Now I know. You're nuts in the head."

"Climb."

They climbed.

Four flights. Then down the hall.

Spivey stopped in front of a door. "We got a secret knock."

"Use it."

He rapped his knuckles against the door. Three and then one. Loud. After a few seconds he repeated it.

Sand nearly died thinking the hood was showing a lot of enthusiasm, considering the circumstances.

It was that neat. That professional. Little Spivey had acted too much like a punk, too much like a rookie with a big mouth and a small brain. He had put on a good act and Sand had gone for it. He hadn't pushed the assassin this far! He had been led all the way!

Only the dame spoiled it.

She opened her door. She looked right at Spivey and didn't know him from beans.

Sand heard the door open on the other side of the hall, the door behind him, and he knew he had been sucked in. Hell, it was the same dodge he had used to pull Richie into the auto graveyard, just a different twist. The code knock had brought Rawlins to the door all right, only Sand was at the wrong door.

But the dame opened the door, and he had that much warning, that split-second warning.

He did a backward dive, like going into water, swinging the .45 to his left as he went down. Behind him Rawlins was already triggering off his first round as his target moved. The slug caught Spivey in the small of his back and broke him in half.

The dame screamed, the sound mingling with the blast echoing up and down the hallway.

Sand's back hit the worn carpet hard as a second slug tore a hole in the floor a couple of inches from his head. He felt the sting of splinters digging into his cheek.

The .45 roared and bucked in his fist as he landed. A good shot if he had landed solid. But he didn't. He slid, throwing the shot a few inches wide. It caught Rawlins high in the shoulder and spun him deeper into the room.

Sand made it to his knees and put a couple of blind shots through the open door, forcing Rawlins still deeper inside.

He got to the door on his knees and stopped with his back against the wall. On the other side of the hall the dame was still standing there screaming at the top of her lungs while she tried to cram both fists in her mouth. Spivey was bent practically double at an impossible angle at her feet.

"Shut up," Sand told her.

She seemed to see the gun in his hand for the first time and realized what was going on. Her eyes kept getting wider until the lids nearly disappeared. Then she got some mobility in her muscles and slammed the door shut.

Now there was the silence that follows abrupt violence.

Inside the room, Sand could hear the man's ragged breathing. The slug in his shoulder hadn't taken him out, but it had brought him a world of worry.

One trouble with the situation, Sand decided. The hall was bright while the room was dark. As soon as he moved through the doorway he was going to be a target too big to miss. And he had to move. Time was not standing still.

He located the hall light and remedied the situation. He shot it out.

Then he moved into the room fast.

A lance of flame from the back of the room and Sand had him located. He hit the floor, rolled, got both elbows under him and turned loose a blast at the spot where the flame had been. Then he rolled back the way he had come.

Silence.

The neon sign in front of the hotel kept the room from being completely dark. It cast a thin line of pale light through the window and a short distance into the room.

Nothing moved.

Sand was flat on the floor, waiting for a faint rustle of sound, a sense of motion. On the other side of the room Rawlins would be doing the same thing, smothering the ragged edge of his breathing.

Sand felt something warm and sticky soaking his shirt. The old wound in his stomach had opened up.

His eyes were beginning to get used to the darkness. He could make out the vague outlines of several pieces of furniture on the other side of the room. Not so good. Rawlins' eyes would also be getting accustomed to the darkness. And Sand was in the open. A few minutes more and he would be an outline.

He remembered Spivey's Magnum in his pocket and reached for it with imperceptible slowness. It was the oldest trick in the book, but it was there for a reason. He lobbed the gun in the air and waited for the crash. It came.

Rawlins fired at the sound.

A flash.

Sand turned the .45 loose on it. The hood yelled as a slug mangled his guts. Another slug cut the sound off halfway out his throat.

And it was over.

He closed the door and switched on the overhead light. Rawlins was sprawled behind the overstuffed chair he had been using for cover. The .45 slugs had ripped the chair apart to get to him. His eyes had rolled back to point at his missing hairline. His toupee looked like something bloody trying to crawl off his head.

Sand was turning to leave when he caught his reflection in a mirror. His cheek was bleeding slightly from the splinters buried in it.

But that wasn't important.

What *was* important was that he was suddenly remembering another mirror he had looked into, and remembering that it had a cabinet behind it the way most bathrooms do over the lavatory. And he was remembering an old man who had offered a stranger a drink because he wasn't greedy.

Then he was stepping out of the room into the hallway and moving down it to the stairs, not noticing that the warm blood seeping from his middle had begun to soak through his coat. He had the other thing on his mind.

Half a dozen times on his way out of the hotel he was told excitedly that there was a ferocious gunfight happening upstairs.

He was halfway back to the Blue Grotto when squad cars began to pile up in front of the hotel.

THIRTEEN

HE EXPECTED HYMNS sung in whiskey-soaked voices. Searching for watery soup and straw sandwiches and maybe a little salvation on the side.

But skid row wasn't singing tonight.

"No service," a bum told him. "Place is dead tonight. Some kind of trouble. Civic league probably. Them civic leagues is always causing some kind of trouble."

The light was on inside the Mission, but the door was locked. He beat his fist against it until he heard Marilyn's voice inside.

"It's Sand," he told her through the door. "Open up."

She opened the door and let him in. As soon as it was closed behind him she came into his arms, the feel of her bringing back in a flood of memory everything she had been in his arms earlier. Her lips reached up for his, but almost immediately she pulled back with concern.

"Sand! You're hurt. The place in your side—and your face!"

"It's all right," he said. "Nothing serious."

Then she saw the case in his hand and everything about her got excited. "You found it?" She was already reaching for her bag, eager to start finding out what the stuff was all about.

"Not yet," he said. "It's empty."

The disappointment showed. "I was hoping . . . but I guess it was too much. I asked the men what you wanted me to. None of them could tell me anything. Reverend Garfield is out now trying to find a couple of men who were pretty close to the old man who died. They might know something, but I doubt it. I'm afraid I'm losing hope."

"Don't."

"You were right, you know. Captain Mohannah called a little while ago. Another case has been discovered."

"Well, don't give up—because I think I know where the stuff is."

"Where?"

"Right here." He was already moving past her, heading for the restroom where he had cleaned up one night that seemed a long, long time ago.

"But it couldn't be," she said. "There is no place—"

"Sure there is. It should have come to me before, but I was thinking of it as what it is. But to Sticky it was exactly what it looked like. To him it was mouthwash. And where do you keep mouthwash?"

He was in the restroom, the door open. He reached for the mirror above the lavatory and pulled. In the cabinet behind it there was a chipped glass with somebody's old toothbrush in it and a beat-up safety razor available to anybody who could borrow or bum a blade. And twelve neatly stacked bottles of mouthwash!

He heard the sharp intake of the girl's breath behind him as she saw the bottles.

He said, "This place was home to Sticky. Nobody throws away good mouthwash, and you don't store it under a bench in the park."

The girl was unsnapping her bag again as he turned back to her. She took the pistol out and pointed it at his heart. Her finger was firm against the trigger.

She smiled at him. "Thank you, Sand. I would have never found it in time. I was really worried that it was lost for good."

He hadn't suspected, but he looked at the gun in her hand and suddenly everything fit so neatly in place. All the lines came together to draw such a neat, ugly picture.

"*You* were the first delivery," he said.

She nodded. "Me. Only Fachman stupidly let an old man take it away from him. Years of planning. Years of effort. And he let an old derelict steal it. It is just as well you killed him, Sand. I can assure you he would have been dealt with harshly for his incompetence. Just as you must be dealt with for your competence. It is too bad you are not one of us. We could use a man of your particular talents."

"Killing me doesn't throw the calendar back five days," he told her. "It doesn't make Fachman more careful or Sticky less thirsty. It doesn't erase corpses or coroner's reports or send the feds home."

"Killing you gets me more time," she said. "It gets me time to contact my superiors, and it gets me all those pretty little bottles." She laughed shortly, and the laugh held a hint of the evil that her beautiful face hid so well. "That filthy old man might have done me a favor, you know. I am sure to be rewarded. None of the error was mine. I have spent years establishing myself, working hard, coming down to this horrible place every week to smile nicely at toothless old men who reek of filth and rotten whiskey. It was all part of the plan, you see."

He nodded. "I do see. I see it all. Would you like to hear about it, Marilyn? Would you like to hear how clever you are?"

"Yes, Sand, tell me how clever I am."

He told her. It wasn't hard to figure. He had gathered all the pieces. All he had to do was put them together.

"The charitable Dr. Street, the derelict's angel. As you said, you worked hard. Just as other warped minds were working in some hidden laboratory to create those little bottles of death. When everything was ready, somebody had to deal it out. This was the perfect place. You were the perfect person. Who would ever suspect an angel of mercy?

"Bums. Drunks. No family. Nobody to give a damn. Get it firmly started before the authorities get wise and there would be no stopping it. It probably took years to create the weapon, more years to perfect the antidote. It would take at least as long here. Except that no years would be available. The spread would be too rapid. Start it down here and in a month it would wipe out the city. Wipe out the city and you could dictate terms to the rest of the country. Hell, to the rest of the world. That is the way it was to work, wasn't it, Marilyn? The beautiful, charitable Dr. Street, sitting right here in this Mission feeding death to every bum willing to sing a hymn for a bowl of soup?

"That was the way it was supposed to work, but Fachman goofed and it got loose. That wasn't good. Everything could be ruined. It had to start fast. There could be no time for study, no time for our scientists to isolate the cause and begin a search for a cure. You got a stroke of luck when I called you after finding Sticky's body. No wonder you got there so fast. You had to. You put on a good act. Or was all of it an act? After all, you had never seen this stuff in action before. One thing I should have put my finger on but didn't. That shot you gave him, the one that turned out to be formaldehyde instead of adrenaline. The medical examiner considered it an excusable mistake under such extreme circumstances, though unfortunate because of the damage it did to the body. But he also pointed out that Sticky had been dead for hours. He recognized it at a glance. You would have, too. And you don't shoot adrenalin into a body that has been dead for half a day."

"I really thought I handled that very nicely," she said.

"Yeah, you're a real pro. You're right up there in the big leagues. You must have graduated top of your class in deceit. Like feeling around until you learned I was on the right track and then getting in touch with me to offer your helping hand. And your body. You had every intention of finding the stuff if you could. But in case I beat you to it you wanted to be around when I did."

She smiled again, pleased with herself. "And I was. Here I am. Pretty smart, aren't I, Sand?"

"Not smart enough not to recognize Fachman's attaché case when I came in here. Aside from being his carrier, it must also have been his identification. A small group of misfits recruited to the cause and waiting for their antidote— they recognized it. It was all the calling card needed to walk right in and sip punch with the group. Of course they had no part in the action. But every team needs a cheering section. The work was left up to the hardcore crew, the pros like you and Fachman."

The gun in her hand was still trained on his chest. It hadn't wavered an inch. It was a snub-nosed .32 revolver, one of the lightweight models. For power it didn't compare with its bigger brothers, but this was a girl who would know just where to put that first shot.

"Now do you want me to tell you what I'm going to do, Sand? Besides kill you, I mean. Which is something I really don't want to do. We were so good together in bed."

"It's your turn," he said.

"Actually, I will act on orders from higher up, but I know what those orders will be. Now that Fachman's mistake has been overcome, nothing is changed. Not really. The authorities will get into the picture a little sooner than originally anticipated. The end result will be the same. In a few months we will agree to accept the unconditional surrender of the United States. The other countries will follow."

He didn't believe it. But she did, and the people she worked for did, and a lot of people would die.

"I have to shoot you now," she said with just a hint of regret. "I've already got my story ready for the police about how it happened. You can thank your friend Captain Mohannah for giving me the idea, telling me all about you this afternoon. Everybody wants to kill you it seems. I'll simply have to tell them somebody did. A tall man with a mustache maybe. That will sound good."

The funny part of it was, she would probably get away with it.

She smiled at him again. "Goodbye, Sand."

Her finger was tightening on the trigger when the knocking started at the door and the Reverend called to her to let him in. Maybe God *does* work in mysterious ways.

Sand threw the case. The case that brought the bottles. The case that started it all. It hit the hand holding the pistol and knocked it to the side. The shot went wild but she held onto the gun, swung it back. Her eyes got wide, puzzled. She really couldn't believe she was looking down the barrel of the .45.

Sand said, "You lose, Marilyn."
But the roar covered up the sound of his voice.

CON'S WIFE

Ennis Willie. Now there's a name to conjure with. Conjure what? Why, visions of a time just past, when spinning drugstore racks and newsstands held more than a handful of books and stories that were, as those same magazines said, "the kind men like," stories whose protagonists were direct descendants of Race Williams, Two-Gun Terry Mack, and Mike Hammer. These were the Tough Guys, and Ennis Willie's Sand was one of the last of them. In "Con's Wife," Sand demonstrates all the qualities that readers had come to expect. He's an outsider, but loyal to his friends (even when they're dead), and he's remorseless when seeking revenge: "Sand was now part of the story, part of the outcome. For somebody this was not going to end well." When an ex-con is murdered for money that he doesn't even have, Sand deals out his own kind of justice. Mike Hammer would understand.

Bill Crider

H E HAD THREE EYES. They were round holes that stared blindly up at the black night while the smelly fog hanging close to the alley floor swam in them. The third eye was in the middle of his forehead, small and black–like a bullet would make going in.

The man looking down at the body was known as Sand, a man built of cold eyes and old hatreds, a man of many enemies and few friends. Dead bodies to him, like the medics and cops standing around him, had long since become routine. His face was a mask showing no emotion, but he was remembering again the phone call and the urgent tone in the voice of Buddy Padula just hours ago.

"I need your help, Sand. I know I don't deserve it, but I need it. I need somebody with muscle. I'm out of my league. It's Valerie. I . . . I can't handle it myself . . . an ex-con just out of stir. Maybe we could meet?"

Yeah, they could meet. But he never made it.

"Small caliber, close range," Max Mohannah said. Max was a big boned cop going pudgy from spending more and more time behind a desk as he rose in rank. They had come close to being friends a couple of times, these two, but that was a wide street to cross. "What's your connection with him, Sand?"

Sand straightened up. He was tall, with a cat-like smoothness of motion that some found disturbing, or frightening, depending on who's what. He lit a cigarette and offered one to the homicide captain. "No connection, Max. Just a kid I knew once."

Max got a look on his face. "Sure, that's good enough for homicide, but don't count on everybody downtown rolling over to purr. He was robbery detail's only lead to the eight hundred grand he stole and stashed before they tagged him and tucked him away in the pen. They've been waiting and watching for him to pick it up. You don't think the only reason he was on the street so soon is good behavior, do you? Anyway, he won't be picking up any missing cash now."

"Maybe there was no money for him to pick up, Max. He claimed it wasn't his job."

"Yeah, a bum rap." Sarcasm crawled across his face. "He worked for Pillman Industrial at the time they were looted, with reasonable access to the dough. Add a few reams of circumstantial evidence. Throw in his previous record. Plus he couldn't come up with any alibi. It should happen to them all. Even his wife couldn't furnish him with one because she was out with friends the night it happened. He was guilty as sin. He went to the pen knowing the dough would be waiting for him when he came out—and not a bad payday."

Sand didn't argue. Maybe the Pillman job had belonged to

Buddy Padula, maybe not. Something else had been digging into him when he called. Now he was dead, shot between the eyes on his way to meet with the great Sand. This was a story that would travel. Sand was now part of the story, part of the outcome. For somebody this was not going to end well.

"Any witnesses, Max?"

"Sure, dame saw a man in coat and hat hurrying this way just before the shot was fired. Not Padula, because he's not wearing either. Nothing else except that the hurrying hat wasn't very tall." He lifted a sheet on his notepad to see if there was more, then flipped the sheet back down.

The white coats loaded the body in a van, mumbled something to the police captain, and went screaming off with it. Then the cops left and he was alone.

He stopped in a bar on the corner and ordered a beer from a slob in a dirty apron. Buddy's apartment was only a block away, but he wanted to give the cops time to do their stuff. Besides, it gave him a little time to think.

He hadn't seen Buddy Padula in the five years since he married Valerie, a beautiful young girl from the world outside, the world that knew about crime and corruption only as much as you can see from a distance. Buddy had picked up a small-time record and was a mobster wannabe. It was Sand who told him it wasn't a good idea, the same Sand who split with the mob a couple of years later and now used the .45 tucked under his arm to keep on living long after the odds had lapsed. Buddy had promised to go straight. Less than a year later he was in the pen for the Pillman score and Valerie was doing four years in their third floor walk-up.

Credit where credit is due—Valerie had waited. A few weeks ago her husband got out on parole. Now he was dead with a bullet in his head.

Sand dropped a bill on the bar and raked in his change.

~ ~ ~ ~ ~

The building with the Padula apartment was sliding downhill

with the rest of the neighborhood. If Buddy had eight hundred grand he wasn't flaunting it.

Valerie Padula was still beautiful. It was a beauty that didn't come off a cosmetic counter or dull under the burden of being a con's wife. The slacks and loose blouse didn't hide the perfect fullness of her figure, and the eyes already red from crying only softened the loveliness of her face.

She took one look at him and ran back into the apartment.

A moment later she came at him with a knife!

It's difficult to defend against a knife attack with bare hands but in Valerie Padula's case Sand chose not to knock her over the head with his gun barrel. She was a woman shaken and stunned by the death of her husband. He tried to take it away from her without hurting her, but she wouldn't have it that way. He twisted her arm up behind her back and pulled her tight against him. Her breasts struggled against his chest, and he could feel the frantic racing of her heart as she fought.

He lifted the arm higher behind her back and his fingers laced around her wrist began to squeeze until she gave a short cry of pain and dropped the knife.

He let her go and there was a minute when she almost grabbed up the knife again. Then a dam inside her broke and words and tears began to spill out. "You killed him!" she screamed. "You did it. You and all the others. Murderers and thieves. He could have been decent! He could have been . . . if everybody had just left him alone." She tried to get a grip on herself. The hysterical quality of her voice settled into a bitterness.

"I suppose you want the money too. Everybody wants the money. Everybody wants it and nobody will believe there *is* no money because Buddy was innocent. No matter how many times he told them, nobody would believe it."

"He called me earlier." Sand said. "Do you know anything about the call, what he wanted to talk about?"

"What difference does it make? He's dead now."

"Listen to me. He asked for my help. Alive or dead doesn't have anything to do with it. Not with me."

Her eyes swept up and down the dingy hall. She didn't try to hide the resentment and anger he saw there. "Let's go inside the apartment. The walls in this place have ears, and this hallway is like an echo tunnel. There's a head pressed against every door you can see right now. Inside isn't much better, but I guess it has more decorum."

Inside the apartment with the door closed he asked the question again. While she hesitated his glance took in the apartment. About what he expected, but certainly not what she had expected on that happy day five years ago.

"Okay," she said. "Everybody in the building already knows. We had an argument about it just before he left. I guess it was when he left to meet you, if everything the police told me is right."

"What was the argument about? He wanted to talk about you. Start there."

It took another minute, but she nodded, weakly at first and then resolutely. "Yes. I . . . I told him not to, that things would work out. But he wouldn't listen. Oh, *God*, and now they have murdered him."

"I have to know specifics, Valerie. I need names. I need to know who, what, everything. I have to move quickly, before I start stumbling over the police and the rats have time to hide. Do you understand me?"

She nodded again. "Yes, I understand. I denied it at first. I told him not to listen to rumors. I thought it would stop once he got home but then it didn't." She seemed to be talking to herself. "Mr. Derkson wouldn't have killed him. Maybe one of the others, but not—"

"Who is Derkson?"

"Buddy's parole officer. That was why Buddy called. Mr. Derkson . . . made several passes at me. He told me I would be wise to do what he wanted me to, because if I didn't he could send Buddy back to prison. The last time, he nearly forced me to the bed. Each time he got more aggressive—I think because he knew I had kept quiet about the times before. So tonight I had to tell Buddy, before it went any further. He called you because you know people in high places.

He knew if he tried to do anything to Mr. Derkson himself he would just end up back in prison."

"That's one name," Sand said. "Who are the others?"

"There was a man named Haggard. He talked to Buddy twice and the last time Buddy seemed kind of scared when he left. Then there was a woman. On the telephone. Buddy called her Viv, I think. He never let me get involved, but it was always about the money—the money nobody would believe he had never seen."

Haggard was a local goon, a low-level muscle who at one time or another had taken orders from most of the racket bosses. The name of the dame could fit any of a thousand broads. But Buddy had been out of circulation for years, and with a wife like Valerie Padula at home he wouldn't have been chasing, so the name probably came from somewhere way back.

"More names," he said. "The more I have the faster I can move."

"That's all the names. I think there were more, but I never heard them."

He nodded and turned toward the door.

"What are you going to do?" she asked. The dislike for him was still in her voice, but it was crowded now by curiosity.

He said, "Somebody killed a friend of mine."

What more was there to say?

There was a thing that came into her face, like maybe she was remembering some of the stories about this strange man with the deadly eyes, or suddenly seeing a glimpse of the man behind the emotionless face. She seemed to shiver a little.

~ ~ ~ ~ ~

Derkson lived in a first floor front apartment in a brownstone that hadn't yet begun to crumble. He wasn't home.

"Went out earlier today," the landlady told him. "Hasn't come back yet."

"You know if he owns a gun?" Sand asked.

She got a kick out of that. "Mr. Derkson? Why in the world would he have a gun? He wouldn't hurt nobody. A nice man, Mr. Derkson."

Haggard was next. The trail led through half a dozen bars and a noisy pool hall, with enough time between each to knock off Buddy Padula if it were on the agenda.

"Nope, Haggard left out awhile ago," a lumpy cashier at the pool hall told him. "Said something about saving a few bucks for Mary-Janice."

"What is a Mary-Janice?"

"Mary-Janice Williams. She's a hooker. Got a pad just down the street."

She had a pad and inside she was giggling like crazy while she kept telling "Haggy" how he should take his time and not rip nothing.

Sand kicked the flimsy door open and the giggles disappeared under the louder sound of splitting wood. The bottle blonde's eyes got wide and quick hands reached for a thin slip to cover up what her boy friend had paid for.

Haggard, long and full of big bones, got untangled from the broad, his wide nose flaring, and went for the rod inside his coat.

Sand took him quick and easy. He smashed his nose and drove a fist in hard just under his rib cage. Beer breath made a sickly sound coming out his throat. He took the gun out of the hood's hand and held it in position to slap it against the side of his head.

"While you still have your teeth, Haggard, give me the story on Buddy Padula."

"I didn't blast him," he wheezed. "I got the word already, but I didn't have nothing to do with it."

"You were bugging him about the dough from the Pillman job."

He shook his head hard. "Not about the dough. He was nosing around since he got out of stir, asking a lot of questions. The word was he shouldn't stir the pot. I give it to him, twice I give it to him. But I didn't blast him."

"You're on a salary, Haggard. Who paid it?"

"I can't—"

"Say good-bye to your teeth."

"Okay. Okay. Wilson, Delmer Wilson. He come a long way from the west side, but he's got his fingers in a lot of pies. He paid me for a piece of work and I done it. Far as I know, he didn't want Padula rubbed. He just wanted him quiet."

Sand snapped the clip out of the butt of the hood's gun, jacked the shell out of the chamber and tossed all of it on the bed. The dame was still standing there with her slip in her hands, a frozen statue with two shades of hair and thighs just beginning to run to fat.

"Have a nice day," Sand said.

Sand knew Delmer Wilson by reputation, a tough punk from the west side who had made good and gone to a lot of trouble to smooth out his rough edges. Occasionally you caught a reflection of Wilson and a stunning wife staring up from the society pages, but he still kept an army of goons hanging around his penthouse apartment headquarters.

One of the hoods had nice pearly teeth. He liked to smile and show them off. He smiled. He said, "Mr. Wilson isn't seeing–" And then his mouth was just a bloody gash and teeth were falling like rain all over the foyer.

Pearly had a buddy. Buddy got his Adam's apple nearly sliced in half. He piled on top of his toothless friend. Sand stepped over them and went through the door they had been guarding.

Wilson sat behind his desk with a grin on his handsome kisser. "I've been expecting you, Sand," Haggard called. "I didn't really expect those two outside to stop you. That's why I arranged to have a gun trained on your back."

It was the hood's clever move of the day. There was a curtain behind Sand and if there was a gun back there that was the only place it could be. He heard something move and knew he was right. It gave him a fraction of a second while the gun was coming through the curtain. In that fraction of a second the .45 jumped from its holster to Sand's hand almost of its own accord and was staring Wilson right between the eyes. Fast. So fast the guy behind him made a surprised squawk in his throat and Wilson nearly ripped his tonsils out yelling at his man not to shoot.

A standoff. But Sand had the edge; he had walked with death and he had talked with death and fear of death had turned to scorn. Wilson saw it and he was scared.

"Let's talk about Buddy," Sand told him.

"I didn't bump him. We were pals from the old days. We come up in the same neighborhood."

"You came further."

"I was smarter. Buddy was always trying to reform, to be a square. You can't make it once you ever touch a dishonest buck. They never let you."

"That what you sent Haggard around to tell him?"

"The message was he should stay out of my territory. Wherever he went you could count on cops. They had him on the end of a string, counting on him to lead them to the Pillman dough. Cops are bad for business. Twice I had to send the message, but he wasn't important enough for me to have him smeared."

It made sense, but if Wilson were going to lie he would come up with one that made sense.

Sand gave him a smile that wasn't a smile at all, and the hood behind the desk turned a little green.

He started backing toward the door. The guy with the gun just stood there waiting for orders and hoping like hell he didn't get any.

His hand on the knob, Sand gave him the word. "If I have to come back, Wilson, I'll break you and your whole setup into pieces small enough to flush."

He stepped over the two hoods pretending to be asleep in the foyer and went to the elevator.

The blonde was waiting for him downstairs, a stunning creature built of flowing lines and sleek contours. She was one of those broads who walk around naked no matter how much clothes they have on. When a man looked at her he saw soft light and pale flesh with shadows and peaks and satin electricity.

"My name is Vivian Wilson," she said. "I heard you talking to my husband."

Valerie had said a woman Buddy called Viv.

"It's terrible about Buddy," she said, and meant it.

He took her arm and led her outside. He whistled down a cab and told the driver to do a slow one around the block.

"Tell me about it," he said to the girl.

"You mean about me calling Buddy to meet me, I guess. Actually, it starts a lot further back. We all grew up together, Delmer, Buddy and I. Only in those days it was me and Buddy who were sweethearts and Delmer was just another kid on the block." Her beautiful face got a little wistful. "We even had our own special place. We called it our hideout. The tallest chimney on the tallest building on Gentry Street. Funny how things stick with you even after you grow up. When I called Buddy and told him I wanted to talk to him, it was the first time I had thought of the hideout in years."

"What was your message? That your husband was after the dough?"

"Delmer wasn't looking for the money, Mr. Sand. Buddy was the one looking for it."

"Keep talking."

"All I know is that Buddy was already working for Pillman Industries when we broke up. He talked a lot about his work. He got married. I got married. And Delmer was always very interested in things Buddy had told me about the company. It was odd I always thought, because Delmer is very jealous. He would like to think he is the only man there has ever been in my life."

"Your message to Padula?"

"That he should go away, as far away as he could. He was no match for Delmer, not before he went to prison and especially not now."

The cab was back in front of the hotel. Sand silently opened the door and let her out.

~ ~ ~ ~ ~

Back to the brownstone and the first floor front apartment. This time Derkson was home. The lights were on.

Sand used his knuckles and waited. Nothing. The parole officer wasn't answering his door.

He forced it open.

It was easy enough to see why Derkson wasn't answering his door. He was face down in the middle of the floor with two small holes between his shoulder blades.

In a corner of the room a fire was burning. As he looked at it, it licked up at the curtains of the closest window, flame skittering up the length of the material like a frightened snake. The fire had been built with the covers off the bed piled in the corner. A couple of minutes later, and there would have been nothing left here to find but one big bonfire covering up a murder.

He snatched the burning curtain down and dropped it on top of the spreading fire. Then he took the mattress from the bed and used it to smother the flames.

Derkson should have been dead, but he groaned weakly when Sand rolled him over. He had expected a younger man. He was gray, everything about him, his hair, his face. His breathing was too ragged to last long.

"Who got you?" Sand asked him.

But the only answer was a death rattle.

Sand cursed. Derkson wouldn't be doing any talking. He pushed the lids down over the gray man's lifeless eyes and began a search of the room.

The dead man's pockets turned up nothing interesting, and neither did the rest of the, room. Except for a note pad beside the phone. Apparently Derkson had a habit of jotting down reminders to himself. The pad said he had been due at a prison fifty miles away at four-thirty in the afternoon to take part in a full-scale tour. Sand went back to the stuff he had taken from the parole officer's pockets and came up with the stub of a round trip ticket. A call to the bus station got him the schedule and proved Derkson arrived back in town about thirty minutes before he got home and caught two slugs in the back.

He got out of the room with its corpse and smoke and pungent smell of burning. He left the door open so the dead man would be discovered sooner than later.

Put the pieces together and if they fit the picture is there. That was the way it usually worked. But not always. Sometimes it took that piece that didn't fit worth a damn.

~ ~ ~ ~ ~

It was the tallest building on Gentry Street. A lot of stairs and a wide flat roof. The tallest chimney on the tallest building on Gentry Street. And a killer minutes ahead of him.

He saw the figure bent there at the chimney, saw the hat and coat the witness had described to the police, and heard the scraping of nails as frantic hands searched for what they had killed for.

He said, "Give it up, Valerie. It isn't there. It never was."

Yeah, his wife, dressed up in the hat and coat Buddy had left behind tonight when he rushed out of the apartment. The hat and coat Valerie Padula had slipped into when she went after him. When Buddy turned around he probably thought how comical she looked bringing them to him. He was probably still thinking it when she shot him in the head.

She was on her feet now, and he could see her eyes shining in the dark like those of a cat. That was the way she had come to her feet when she heard her name, quick, like a surprised cat.

"Sand, I can—"

"Explain, Valerie?" He laughed at her there in the darkness, a sound without humor. "No explanation is necessary. You were like everybody else, you wanted the money. Sure, you waited on Buddy those years he was in prison—the beautiful young wife from the decent side of humanity who would stand with her husband no matter what he had done. You waited—but somewhere along the line it became the money and not your husband you were waiting for.

"But after he came out of prison there was still no money.

You wanted him to pick it up. You could smell it, taste it. You had to get your hands on it before one of the other jackals did. So tonight you pushed him with that lie about Derkson wanting you and threatening to throw him back in the pen. Only you went further. You threw in an alternative on the money. You insisted on knowing where the money was in case something happened. And this time he was in too big a hurry to argue, so he gave you a place. The place he would come up with on the spur of the moment. Then he called me and you saw how easy your lie could come apart, how easy it could be to lose the money when you were so close to it. He had gone less than a block when you left the apartment behind him. That was how long it took you to decide which you wanted most, your husband or the money you thought he had stolen."

He pretended he didn't see her slowly reaching for the gun in her pocket, the gun she had used to kill twice.

"You would have come here after the money before now, but first you had to correct a mistake. You were a little flustered when I showed up. You had to give me some kind of story and the only one you could come up with was the line about Derkson you had given Buddy. As soon as I left, you knew it was a mistake that would have to be corrected. The parole officer hadn't been making passes or threats. You had to make sure he didn't get a chance to make any denials. It almost worked. But there was a matter of ticket stubs and a prison fifty miles away. You had to be lying about Derkson because he wasn't even in town. It made you the killer, Valerie."

Her hand was nearly touching the gun now, but he had one more thing to say, the irony of it all. "Buddy was a patsy, Valerie. He never had the money. But nobody would believe him. You said it. Not even his own wife."

Her hand dipped and the gun came up! Sand shot her once below the navel.

Funny the way a .45 slug works sometime. Shoot a heavy man in the arm and knock him sprawling. But she didn't go down. The impact slammed her back maybe a dozen feet, but she was still standing, shock and incredulity spread out on her face. Learning what it was like on this side of the line. She tried to lift the gun. The second blast knocked her back again, but still she didn't go down. They were close to the edge of the roof now. The third time he pulled the trigger she disappeared.

FLESH HOUSE

I read my first Ennis Willie and my first "Sand Shocker" way back in the 60s. Not my last, though. I've consumed the others, all except a couple of elusive titles, in the years since. Willie is addictive in the same way and for the same reasons that Spillane and Peter Rabe are addictive. Sand is something of a cross between Mike Hammer and Daniel Port, in fact, and he can hold his own with both of them in a brawl or a shootout or a bedroom. Hard, man, hard.

The Sand novels may be short, but they're packed with action, incident, surprises. The same is true of "Flesh House"; there is enough material here for development into a full-length book. And like the novels, it moves at lightning speed. You'll never read a faster—or harder—4000 words anywhere.

Bill Pronzini

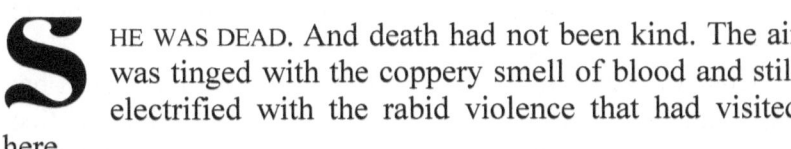HE WAS DEAD. And death had not been kind. The air was tinged with the coppery smell of blood and still electrified with the rabid violence that had visited here.

The fat man looking down at the body was Max Mohannah, captain of homicide. He took the bad-tasting stub of what had been a good cigar from his mouth, stared at it with a disgusted expression and shoved it back between his teeth. He turned to watch the tall man cross the brothel's large parlor and enter the small room with the murdered madam and half a dozen busy lab men.

His name was Sand. He was not a likeable man, not by anybody's standards. He was tough and he was hard, and he had once used those qualities to fight his way nearly to the top of a national crime organization. Then he had quit when the stink and corruption got too strong. Now he used these same qualities to stay alive. Nobody quits the organization and lives—it was like a slogan. They had sent their gunnies after him and he had chopped them up and sent back the pieces. But there would always be more. The line of killers is long—and the pay is good.

Max took the cigar stub from his mouth again. "She was still alive when the squad boys arrived," he told Sand. "She asked for you several times—kept on asking. It was all they were able to get out of her before she died." He shrugged. "So here you are."

They were not friends, these two—the gap between them was too wide. But they knew each other well.

Sand looked down at what was left of Mopsie Steiner after the knife was through. Flesh had been her stock in trade, but she had been human. A person. Even a loyal and kind person. He had to suppose she had been a lot of things to a lot of people, but to him she had been something good.

"Looks like a joy kill," the detective captain said. "Some guy who gets his kicks with a blade. Stabbed repeatedly, but none of the wounds appear to be more than an inch deep. Must be a hundred of them and still she was alive when we got here. This took a long time. She certainly had enough time to recognize the killer."

That was the way it looked, but that wasn't the way it had happened. This had been the brothel madam's private office. Nobody came in unless they were invited, and Mopsie had been in the business too long not to spot a weirdo a mile away. Why the knife? Why the shallow stab wounds? Sand didn't understand what he saw. He didn't understand the knife. He didn't understand the rage.

"She has a son," Sand said. "Only relative, far as I know, but I don't think he's been around since she sent him off to college years ago."

"We'll find him," Max said. "You got any idea why she asked for you? Same amount of energy and she could have described the killer, maybe even given us his name."

Sand shook his head. He didn't know. It would be a thing to find out. "What about the girls she had working here?"

"It was a woman who called in, probably the first to arrive for work. They'll be in the process of scattering now. None of them will want a part in a thing like this." He stopped as Sand turned to the door. "You going already?"

"Things to do."

"Sure you do," Max said.

Sand turned to go again, but Max wasn't through.

"You want to know why I think she wanted you here, Sand?" the police captain said. "You. Not the police. Not a priest. You. It was because the police, assuming we ever catch the person who did this—what does she get out of it? Justice? Revenge? Closure? This was personal. She new the person murdering her. She could have given us a name. But she didn't want the police catching him and tucking him away in a cell, and she didn't want the police getting in the way. She figured you don't need a name. You'll find a name. She has given you a mission, and what I saw in your face when you turned to go was a man on a mission.

"I know from years of watching that you don't take orders from anybody. Isn't that what your whole life has been about? I don't know what Mopsie Steiner did for you or when, but I think this is payback time. She knew you would figure out what needed to be done. And she knew you would *do* what needed to be done. I might not like you or much that you've ever done, but one day we have to sit down over a cold beer and you tell me what this woman did for you that she knew she could talk to you from the grave."

"That's a lot of words, Max, for a man who lives by the grunt."

The police captain realized something was missing and found the chewed cigar stub and stuffed it back into his mouth. "Yeah, ain't that the truth."

~ ~ ~ ~ ~

Outside, the world hadn't changed. Still slick black and smelling of damp and exhaust. A woman dies, a woman who has been your friend since a night long ago when she chose to go against logic and reason and put everything on the line to help a young man stay alive another night, and maybe the day after, nothing more. Still, the night doesn't change. But you change. If your name is Sand, and you know it is the small but grand gestures that count, made without caution or regret when the moment is at hand. These are the things that can't be repaid until they must be repaid. The night is the same. But the debt is due.

The first one was a girl. Third floor of a nondescript apartment building in a nondescript neighborhood. The girl was not nondescript. She was a leggy blonde with a lot of chest and not much of a disposition.

She looked at him through the crack allowed by the night chain, made a small sound in her throat, and tried to slam the door closed again.

He straight-armed it, and the door and the girl both went inward, the night chain pulling out of the wall and dancing against the splintered door.

In the middle of the disarranged room she caught her balance and stood glaring at him defiantly. She wore a bra and half-slip and was still in stocking feet. That was as far as she had gotten. On the bed, still open, were two half-filled suitcases.

"Going somewhere, Ginger?"

That was her name. Ginger Dacus. She had been second in command in Mopsie Steiner's house of flesh. Right now she was a package of anger and fear.

"You know damn well I'm going somewhere. Mopsie's dead. It's me I've got to look out for now."

"You called the police?"

"Sure. I came in and found her. I called the cops and then spread the word to the other girls."

"Who did it?"

She shrugged. "How should I know? Probably somebody after dough."

"Not the way she was killed. Dozens of stab wounds, none of them deep. Somebody didn't like her. Who?"

"You knew her, mister."

"Not for a long time. I haven't been around. Somebody close must have seen this coming."

She shook her head. "You're way off track, Sand. Mopsie didn't pick up any new enemies lately, not that I know of. The only trouble she's had is with this one guy who came to the house to see her a couple of times. They had some loud words. But he was a relative or something, I think. I never caught his name. I asked Mopsie, but she told me to mind my own business."

He said, "Okay, finish packing, Ginger. Have a nice trip."

That caught her by surprise. "That's all? I can go?"

"You're free as a bird, and it's time to fly. Mopsie says so."

The next stop was another apartment hotel, but representing a big leap in style and class. The name engraved above the pearl button read Joseph S. Wangstrom.

Not too many years ago Joseph S. Wangstrom had been a punk kid called Joey Steiner who got a kick out of hanging around his mother's place of business. These days, according to the society pages, he was an up-and-coming young attorney with a political eye. Sand hadn't bothered to mention to Mohannah that the boy had changed his name. He wanted to reach him first.

He reached for the button just as the door opened and the blonde rushed out. She saw him in time to let out a short startled sound, but not soon enough to stop before her lush breasts were warm cushions against his chest. She started saying something apologetic, then looked up at him and let it hang.

She was young and pretty and rich. She was also the daughter of the state's Lieutenant Governor.

"I know you," she said when she got her voice back. "You're a killer and your name is Sand. My father pointed you out to me once." She studied him more intensely for a moment. "Are you here to see Joseph?"

"Joey, yeah, I'm here to see him."

He stepped past her and inside. Joey came from one of the other rooms wearing a tux and carrying a half empty glass in his hand. He was saying something to the effect that he hadn't expected her back so soon when he got a good look at Sand. The blood ran out of his face in thin streams, leaving it pallid and striped. His eyes traveled from Sand to the girl and back.

Then he dropped the glass and took a swing.

Sand pushed it aside and hit him low in the gut. Joey boy had changed a lot in the last few years, but it was all front. Punks don't change.

The girl was still standing in the open doorway. She didn't scream or go into hysterics at the sight of this little interplay. That much was to her credit.

Sand said, "Tell her to run along home, Joey. We've got a little talking to do."

Joey's raised his head from where he was bending over his hurt gut. "It . . . it's all right, Marina. Everything's all right. You run along or you'll be late meeting your father."

She didn't like the idea, but she left.

There was a bar against one wall. Sand poured himself a drink while Joseph S. Wangstrom finished pulling himself together. Then, "Why the punch, Joey?"

He was standing straight now. He checked his tux to make sure he again looked the part of the brilliant young attorney. "Why the hell do you think? A notorious criminal suddenly walks into my apartment—I wasn't sure what you might say." He pointed a finger at the closed door. "Marina is my fiancée. She wouldn't have understood."

And her father wouldn't have understood, Sand thought. He said, "I hear you've been having arguments with your mother, Joey."

He got surprised. "How—"

Sand tasted his drink. "Tell me about it."

"What the hell is there to tell? The same old thing. I wanted her to give up that place of hers. Do you realize what it would do to me, my career, if anybody important even suspected that—"

"You remember when you used to wear a gang jacket and carry a switchblade, Joey?"

Joey laughed mirthlessly.

"That was a long time ago. I made something of myself." He pulled a small penknife from his pocket and held it up like a souvenir. "I haven't carried anything bigger than this for years. And I'm not through yet. Now that Mopsie is selling out and going away there's no limit to the heights I can reach."

Nothing showed on Sand's face. "Your mother is selling out?"

"Yes. I convinced her it would be best for both of us. She's going away for a long vacation, probably to Europe."

"Who's the buyer?"

"A man named Lopass, I think she said."

Sand knew him. It fit. All but Mopsie giving up her place—but, then, she had made a lot of sacrifices for her kid.

The telephone rang and the young lawyer picked it up. He mumbled, "Yes" into the instrument a couple of times and then listened. His face lost most of the color it had regained. Sand figured it was probably the police with the news until just before he hung up when he said, "Yes . . . yes. I'll meet you then."

Sand hated to tell him. He hadn't been much of a son, but that didn't make it any easier. He said, "Your mother won't be taking that vacation, Joey. She's dead."

~ ~ ~ ~ ~

The girl was waiting for him by the car when he came out, a light breeze dancing slowly about her, its fingers playing with the hem of her skirt.

"I thought you were in a hurry," he said.

She shook her head slowly, and there was a thing in her eyes as she looked up at him. "Not any more. You did something to me up there. I didn't realize what it was at first, but now I do. You want to know what you did?"

"No."

"You made me a *woman*. I thought I was a woman, but I wasn't—not until I took one look at you and a floodtide of woman juices started rushing frantically through my veins. I guess there's something about you that makes you affect women that way, perhaps because of the things you've done or the things you're capable of doing. What would you say if I told you I think I'm in love with you?"

"Your father wouldn't like it. Neither would your boyfriend upstairs."

She shrugged slightly and her breasts moved. He remembered their warmth against his chest.

"I'm a big girl," she said, "and sometimes even a rich girl has to make a decision very quickly and very permanently. I've decided on you."

A man can be tempted. A lone man tired of watching his back; a man who has lost a friend.

She pressed a note into his hand. "This is my phone number. I'll wait." Then she was gone, and he stood there a moment longer before climbing in the car.

Lopass was a moneyman. He had made his dough legitimately and bought his way into the rackets. His penthouse apartment was unpretentious as penthouses go, but he did keep a beefy bodyguard named Jeff at the door. Without speaking, Sand hit him right between the eyes with a blow that bounced his head off the door before he toppled facedown into the carpet.

He kicked the door to pieces and found Lopass huddled in a corner trying to pretend that was rye whisky running down his pants leg.

Sand didn't bother showing him the .45 he always kept under his coat. Lopass knew it was there. He just let the chubby hood watch his eyes until his flesh began to tremble, then he said, "You do it, Lopass?"

"*No! I didn't do it.* You . . . you mean the dame at the whorehouse, Mopsie? I didn't do it. I swear. I just heard about it. I don't know nothing from nothing. Honest!"

"Way I hear it, you had business dealings."

He jerked his head up and down fast enough to sling beads of sweat off his forehead. "There was some talk of me buying her out, yeah. It was practically set. But she called it off."

"When?"

"Tonight. At her place. Couldn't have been more than a few minutes before she got herself killed. But I didn't do it, if that's what you're thinking, and I can prove it,"

"How, Lopass?"

"By the dame that was coming in when I left—a big blonde with a frontage like ripe cantaloupes."

That would have to be Ginger.

Sand said, "She was coming in as you left?"

"I told you. I can prove it, I tell you."

But Sand was no longer listening. He turned and walked out, stepping over the big bodyguard asleep on the job.

Behind him Lopass made small retching sounds as he tried not to throw up.

Lopass said Ginger saw him leave. Ginger hadn't mentioned it. Bad girl, Ginger. He went to find Ginger.

He didn't really expect to find her home. She had been in too big a hurry before. But he went back to the nondescript building with its nondescript apartments and pounded on her door until he was sure no one intended to answer, then he forced it open.

The girl was gone. Her bags were gone. The junk she had decided to leave behind was scattered all over the place. She wouldn't be coming back this way.

The phone was by the bed and the directory was on the floor where it had been dropped. Sand picked it up and started going through it, checking the listings for airports, train and bus terminals. It's a habit some people have, and she had it—marking the number to keep from losing it as she dialed. She had called a bus terminal three blocks away.

The place belonged to one of the smaller bus lines and was as unpretentious as the rest of the neighborhood. A couple of dead buses parked out back, nothing moving. The waiting room was half dark and divided from the ticket counter by a row of magazines. The guy behind the ticket cage was absorbed in a newspaper and didn't look up as Sand came in.

It looked as though he was too late, but then he spotted her sitting alone in a dark corner of the waiting room, her back to him. He moved past empty seats to her side. She had a lot of explaining to do. A lot of questions needed answers, and she had to have them. He reached out and caught her chin in his hand.

And two staring, dead eyes swung to face him!

He caught her body and kept it from falling out of the seat. She hadn't been dead long, but she would be dead from now on. The marks where the fingers had slipped around her throat were purple.

He pushed her back in the seat and took a long, appraising took at her. Then he actually sighed. "Too bad, Ginger. You should have just flown away."

The guy behind the ticket cage still hadn't looked up when Sand left.

~ ~ ~ ~ ~

This time he rang, and the voice told him to come in. Joseph S. Wangstrom hung up the phone and looked across the room at him. "That was the police, a man named Mohannah. He wanted to know if you had already been here. I told him yes, that I thought you must be looking for the killer."

"No more. That part of my job is done. I found him."

"Lopass?"

"You, Joey."

He turned white again, and his hands began to tremble. "You . . . you must be crazy!"

Sand shook his head slowly. "A matter of motive, Joey. It was the thing that didn't make sense. Lopass wanted her place, but killing her wouldn't get it for him. Ginger had no motive. Nobody else could have gotten close enough to her to do the job. Nobody but you, Joey."

"I tell you, you're—"

"You were afraid," Sand continued. "Afraid somebody was going to find out who your mother was; then you would no longer be the up-and-coming young politician. You couldn't have that. You talked her into getting out. Enter Lopass, the moneyman. But somewhere along the line something must have sunk in for Mopsie. She always wanted a lot for you, boy, but now it occurred to her that you were kicking her out of your life for good. She couldn't help you anymore. So she changed her mind about selling.

"Lopass came—listened to Mopsie tell him the sale was off—and left. He passed Ginger on the way out. That places you inside, Joey, to hear her say no to you for the first time in your life. You went berserk. You killed her. Not a psycho kill like the police still think. Sure all the wounds were shallow. You said it yourself—the only knife you've carried for a long time is a small penknife.

"And Ginger? She was a witness, a witness who knew you. With Mopsie dead she had to clear out, but she felt you should do a little paying. I figure it was Ginger on the phone when I was here before, telling you where to bring the payoff. You must have peeled out of here as soon as I left. You had to get to her before she had a chance to talk to anybody. She would have been nervous on the phone, and nervous people talk too must, even when they don't intend to. You had to shut her up fast, and letting her blackmail you was never in your plan. If she had known the old Joey she would have known that. You had to shut her up for good. By the time I reached her she was dead, and you were probably already back here, ready to pretend you never left. Feeling your hands suddenly around her throat was all the payoff she got. But the facts were already in, Joey, with only one thing needed to tie it together, and I had it all the time; Mopsie Steiner gave it to me."

The killer's hand moved from the phone slowly to the top of the bar. Underneath would be a gun. Even politically minded attorneys own guns. He said, "Mopsie's dead. She couldn't tell you anything."

"She called for me as she was dying," Sand said. "Why?

Not to find her killer. The police were there. She could have told them the name of the killer. She called for me because she wanted me to *protect* her killer! Who else but you, Joey?"

No more room for denial. It was all there.

Joseph S. Wangstrom said, "You were her friend, Sand. She wanted you to protect me—you just said it yourself. She wouldn't want you to turn me in."

Sand got ready to leave.

"I'm not going to turn you in, Joey. I'm going to go out and get drunk and try to forget that scum like you exist."

Sand turned slowly and took a couple of steps toward the door. Then he turned back and shot the man behind the bar just as the gun cleared its polished surface. The force of the slug slammed him against the wall and held him there with disbelief spread all over his face. That was the way he died.

Once a punk, always a punk, Sand thought. And a punk who can't trust his own mother can't trust anybody.

~ ~ ~ ~ ~

He took the elevator down, and outside the night was no longer the same. It looked the same and even felt the same, but it was cleaner now. He took a deep breath. Everything was as well as right would allow.

As he walked toward the car he thought about the girl who had stood there before and the note in his pocket. He took it out and held it in his hand. A man can be tempted . . .

THE UGLY REDHEAD

For a while there, I was beginning to wonder if Ennis Willie was a hoax.

I first encountered the name of this author in a Mystery Scene article by Ed Gorman, praising a series of novels written by Ennis Willie in the early sixties. I'd never seen any Ennis Willie books, never even heard of him before. Then my friend Steve Mertz chimed in, also praising Willie's work. Not long after that, I began to hear speculation that this obscure but evidently excellent author was either a.) Black or b.) Mickey Spillane. But I'd still never seen any Ennis Willie books, and it's about then that my cynical, suspicious nature began to get the better of me. What if, I asked myself, Ed and Steve simply got together and made up this Ennis Willie fellow and all the great books he was supposed to have written? Admittedly, this didn't sound to me like something Ed and Steve would do. Both men can be hilariously funny, but they never struck me as the practical joker sort. And when it comes to bibliographic matters, I trust them to be serious and diligent in anything they write.

Still, there was that little nagging doubt in the back of my mind . . .

Well, no more, of course. Ennis Willie does indeed exist, along with the books and stories he wrote, and we're all the better for it. Because Willie's prose paints one of the most vivid, compelling portraits of the underbelly of life in the early Sixties that a reader will ever encounter. It's a world of seedy bus stations (the sort where many of Ennis Willie's books were sold, no doubt), sleazy strip joints, bars that cater to the losers of the world, and squalid rooming houses full of the smell of old food and desperation. A world where anything can happen and often does, all recounted in lean, fast-moving prose that seldom pauses to let the reader catch his breath.

Yes, Ennis Willie is real, and so is his work.

~ ~ ~ ~ ~

"The Ugly Redhead" is the final story to feature Willie's only series character, the man called Sand, who left the mob only to find himself dogged by a series of ruthless underworld killers who want to rub him out. Since this story is the finale of Sand's odyssey, it's appropriate that its plot goes right to the heart of the series. In other Sand stories, he is called on to solve the murders of friends of his and avenge their deaths. That's true in "The Ugly Redhead" as well, but this time the stakes are not simply vengeance. The outcome is vital to Sand's continued survival as well. As always, the story is well constructed, with enough twists and turns for a longer yarn. Willie tells it in his usual hard-hitting, stripped-down prose and brings everything to a violent but satisfying conclusion. The world of "The Ugly Redhead" isn't a pretty one, but it's one that the reader will never forget.

Now I know why Ed and Steve remembered Ennis Willie for all these years.

James Reasoner

I T WAS ONE OF THOSE NIGHTS when the fog rolls in to hug the docks in a damp, vapory caress; a night when the world should roll up and hide its sorrows. Nothing should happen on a night like this . . .

The tall man did not mind the solitary aspect of the night. It fit his nature. His thoughts were more clear on a night like this. The mob had a new crew on the way to collect the bounty on his head. Who would it be this time? How many? And he thought about the plane that would be warming up three hours from now, the plane that would take him away from here.

He heard the staccato click of high heels behind him, but he did not lift his hands buried in the pockets of a trench coat or turn his head. The fog was too thick and it was none of his business. Some dame hurrying to keep a date—or just hurrying. Whenever Sand walked it was usually here close to the docks, and it was always a good idea for a woman alone to hurry.

The footsteps got closer and when they were close enough for her to pass she reached out and tugged at his sleeve and nearly got herself killed. When he moved it was with a sudden, practiced flow of motion that had his hand already on the butt of the .45 automatic under his arm.

"Sand?" the voice said.

He stopped. He could see her now. A few feet away a street lamp illuminated the fog. She seemed almost to float in the drifting mist. A redhead with a nice figure and long, tapering legs. The face belonged to somebody else. It did not go with the striking body composed of breathtaking curves and screaming sensuality. The face belonged to a trick mirror in the House of Horrors. One side of it was lower than the other, the flesh rippling like water in a stream, one corner of what should have been a ripe mouth twisted grimly downward,

"I know I'm not pretty," she said, either reading or anticipating his thoughts. "The ugly redhead, that's what people call me when I'm not around. But that's not important. Are you Sand?"

"That's what people call *me*,"

She looked hard into his face and nodded, "I guess you are. Herbie said I would know. He said if I looked into your face I would see a killer there."

Herbie would be Herbie Cole, a skinny little guy with a chronic cough who was always around to run favors for the racket boys. It was Herbie who had called Sand earlier tonight to give him the word the mob was ready for another try. *Nobody breaks with the organization and keeps living, they had told him; nobody is that tough.* They had tried for him before and failed. Now, according to Herbie, they were coming again.

"I'm Sabrina Cole, Herbie's sister," she told him. "He sent me to find you. He says he has some more information for you that might change everything, but he was afraid to bring it himself. He says for you to come to his place. He said you would come."

"He was right. What about you?"

She stood where she was, shook her head from side to side. The drifting fog seemed to magnify the deformity of her face. "No. I've got to get back to the Bird Hut, where I work. Besides, who would . . ." She let the thought tail off. Then she turned and hurried away, back the way she came.

~ ~ ~ ~ ~

Sand flagged down a cruising cab a few blocks over. He had never been to Herbie's place but he knew it, a single room in the rear of a rotting brownstone.

Herbie's information would be the identification of the shooters. Sand didn't like to run. Herbie knew that. Running can get to be a habit. But you can't fight shadows. With names, maybe he wouldn't need the plane.

The cabby found the address in the fog. Sand handed him a bill and climbed out. Nothing moved on the street but the fog. Inside the building was the smell all these old buildings had, the smell of many humans and many years.

At Herbie's door Sand knocked, and when there was no answer he twisted the knob and pushed the door open, wondering what would make the little guy go out after the message he had sent.

The answer was leaning over the edge of the bed. Herbie hadn't gone out. He was dead!

Somebody had slit his throat. He was face down, both his arms hanging off the bed. Some of the blood had soaked into the mattress, the rest making a pool on the floor. That much Sand could see from the open doorway with the help of the hall light behind him.

He stepped inside, pushed the door closed and turned on the naked bulb in the center of the room.

The little man on the bed had talked to Sand only a couple of hours ago. "A favor," Herbie Cole had called it when he refused to accept the C-note Sand offered. "We're friends, sort of," he had said, "much as a ignorant nobody guy like me will ever get to being friends with the great Sand." Not long after that the little guy must have latched onto the additional information. By then he was scared; probably he knew somebody was onto him. Still, he gave it a try.

Sand walked closer to the bed and looked down at the dead man. "You were a friend, Herbie."

He had started to turn away when he saw it! On the floor next to the bed Herbie's finger had written in his own blood: S-A-N-D.

Only Herbie hadn't written it. Sure it looked that way, but there wasn't a chance. Because Herbie had been illiterate—he couldn't write.

Things started bouncing around inside his head then, but before he had time to pin his thoughts down a banging started on the door behind him. Not knuckles, but a stick. And a voice called out, "Open up. Police."

Yeah, that made sense, too, Sand thought. Somebody had gone to the trouble to make it look like the dead man had written a name with his own blood in those last few seconds of his life. What was it he was trying to say? The cops wouldn't even strain at it. What else would a man write after having his throat cut? The name of his killer.

"Open up," the cop said again.

Sand was already crossing the room to a window. He raised it. "Coming," he said to cover the noise. "Coming." Then he climbed out into a narrow alley filled with fog and the smothered stench of garbage.

He was half a dozen blocks away before he heard the wail of sirens that would mean the first cop had found Herbie and put in a call to the precinct.

A cab happened by and got itself a passenger. As Sand crawled in the back seat the driver said, "Lot of sirens.

Somebody must of got bumped. Too bad a night for one of those teen-age gang fights."

"Yeah," Sand said. "You know a place called the Bird Hut?"

"Sure."

"Let's go."

~ ~ ~ ~ ~

The Bird Hut got its name from its Polynesian motif. Synthetic tropical plants everywhere; ferns, rubber plants, even a couple of ceiling scrapers pretending to be coconut trees. If you had a big enough imagination or weak enough eyesight the effect was there; otherwise, it was just a third-rate night club struggling to hide itself.

The headwaiter was a fat guy in native dress who lacked the tan needed to pull it off. "Table or bar?" he asked.

Sand shook off the question. "You know a little guy named Herbie Cole, always coughing?"

"Sure. Everybody knows Herbie. He's around here nearly every night—likes to catch the floorshow. He was around earlier, but he's been gone a good while."

"Where do I find his sister?"

He got a funny look on his puss. "You don't, mister. Herbie don't have no sister."

Sand didn't let it throw him. "A redhead. Her name is Sabrina."

"That we got, a redhead named Sabrina. She's the reason Herbie and all our other customers like to come around. She's part of the show. A terrific build. Does this thing at the end where all her clothes fall off all by their self—"

"Where do I find her?"

"She's in back in her dressing room. Only you ain't supposed to—"

Sand left him standing there with the words still spilling out his mouth and crossed the wide room, skirting the tables, and pushed through a curtain stretched behind the stage. Backstage nobody had made any effort to create an exotic atmosphere. Junk was scattered everywhere. He spotted a room with a star painted on the door and headed for it. The room wasn't actually part of the building. It sat there like an oversized refrigerator crate, its walls built of some kind of thin fiberboard.

The guy who tried to stop him was big, part of the act that went on for the customers three times nightly, decked out in a bright lava-lava with his chest bare to show plenty of muscle. He said something like, "Hey, buddy! You can't—" and shoved a big palm at Sand's chest.

Sand caught the guy's wrist, twisted his arm up behind his back and slammed him face-first against the wall. The guy was still standing there on weak knees trying to shake his brain back into place and figure out his fascination with the wall when Sand started making tapping sounds on the door with the star.

"Come in," a voice on the other side called. It was a feminine voice. A *very* feminine voice. A voice not unlike, Sand suspected, the one that called Ulysses and crew onto the rocks.

He came in. The girl was sitting in front of a mirror at a dressing table, a robe wrapped about her generous body that didn't cover much more than the thing nature boy outside was wearing. She looked at him in the mirror, turning her face into a question mark.

She was a redhead named Sabrina, but she wasn't the one he had talked with on a dark street not more than an hour ago. This one had no twisted, ugly face. She was, in fact, probably the most beautiful woman he had ever seen.

"Your name is Sand," she said after that first moment had lasted a little too long. "I've seen your picture in the paper. I'm Sabrina Webber." The quizzical expression was still on that beautiful face.

He said, "I hate to break it to you this way, baby—but somebody has been going around using your name. You know Herbie Cole?"

He was going a little fast for her, but she nodded that flaming head of hers. "Sure. I know Herbie. He's around nearly every night. He's nice. I like him. But before tonight he's just been part of the furniture. Now I'm beginning to wonder why all of a sudden he's important enough to have people asking about him, the famous Sand—and the other guy earlier."

"What other guy?"

"I heard one of the waiters mention his name after he left." She pursed full red lips as she tried to think of it. "Spade something. Spade Spradler, I think."

Spade Spradler was a hood out of Chicago. That would be one of the names Herbie wanted to give him.

Sand crossed the small room and leaned an arm on the dressing table. As he did, the girl let out a short scream and reached out quickly for one of the dozen or more containers filled with various creams and liquids.

"What's the matter?" he asked.

She gave a heavy sigh that moved her large breasts beneath the robe, then managed a weak smile. "Just nerves, I guess." She held the container slightly out from her body. It was open and filled with a colorless liquid. "This is the stuff I use in my act to make my costume fall away. Acid. A precise amount on a cord of a certain thickness and I can time the fallaway to the second. I dropped the top on the floor before the last show and haven't gotten around to looking for it yet. I guess I better put it somewhere. What this stuff does to meat . . ."

The dressing room had a second door built into the side, a three-inch ledge above it. Sabrina Webber reached up and sat the bottle on the ledge, in the process proving she wore nothing but skin beneath the thin robe.

"Don't you think it might be a better idea to start a search for the top?" he suggested, "It's liable to get jarred off of there."

"Uh-uh. Nobody ever uses this door." Manicured fingers snapped a lock closed, "That will make sure." She glided back to him, sex personified and in motion. She didn't stop until the tips of her breasts were nearly scraping his chest, and her voice came out in a hopeful caress. "Now what was your next question, Sand—what time I finish my last number?"

He thought about the plane and the fact that he still didn't know the names except for Spradler, and Spradler was brawn and not brains. Then there was the other redhead, the one with the twisted face, who wasn't Herbie's sister because he didn't have a sister. And Herbie, his throat cut with his dead eyes staring down at the floor where somebody had written a name with his finger and in his blood. The cops would know the name; and if they worked fast they would also know about the plane before it had a chance to get off the ground.

"Some other time," he said. "Right now I'm more interested in the man who was asking about Herbie. Maybe if I talk to the same waiter he talked to I'll get some idea where to find him."

"Herbie?"

"Spradler."

"The Broadmont. He asked the waiter to call him there if Herbie came back before he found him."

Sand started for the door and she followed him. He opened it and turned back. She was still close, her breasts nearly rubbing his chest.

She gave him a big smile full of promise. "An hour and a half," she said, "is when the last show will be through. That's another time. Maybe you can make it."

"It would be nice," he said.

"Now aren't you the one for understatement," she said. She added a faint smile, half flirtation and half invitation, that followed him like the warm tug of her siren song as he stepped outside and grabbed a cab.

~ ~ ~ ~ ~

Spade Spradler would be used to a little more class than this flea trap, but it had probably been chosen for him by someone who didn't want the word to spread too quickly that he was in from Chicago.

Sand learned the room number he wanted from the desk

clerk. Yes, Mr. Spradler was in, he was sure, because he had just called down with the usual complaint about the TV signal.

Sand took the stairs up to the third floor, found the door he wanted and gave it a couple of taps with his left hand while he filled his right with the warm butt of his .45.

"Yeah?" the voice asked from inside.

Sand didn't know Spradler well enough to be familiar with his voice, but it was mean enough and nasty enough to fit.

"You call about the TV?"

"Okay," the voice said, "come on in."

Sand twisted the knob and pushed the door inward. Spradler sat on the edge of the bed in a pair of boxer shorts, scratching a broad, hair-matted chest like something kin to an ape.

Spradler played his part well. He had no gun showing; he even managed to look surprised. Sand was inside the room with the door closing behind him before he sensed the trap. The hairy hood was good, but he wasn't good enough to keep his eyes from shifting to the second man, the one behind the chair on the other side of the room.

Sand was already turning when the guy behind the chair got off his shot. The slug caught Sand just under the rib cage and sliced through about two inches of meat as it kept him spinning in the right direction. The second hood's head was the only thing showing, that and the gun hand resting on the arm of the overstuffed chair. He was squeezing off another shot when the big .45 roared and bucked in Sand's fist and the hood suddenly wasn't there any more. He was gone— like a duck in a shooting gallery, except for part of his bleeding skull embedded in the wall.

Sand went down on one knee and spun back toward the bed in time to see Spradler had found a gun somewhere and was busy aiming it. Sand shot him in the belly just above the elastic of the boxer shorts.

By the time Sand reached him the hood had already begun the slow process of dying hard, the way you do when your gut wound is bad enough to let your intestines start crawling out. Sand grabbed him by the hair and snatched his head up. His eyes got bright with the stinging pain. The pain from down below hadn't started yet; from the chest down he would be numb right now, but the pain would come.

Outside this room the hotel had been turned into a bedlam of running, yelling people. It would take them a few minutes to locate the origin of the shots, a few minutes more for the cops to arrive.

"Talk, Spradler, and talk fast," Sand told him. "Who else did the bosses send besides you and your buddy? Who's the brain?"

"Nobody. They didn't send nobody else. We was to get our orders from here."

"A name."

The hood managed a grin in spite of his troubles. "I ain't that stupid. There's a chance I could pull through if a doc gets here in time. I ain't doing no squealing."

"Another question, Spradler. Whose idea was it to kill Herbie and plant the frame?"

"What the hell you talking about? I don't know nobody named Herbie—"

On another street the familiar sound of police sirens sliced through the foggy night.

Sand left the hood bleeding to death on the bed and made his way down the fire escape. Uniformed cops were already entering the lobby of the hotel when he walked away.

~ ~ ~ ~ ~

At the Bird Hut things had changed. The star of the show, the gorgeous redhead named Sabrina, was holding the rapt attention of every pair of eyes in the room. Only the guy in the lava-lava paid him any attention. He glanced up, recognized him, and went back to looking. Nobody wanted to miss the end of the act, when the clothes would fall away from that magnificent body.

In the meantime they were getting their money's worth in

the warm-up. She had plenty and she was moving it erotic-
ally to the rhythm of the music and to the humming sound
coming from her own luscious throat. The flames of her hair
fell down past her face to her shoulders and beyond while
her hips swayed and her breasts made movements of their
own as though urging on the finale.

Sand skirted the crowd as he had earlier and went backstage. He was waiting in her dressing room when the club
exploded with whistles and applause—the act was over—and
a moment later when she rushed in holding several pieces of
clothing against her breasts and middle but unable to do anything about the view from the rear.

He was leaning against the wall next to the door. She
didn't see him until she slipped into another outfit behind a
small screen and turned around. She saw him and made a
small startled sound. Then she saw the blood from the slug
he had caught in the side and her beautiful eyes got wide.

"Sand! What in the world—"

He said slowly, "It didn't work, Sabrina. You warned
them I was coming and they nearly pulled it off, but not
quite."

She wanted to pretend she didn't know what he was talking about so he told her the whole story.

"You are the one the organization selected for the job, Sabrina. They knew I wouldn't be expecting a woman. Herbie
was always hanging around the club. This was where he
picked up the news that the organization was ready to try
again. You said it yourself, he was like a piece of the furniture—so somebody talked a little too much without considering he had ears and without knowing Herbie was a friend.
Only he didn't know *you* were the one. If he had, he just
might have kept it to himself. But I'm prepared to give him
the benefit of the doubt.

"After he talked to me Herbie made a mistake. He told
you the whole bit. So you altered your plans a little. The organization had sent a couple of brawn boys to do the work,
but you left them sitting in their hotel room while you did
things fancy. First you let Herbie take you to his place,

where you slit his throat and used his finger to write out my name in blood. A pretty frame, especially if the cops should happen to catch me right there in the room with him.

"The ugly redhead, that was you. I should have guessed. With all that junk over there on your dressing table you could make yourself look any way you wanted. Was it a slip when you told me where you worked? No, I don't think so. It was a hook to bring me right here to you in case Plan A failed. If the cops you sent to Herbie's place missed me, by the time I got here you would be a different redhead.

"While we were talking you came up with the other idea. You told me where to find Spradler, then called the two hoods who had been sent to help you and told them I was coming. The trap was good, but I kill hard, baby. And your boy pointed the finger right back at you. You were supposed to know about him because he came around asking for Herbie—but Spradler had never heard of Herbie!"

There was no room for denial. It was all there, and the stricken expression that had crept into the features of that beautiful face meant she knew it. She knew it was over. She ran.

Sand was standing too close to the door she had entered. There was only one other way out, the second door—and she went for it!

Maybe Sand saw it in time. Maybe he could have stopped her. Maybe he thought she would remember she had locked the door when she put the open bottle of acid on the ledge. A dozen things.

She snatched at the knob and the flimsy wall of the dressing room shook as the door held. Then the girl was staring up, watching the bottle topple off its perch to spill its fiery substance into her face.

She screamed. And then she continued to scream, over and over without end as she again became the ugly redhead.

TOO LATE TO PRAY

Ennis Willie is a writer whose work primarily appeared in the soft-core "adult" ghetto paperbacks of the 1960s. Like many other writers—some of whom left that ghetto and went on to greater things like Harlan Ellison, Robert Silverberg, Lawrence Block and Donald Westlake—there were also some who never left it like Willie. It's a real shame because the hard crime reader and fan have missed out on his fine writing, incredible stories and memorable characters only because of the sleazy marketing and cheap formats these works appeared in. Ennis Willie deserved better and thankfully this new book in some measure will remedy those shortcomings.

In this story, Willie's protagonist, Sand—he uses just one name and there's no need for any more than that because everyone knows who he is—is the quintessential outsider hero, the ultra tough guy. He's a gangster who wanted out of the Mob and left—but now he's back! You see, an old flame has been snuffed out and Sand is back to find her killer, even if it kills him, which it just might. Then he's going to send that killer straight down to hell and we get to go along for the ride.

As Sand himself puts it, "For a man like me, revenge is law."

The story is brutal, fast and violent hard-boiled fiction, satisfaction guaranteed!

Gary Lovisi

ONE

THE PLANE CIRCLED the field for the better part of an hour trying to find the landing strip through the dense overcast.

The tall man named Sand looked out at the night through the window beside him and thought of nothing.

Across the aisle a woman who had watched him intermittently throughout the flight thought that he looked tired. A business executive, she decided, probably returning from some top-level conference in another city. She wished she could hear him speak, knowing his voice would be as impressive as his appearance. The beginning of gray at his temples was probably premature, but it was impossible to be sure because of his face. The face was neither young nor old. There seemed to be a hardness about the steel-gray eyes, perhaps because he was tired. She wondered what it would be like to make love to a man like that, not really contemplating it. Her husband would be waiting for her at the gate. She wondered if anyone waited for the man across from her.

They were waiting. They had arrived thirty minutes before the plane was scheduled to land, and neither of the two had spoken during the hour the plane circled the field. They waited because the word had come ahead of him. Sand was coming back. Sand—a legend. Indestructible, some called him. Others said it was partly luck that he had walked over every assassin the organization had thrown at him. Hard, mean, deadly—these were words they all used when they described him.

Others waited besides these two stony-faced men who stood without speaking. In effect, a city waited—everyone who had gotten the word as it sped through the underworld grapevine. Sand is coming back! This was where he had started, this town, where he had begun with a fast brain and a hard core and a burning ambition to reach the top. He had nearly made it when suddenly he decided he wanted out. They had said the only way he could get out was dead, but he had gotten out anyway. He laughed in their faces, and every time they sent their gunnies out after him he sent them back in pieces. The organization hadn't sent anybody after him in a long time, and maybe a few had begun to forget. Now the word was out.

Sand is coming back!

They all wanted to know why.

As Sand stepped into the main terminal he saw them, the fat one whose round face looked a little odd without a cigar sticking out of it, and the other one. The second one was taller and younger but still a long time out of the rookie category; Sand didn't know him. The fat one in a slightly wrinkled suit was Max Mohannah, a detective captain who would have made inspector before now if he'd had a little more polish.

When they were practically face-to-face Sand said, "Hello, Max. Been a long time. You here to meet a friend?"

The fat cop reached in his pocket, found the cigar that was missing from his face and put it there. "Not exactly," he said. "Waiting for you."

"Oh?"

"Word was out that you were coming back. Thing like that makes a person wonder. You got a lot of enemies here. A man doesn't usually go where he's got a lot of enemies."

"Maybe I've got a few friends here too, Max."

He chomped on the cigar and scoffed around it. "You got no friends, here or anywhere else. The whole damn world is divided up in cliques, and you don't belong to none of them. That makes you a man outside, Sand—and a man like that ain't got no friends."

Sand almost grinned at him. He and Max Mohannah had a history together. A mixed history, to be sure, but a history nonetheless. They trusted each other to the extent their positions allowed and had come close on occasions to friendship. On the latter, the police captain remained in denial.

"You're getting philosophical, Max."

"I'm just talking sense. Nobody likes an ex-hood."

"And yet you came out of your way to meet me."

"I came to find out why you're back where you don't belong."

"I thought you kept your ear to the vine, Max."

"The vine don't know squat. Nobody does. But there is one thing everybody knows—wherever you go, trouble comes right along behind. From here, I can smell trouble on you. You're here for a reason, and you never have a reason that doesn't involve blood on the floor."

Sand shook a cigarette loose from a half empty pack and lit it, saying nothing, a casual insolence in his movement.

"You ain't going to say?" the fat detective captain asked.

Sand shook his head, smoke drifting out his nostrils. "Afraid not, Max."

"Yeah. I sort of figured that's the way it would be, so I brought along a warning too. Walk softly, Sand. You know me and I know you, because we've had dealings before. You know I don't talk just to exercise my tonsils. Walk damn soft. I like to keep everything neat. I don't want any extra corpses littering up my town."

He turned abruptly and walked away. The other cop, caught off guard, spun on his heel and rushed to catch up.

Sand stood where he was until the cigarette in his hand began to burn his fingers.

There will be corpses, Max. At least one and maybe more—maybe a whole string of them before this thing is through. Because the first corpse is already in the morgue. Not an important corpse to you, Max, or to this lousy town. Hell, you probably don't even know she's dead. But I know, Max, and that's why I'm back. To me she was important.

His bag was waiting for him.

Outside he had his choice between the airport limousine and line of cabs. He took one of the cabs and gave the driver the name of a hotel.

"You'll never get in," the driver told him. "Not unless you got a confirmed reservation. Jaycees and some kind of fruit growers association decided to have a convention the same time. All the better hotels are about to bust their seams."

"I'll get in," Sand said.

He got in. He hadn't been gone that long. The manager of the hotel looked, acted and wore the title of vice president. Yes, of course, there were accommodations available for Mr. Sand.

Sand shook off the bellboy and carried his own bag.

In his room he engaged the night latch and opened his suitcase as he peeled off his coat. He turned the television on and switched the channel to the local news. The shoulder rig with its holster hugging the big .45 automatic, he laid across the foot of the bed.

A shower came next. Hot—then cold. When he had toweled himself dry he climbed into fresh clothes and strapped the shoulder rig in place. As he pulled his coat over it he caught his reflection in the mirror.

They never let you take it off, do they Sand? It's a part of you now, as necessary as the hand that holds it. Always there. Always ready. The day you forget is the day you die, because the organization is still waiting, still waiting for you to make a slip or grow weak.

Downstairs he caught a cab and gave the driver the address he wanted. The guy's face didn't change expression as he recognized the address. With two large conventions in town, his hack probably knew the way by heart.

It was a long ride. It took the better part of an hour to get out of the heavy traffic, made heavier by the overcast that had settled to the ground in patches of fog. The traffic thinned as the tall stores and office buildings became apartment buildings and then tenements. The sounds disappeared and so did the lights until there was only the street lights fighting a futile battle against the fog and the blast of a car horn a couple of blocks away that kept blowing because it was stuck and its owner was probably inside somewhere piled up in the hay.

The house he wanted was built away from the street and inside a wrought iron fence that had once spelled class. The

first owners were dead and their successors had moved uptown when the neighborhood started coming apart—add to
that the toll taken by time and subsequent tenants and the
place still managed to retain a certain air of fallen gentry.

"Wait for me," Sand told the driver.

"Mister, you could run up a hell of a tab."

"Wait for me," he repeated.

He moved up a cracked concrete walk to the large double
doors and touched his finger to a call button.

A skinny kid battling acne opened the door. He had a grin
stretched across his face and something pinned to his coat
that said he was an honorary fruit grower. When he got a
look at the man in the doorway the grin started to jerk and
died a slow death. The kid was scared without really knowing why he was scared.

He knew this was the one they called Sand. That was
enough.

Sand moved past him and inside.

He was in a large parlor with a bar and music and conventioneers scattered about. Everybody having a casual good
time and nobody particularly interested in one more arrival.
The girls covered practically every age above puberty and
every nationality you could think of, some of them almost
dressed and some almost undressed. Most were smiling and
some laughing as they responded to the hands of whichever
paying customer happened to be interested and closest. But
the laughter was difficult to find in their eyes. There was a
time, long ago, when he would not have seen that.

"Mopsie Steiner," Sand said.

The skinny kid looked like he could still be in high
school. He made a show of craning his neck around the
room. "I don't see her anywhere."

"Find her."

Then he walked across the parlor, the people in this room
beginning to notice him now, men who didn't know him
stepping quickly out of his path, the eyes of the girls following him. Perhaps it was the way he walked—like a warrior,
or something about his face or the gray steel of his eyes, dis-

tinctive because they seemed to tell nothing of the man while actually they told it all.

On the other side of the parlor was a door opening into a smaller room. He twisted the knob and walked inside. There was a desk and a sofa and even a couple of file cabinets against one wall. Mopsie Steiner had always run her house like a business. A lucrative business.

He sat on one corner of the desk and smoked while he waited.

It didn't take long.

Mopsie hadn't changed, and that was strange for he hadn't seen her in a lot of years. A plump blonde with enough sense to come in off the street a long time ago and eventually to get off the turf altogether and let other girls do the work that would make them stale at thirty and old at forty. Her place had been one of the biggest in the days when houses were the rule and not the exception. Her surroundings had aged and grown more seedy, but she was still the same Mopsie who had been his friend, was still his friend. It showed in her eyes as she looked at him.

She stood there in the open doorway for a moment and then she closed it behind her.

"I heard you were back, Sand, but I wasn't really sure. Because of the letter I wrote?"

"Because of the girl, Mopsie. Because somebody killed her and nobody but you and I give a damn. Because if she died here she slid too far too fast, and that means somebody was pushing. Whoever it was, I'll get. The one who used the knife, I'll get him too. Maybe they're the same. However it is and whoever it is, I'm here to hand him his ticket to hell."

She nodded. She understood.

"You'll want the diary," she said. "Lots of names in there, even yours, but it doesn't really give any idea who would have done it." She walked around behind the desk and opened the middle drawer with a key. She took the book out and handed it to him. It was a five-year diary bound in imitation leather with a small lock, the kind that can be bought in any stationery store. Five years—so it probably began about the time . . .

The name was stamped into the imitation leather.

Delia Shannon.

A petite redhead with too perfect a body and too many illusions about life—a heart so filled with enthusiasm for living that she had managed to give a little of it to a tough hood up to his chin in slime. That was five years ago. She had been a lot of things since then; most of them he didn't even know about, but he would learn.

Five years.

She had been so warm.

And a slab in the morgue is cold.

TWO

THE LOCK ON THE DIARY had been broken. Sand opened it and flipped the pages. He did not try to read it here; there would be time later.

"How did she get to you, Mopsie?"

She made a slight shrug with her shoulders. "From a bum named Jessey Jollie, a real nothing guy. He's a small-time hustler willing to do anything to turn a buck. Somehow he got hold of the girl and had her cribbing out of a rented room in a dump down on wino row. He's a drunk, and she was boozing bad. I guess she felt that made them compatible."

He held up the book. "She leave this Jollie character out?"

"It ends about three months back. That must have been a little before she tied up with him. She didn't start a new one, far as I was able to tell. I guess she just didn't have the ambition."

"How long was she with you?"

"Maybe a month before I found her with the knife in her. When I heard where she was and found out how things were I talked her into coming here. It took a while to dry her out, and even then she was kinda like a rag doll."

"Was Jollie still in the picture?"

She shook her head. "No. I gave him her money for the first couple of weeks. A good pimp can come in handy in this business. A good pimp keeps his woman in line and working and reasonably happy, only Jollie didn't have the talent to be a good pimp. I told him to beat it and not to come back. He squealed, but he went. She didn't really care one way or the other. She just went around in a trance until . . ."

"Until when, Mopsie?"

"Well, during that last week she began to show signs of straightening out. I actually saw her smile a couple of times, and she was starting to eat without being prodded."

"Why?"

"A guy, I guess. Almost always it's a guy. That or religion. Only with religion you don't get the smiles."

"Who?"

"I don't know. Probably one of the customers. It happens sometimes. Couldn't have been anybody on the outside because she never went out. After Jollie was gone, she moved her things into one of the rooms upstairs."

Sand lit a cigarette. "Which customer?"

"She had her share of Johns. She still had most of her looks, and the damage the booze was doing to her body hadn't quite reached the surface. Could have been any one of them. Like I said in my letter, I found her in her room when she didn't come down for breakfast, the knife sticking up in her chest."

"Maybe the guy making her smile also made her dead," Sand said.

"Could be. I don't know. All I know is that suddenly she's happy and then she's dead. I asked the other girls if anybody stayed with her after the place was closed, but none of them know. That's what they all say and I believe them. Delia was friendly enough with the other girls but she was too filled with her personal sadness to bond with any of the staff."

He held up the book. "So we have this."

"And it's nothing. I told you, the last page was written three months ago."

Sand looked at the book in his hand, contemplating it silently for a long moment before he said, "You're wrong, Mopsie. It's a map, a five-year map complete with names and dates. No X marks the killer, but I'm going to follow this map, and by the time I reach the end I'm not going to need any mark."

For the barest instant there was concern in her face. "There are a lot of big names in that book, Sand. Not lately . . . but early on."

"Names are people, Mopsie. People have bones, and bones break. When bones break people squeal. That's what I want to hear; I want to hear what comes out when they squeal."

"It's going to be bad, isn't it?"

"Yeah, it's going to be bad."

"They'll know you came here, that I helped."

"You scared, Mopsie?"

She shook her head, a light smile touching her lips. "You know me, Sand. I never had the sense to be scared. You going now?"

He had pushed away from the desk.

"People to see. She was really a good kid. She didn't deserve life the way she got it. The one who shoved the knife into her chest, he only finished the job. It began a long time ago, and every son of a bitch who kicked the props from under her dropped her a level lower, a little closer to looking up at the ceiling with a knife in her chest. They all played a part—they all get a piece of the action."

"They'll try to kill you."

"I die hard."

"Syndicate hoods, all of them. That's what you'll find in that book because that's who she hung with. They get smaller until they shrink to the size of Jessey Jollie, but they start big. The organization won't stand for anybody shoving their boys around, Sand—not even you."

"We'll see." He started for the door. "By the way, the kid who let me in—isn't he a little young for the job?"

A smile touched her lips, and for a moment there was a hint of pride in her eyes. "He's young all right, and a little foolish sometimes. I've told him before to stay out of sight, but he never does. That's Joey, my kid. You would never know it by looking at him but he goes to college now. Not local either. Ivey league. He ranked in the top two percent on his SATs. His father was very brainy. I guess that's where he gets it."

Sand nodded. He seemed to recall that she had a kid. She had always tried to keep him as far away from this kind of life as she could. Apparently she was still trying.

"Sand . . ." she called to him as he opened the door to

leave. It was a whisper, but it was also the other. "If you need help . . . remember me."

He knew how much guts it took for her to say it.

"Thanks, Mopsie."

The big brunette waiting for him in the parlor stepped up close and bumped her breasts against him as he closed the door behind him.

"Hey, big boy. You like?"

Two large pillows of perfumed female persuasion trying to climb out the top of her gown seemed destined to topple her forward at any minute.

"What's not to like," he said, "but I'm busy."

"I heard about you," she said. The voice was as big as the rest of her. "They say you're that Sand, the one who bumped off all those guys when they tried to bump you off first and maybe some more just for the hell of it. That who you are?"

"That's who I am."

"Then it's too bad you're busy. I sure would like to get to know a man like that. Maybe you won't be so busy next time. If you ever get back this way, that is."

"I have a feeling I'll be back," he said.

That made her happy.

He left her that way.

The cabby was glad to see him. He was so pleased he got out of the cab with the intention of walking around and opening the door for his passenger. He walked around the front of the car, and that made him a lucky man, lucky he wasn't in the cab; otherwise, he would have been directly in the line of fire.

The loud bark of a heavy caliber pistol began its act while the driver was in front of the cab and Sand still several yards away from it.

Sand heard the roar and saw the windshield of the cab web. He hit the ground with a yell to the driver to do the same. The yell wasn't necessary.

The car was parked across the street. It hadn't been there when Sand went inside.

Even as Sand hit the ground, the. 45 automatic was in his

hand because practice had made it habit, a reflex action performed without conscious thought. The car was already speeding down the street. He raised the .45 and fired once just as the hulking black car passed under the yellow glow of a street lamp. There was the sound that told him the slug had found the car. It lurched to the left slightly, then straightened out. It took a corner on squealing tires and was gone.

He stood there and lit a cigarette. He showed no concern.

The cab driver picked himself up and hurried over. "You all right, mister?" Then the concern in his voice became confusion. "Why the hell you smiling?"

Sand didn't bother to tell him that it wasn't a smile, not really, but an expression—an expression that always came when the battle had begun.

THREE

TOILET WATERS was first—because Sand had a hunch the ambush was his idea. Torbert Waters was the name his parents had given him, but the gangs had always had a tendency toward giving nicknames. Now that he was big enough to wear a respectable front and getting bigger it was Torbert again, except to those who had known him in the early days.

The small, exclusive supper club he owned was called The Waterfall. He thought the name up himself and had been patting himself on the back ever since. If you managed to get in the place, you could rub elbows with a politician who had won despite the way you voted or fannies with some broad you might have seen that afternoon on the movie screen. On the stage you could watch top-rated performers go through their paces while you drank good booze and ate aged steak. The tab was high, but that was what kept out the riff-raft.

At the door a tuxedoed hood named Turkey tried to keep him out. Sand shoved a single finger hard into his gut and watched his eyes bug out as his tongue tied itself into a knot trying not to scream. Everything about the hood was suddenly paralyzed but those big eyes.

Sand said calmly, "Now, I think we must have a case of mistaken identity here, Turkey. If you knew it was me, you wouldn't try to keep me out. You look at me real close and see if you don't remember me. Sand. S-a-n-d. Like the stuff you walk on, except that nobody walks on me. Ask your cousin Herne Gottmam about me and see if he remembers. I hear he's so fat he can't walk without rolling these days. You might say I helped him along by shooting his balls off. Think cousin Herne with balls; then think cousin Herne with no balls. You think hard, Turkey, and maybe you'll remember me."

He had his voice back now, but part of the pain was still there and it edged his words.

"I remember you. Damn right, I remember you."

"Then you wouldn't want to keep me out, would you, Turkey?"

Turkey didn't want any more of what he was still trying to get over. "No . . . No, I guess not."

Sand patted him on the head like he was a kid. "Good boy, Turkey."

He stepped past the hood and into the large room filled with tables and people and surprisingly little noise, despite the fact that everybody seemed to be talking.

For a moment he thought nobody had noticed the exchange between him and Turkey, then he realized someone had.

She was a tall blonde with breasts that filled the top of her gown in an exciting way and hips and thighs that really did something for the material stretched across them. Young enough to be a starlet, but the glasses she wore denied it. Starlets never wear glasses. Even the severe hairstyle seemed to have an air of the practical about it, and that must have meant something too. She was looking at him hard in a displeased way.

He stood there a moment and surveyed the place for other hoods of Turkey's caliber, and then he continued to stand there and wait for the blonde to reach him. She had already started in his direction.

When she was close enough, she said, "I don't know who you are, mister—but I saw what you did to Turkey. My brother owns this place, and I think you should leave before something happens to you."

It wasn't a threat; she was really trying to warn him. She had a nice voice, a voice that made a man wonder why he wasn't making love to her.

"I didn't know Toilet had a sister," he said.

That got a funny look out of her. "I haven't heard him called that since—"

"I knew him before he outgrew it."

"An old friend?"

"An old enemy."

Her pretty lips got a little tight. "From the days when he was a criminal, I suppose. If that's the case, I don't think he would want to see you. He's a respectable businessman now."

She really believed it.

"Honey, you're either mighty stupid or mighty blind. That crumb your brother has watching the door has been indicted for murder three times. The bartender over there mixing a batch of martinis I used to know when his specialty was feeding knockout drops to sailors so B-girls could clean their pockets."

"Would it hurt your feelings, mister, if I said I don't believe you?"

"No. My feelings aren't very sensitive. And my name is Sand,"

That meant something to her. "Not the one—"

"If you've heard about me, I'm the one."

His eyes went over the room again. He didn't see any trouble here. Evidently Waters didn't let his boys use the place as a social hangout.

"All the things I've heard about you are bad," the blonde said.

"All the things I've done are bad. Where do I find your brother?"

"You aren't going to leave?"

"Later."

"Why do you want to see my brother?"

"None of your cute little business, blondie. Where is he?"

"His office is upstairs. If you mean to start trouble, you better not go up. He has some other men with him."

She was warning him again. That bit about her brother no longer being part of the rackets—it was something she was trying hard to convince herself was true, but down deep she knew it was a lie.

"Any friend of Toilet's is an enemy of mine," he said.

"Maybe I'll break some heads while I'm up."

"You'll get hurt."

He gave her something resembling a grin and started toward the stairs. She didn't follow him, though he had a feeling she wanted to.

They were waiting for him by the time he reached the upper level. Turkey was smart enough to know that's what phones were made for. Probably, too, there were standing orders not to force any ruckus in front of the paying customers.

Before you got to the office you had to walk down a short, thickly carpeted hallway and past two more tuxedoed hoods who were a little younger but in the same class with their downstairs cohorts.

One of them was big enough to weigh in at about two-twenty-five, the other one just as wide but not quite as high. Manicured nails and pearly teeth, trim haircuts and formal tailored attire with no scars or tattoos showing. Everybody had class these days. Only the tailor hadn't allowed for the heaters these boys kept stuffed inside their coats. The big lump where a shoulder holster would be sort of ruined the effect.

The biggest one grinned at Sand as he approached. "Where you think you're going, friend?"

Sand didn't like the way he said it. So he hit him, a short, powerful jab to the throat that the hood didn't see coming until the pain was turning bells loose in his brain and his Adam's apple was clogging his windpipe. All he could do was stand there and strangle.

His buddy spit out something that sounded like a curse and went searching for the rod inside his coat.

Sand kicked him in the groin and watched his face turn green and his tongue climb out his open mouth as though it were running from the scream of agony following right behind it. Sand took a step back and kicked again, slamming the scream back down his throat along with some of his teeth. He hit the floor on his back, his mouth a soft bloody hole, but he hadn't forgotten the gun inside his coat. He had it out and was trying to get it pointed when Sand stomped down hard on his arm and listened to the music of the snapping bone. Another scream started then, but it died in a gurgle as the hood passed out.

The other one was still holding his throat, beginning to get a little of his wind back. Sand casually slipped the heavy black .45 from its holster and showed it to him. Then, just as casually, he laid it across his forehead with enough force to send blood spurting out his nose like a berserk drinking fountain.

Toilet had really thought they would keep him out. Otherwise, he would have sent the second pair of hoods out the back way.

Surprise was a worm that crawled all over the racket boss's face as Sand opened the door to his private office.

"Hello, Toilet."

His gag was almost as real as the hood's with the smashed Adam's apple. On about the third try he got some sound out.

"Sand!"

The two boys who had been riding in the car were in the room. The one who was able wanted to make a grab for his rod. He did a double take when Sand shook the .45 loose and taught the punk how damn slow he was. This one was tall and skinny. He swallowed hard as he looked down the nose of the .45 and realized how easy it would be to die.

The second one was sitting on the edge of the couch, his arm hanging down and blood running off the tips of his fingers onto a dinner jacket that would never be the same again. This was the one his slug had found outside of Mopsie Steiner's place, a young one, the pallor of his face saying that right now he was a mighty sick fish.

Toilet just sat there with the phone he had been dialing still in his hand. Probably he had been calling a medic for his boy.

Sand said, "Finish your call, Toilet—then get them out of here."

"Why?"

"Because we're going to have a little talk."

"And if I don't?"

Sand smiled. And the men who saw it felt a cold sensation creep up their spines. It was that kind of smile.

The racket boss finished dialing, said a few curt words into the mouthpiece while he scribbled something on a piece of scratch paper, then handed it to the tall one. The two hoods left down the back way.

Sand sat on the corner of the large walnut desk and shoved the .45 back under his armpit. "I figured they were your boys, Toilet. Who tipped you?"

He would have liked to deny it, but it was too late for that. He shrugged. "Nobody. The rumor was out all over that you were coming back. One of my boys happened to spot you."

"And you told them to shoot me up."

"Wasn't like that, Sand," he lied. "We always got along all right. Why would I want to do a thing like that? The boys took it on themselves."

"Crap. They don't blow their nose without asking your permission."

"What you doing back, Sand? That wasn't part of the word."

"Delia."

All the man behind the desk looked was puzzled.

"Who?"

"Delia Shannon. Strain hard and you might remember her, Toilet. You were engaged to her five years ago."

A look of distaste that might have been real replaced the puzzled expression. "That tramp? I ain't seen her in years. Sure I remember her—a redhead with big tits and a nice little body. She was kinda special right there at first, so I gave her a ring and that means we're engaged. I do it sometimes. What the hell's a ring. But what's your interest? I didn't know you even knew the little slut."

"You kick her out?"

"Naw. She went for somebody else. Paddy Clay, I think it was. You remember Paddy."

Sand remembered Paddy Clay. Organization-wise about the same size as Toilet; he handled the horses, the bets, the fixes, the works. Sand wished he'd had the time to read the diary before he came here. That way, he would have known whether or not the man behind the desk was lying. If he was, it would have saved a return trip.

"What happened to the girl after Paddy, Toilet?"

"I don't know. I got more important things to keep up with. He don't have her any more though. I see him around sometime. I wouldn't have remembered the chick to start with except for that red hair and the ways she could use that hot little body of hers. If you're looking for her, I don't know where—"

"I'm not looking for her, Toilet. She's in the morgue."

"Oh?"

"It's the man who put her there I'm after."

"Well, like I said, I ain't seen her in years. Probably she put herself there. Dames are always committing suici—"

"A knife in the chest, Toilet. A neat job. Right through the heart."

He thought about that, shrugged. "I didn't even know she was dead. What business you got with me I don't know."

"Five years ago she was your woman, Toilet. A few days ago she was murdered in a slum crib. Two ends of a long ladder. Maybe you didn't like her walking out on you. Maybe you're the one who kept kicking the slats out from under her as she fell. Somebody did it, and whoever it was is due a lot of grief. Maybe the same bastard also used the knife. It will be neater that way. Less mess to clear up after I'm through."

The racket boss knew he meant it. He didn't know why, but he knew he meant it.

"I think you must be barking up a wrong tree, Sand. Nobody gives a damn about a dame like that. Hell, they're a dime a dozen."

"I give a damn."

"That I can't figure."

"The important thing, Toilet, is that I'm here. Once the girl did me a favor. It's a debt I owe. I'm here to pay it off with the corpse of the son of a bitch who persecuted and murdered her." He reached inside his coat and saw the hood's eyes get scared with the thought that the .45 was coming out again. Instead, the hand came out holding the leather-covered diary. "You see this, Toilet? A five-year diary, and every page filled. When I leave here I'm going back to my hotel and I'm going to start reading. If you lied to me, I'll be back."

Waters swallowed hard. "I ain't got any reason to lie."

Sand replaced the diary, straightened up. "Tell your friends I'm coming, Toilet. Spread the word. Tell them why I'm coming and what I'm going to do when I find the man I want. And tell them about the book."

He didn't wait for the man behind the desk to answer. He turned and walked out into the hall. The short hood with the broken arm had puked all over the floor. He was just beginning to come around. The other one was still out.

The blonde was still in the club. Her pretty eyes followed him with a look he couldn't quite read as he crossed the wide room and walked outside.

FOUR

THE GIRL HAD BEEN the loveliest thing in the world that night, but the tall syndicate executive standing silently in one corner of the crowded room hadn't noticed her. He had other things on his mind.

The man was called Sand.

The problem that kept his face tight as he drank slowly from the glass in his hand was one that had been nagging him for a long time. More a feeling, really—a feeling of suffocating.

How deep do you burrow in slime before there is no crawling back? How deep before you become an inseparable part of the slime?

The girl was Delia Shannon, but he didn't know that then.

The party? The aftermath of a meeting held here earlier. The meeting had been significant; a gathering of the syndicate hierarchy for the purpose of making a promotion in personnel. Sand was the man, and the job was big, very big. The men who had come here from all over the country to talk it out and make the decision bore witness to that. They were the top.

Or were they from the bottom? Funny thing about the rackets—the lower you crawl the higher you climb. The more corruption you wallow in and the more stink you learn to live with, the more authority you claim.

They hadn't bothered to ask him if he wanted the job. Why should they? It was what he had spent years working for, wasn't it? Sand—tough, competent, resolute, a climber whose value had been proven and proven again. They knew him, and everything they knew was true. But there was the thing they didn't know, the thing he hadn't consciously known himself until it closed in on him like a dark, smothering cloud.

He wanted out.

Yeah.

He had seen and wallowed in too much of the filth that went with the business. Sure, he had gotten rich on the way, but suddenly even the money didn't matter any more.

It was his problem.

Only there was no answer.

So he drank slowly and paid no attention to the dwindling party noises around him. Tonight would be his last in this town. Tomorrow he would leave for Chicago to take over his new position in the underworld.

He walked out onto the terrace, and while he was there the last of the partiers must have drifted out, some to the bedrooms of their women, others to the clubs to catch the last show and have a few more drinks.

When he reentered the room it was empty. He crossed the room to a foyer that ran to the elevator of this penthouse suite. His hand had stretched out to push the button for the elevator when he heard the girl's scream. Not a scream really, but close enough.

It came from one of the rooms off to the right.

When he pushed the door open she was struggling with a man in the center of the room, her hair loose and tangled about her face, her dress torn down the front to reveal a white slip, itself torn to expose one cup of the bra straining at the task of holding her moving breasts as she struggled.

Sand didn't know the man, but he didn't need anybody to explain what was happening. One look at the burning lust in the man's eyes and the fear in the girl's, and no questions were necessary.

Neither of them knew he was there until he said quietly, "Let her go."

The guy froze like he had been kicked in the spine, then turned his head slowly. Sand could smell the booze on his breath despite the distance between them. The drunk didn't know the intruder, and that was his mistake.

"Go away, mister. This ain't none of your business." He

continued to hold onto the girl. She had stopped struggling. Her eyes looked at Sand with a note of pleading.

"I'm making it my business," Sand said. "Let her go." His voice calm and even.

The drunk drew himself up to roar. "I'll let her go long enough to break every—"

Sand closed the distance between them almost in a casual stride. His fist slammed like a battering ram into the guy's heart, forcing the whiskey breath from his lungs. Then, like a pneumatic hammer, Sand hit him between the eyes: One. Two. Three. Fast, precise, crushing blows. By the time the man hit the floor his head had already begun to swell and the top of his face was turning purple.

"Is . . . is he dead?" the girl asked.

"I don't think so. You care?"

"I wouldn't want anybody dead on account of me. He was just drunk. Probably he thought I had led him on. I let him talk to me earlier at the party."

"Did you lead him on?"

"No. But it might have seemed that way. I didn't think about it at the time. I was lonesome. My fiance brought me to the party, but then he had to leave suddenly."

Sand studied the girl. It occurred to him that her dress, before the guy on the floor had ripped it apart, had been a little more conservative, her beauty a little more natural, than you usually expect to find at a party like the one tonight.

"Who's your fiancé?"

"Torbert Waters."

Toilet Waters. He looked at the girl and thought of the hood who had come up through the ranks with him, and something didn't jell. If this girl wasn't artificial enough to belong to the party, she wasn't artificial enough to belong to Toilet Waters.

She seemed to become conscious of the state of her clothing for the first time and tried to pull the material back in place and hold it there.

"Do you know him?" she asked.

"I know him. Let's get out of here."

"But what about him?" She pointed down at the floor. "Aren't we going to get him a doctor or something?"

"No." He took her arm and guided her into the foyer and to the elevator.

"You have a car?" he asked when they were downstairs.

"No"

"I have. I'll drive you home."

"You don't have to. A cab—"

"You're not dressed for it."

He put her in his car and walked around to the driver's side. They were in the light traffic of a night soon to become morning when the girl spoke again.

"You're mad at me for some reason, aren't you?"

"Why should I be mad at you? I don't even know your name."

"My name is Delia Shannon, and I don't know why, but you are."

He fired a cigarette with the dash lighter. "Yeah. I guess I am."

"Why?"

"Because I think maybe you're a decent kid."

"What's wrong with me being decent?"

"The company you keep."

Her eyes fastened on his face a little harder. "Torbert, you mean?"

"Yeah. Toilet to his friends."

"He hates that nickname. Are you his friend?"

"No. But I know him. Maybe I should describe friendship in this world you're playing in. In the rackets everybody you know is your friend. Unless, maybe, the word has come down to knock you off—then nobody is your friend."

She was still looking at him hard. Suddenly she said, "Your name is Sand, isn't it?"

That surprised him. "How did you know?"

She gave a little shrug and the torn piece of her dress got loose from her fingers. She didn't try to retrieve it. "I don't know. I just guessed. Torbert was raging mad tonight before we went to the party. He mentioned your name several times.

Something about you taking over some kind of territory."

"That figures. He wanted it for himself so bad he could taste it."

"Yes. I think so. I'm glad he didn't get it."

"Why?"

"Because I want him to give up what he's been doing. I think I can convince him if he loves me as much as he says he does. It would have been harder if he had been chosen."

Sand almost hated to tell her, but he did. "You're having pipe dreams, girl. Nobody breaks with the organization. Not without getting dead. If you'd been around very long you would know that. And your friend Toilet would be the last one to want out. He thrives on what he is and what he's a part of."

"I can't believe that."

"That's because you're stupid. If you had any sense you wouldn't be playing around with the crowd you are. What's your story, anyway? You come here from some small town hoping to get a break in show business or something?"

Her expression was the answer. "Does it happen that often?"

"Yeah, it happens that often. Most of them aren't as pretty as you, and some of them have talent. Some make it and some don't. Most run back home and some stay behind and get mixed up with scum like Toilet Waters."

"I guess you're right. But there must be exceptions, stories here and there with happy endings. You aren't much of a dreamer, are you, Sand?"

"There's too big a gap between dreams and reality."

"Maybe—except for the lucky ones."

"And you think you're one of the lucky ones."

"Uh huh."

"I hope you're right." He meant it.

"You aren't one of the lucky ones, are you, Sand?"

He flipped his cigarette out the window and lit another one. "I'm alive. After some of the things I've been through, I suppose that makes me lucky enough."

Suddenly she said, "I don't think I want to go home right

now. Could we just ride some place? Maybe we could park somewhere on top of a hill and look down at the lights? Or on a shore and look out over the water? I've always wanted to do that, but I never have. Have you, Sand?"

"Not recently."

"Let's do."

He thought about it. All too soon the sun would be up and a new day would arrive. The plane reservation to Chicago had already been made. They wanted him to step in fast and take over before the operation had a chance to start coming apart. Another step up the ladder. A little deeper in the slime.

At the party he had tried to think and gotten nowhere. Now he wanted to stop thinking, to make himself numb. The hours between this minute and the new day would probably be better with the girl, despite the fact that he had known her name only a few minutes and that she was a stupid kid with big dreams and a louse's ring on her finger.

"Well?"

"Sure," he said. "Why not."

He drove and the girl talked. Then they were parked, with the city spread out beneath them, and she continued to talk. He liked the sound of her voice. He liked the girl. She didn't deserve what she was letting herself in for.

"Let's talk about you," she said finally. "I've already told you all about me."

Actually she hadn't. She had told him about yesterday and the day before and how she happened to meet her fiance. She hadn't mentioned where she had come from or what she had done before she came here.

"Let's not talk about me. It's not a pretty subject."

She nodded her head for some reason. "It's like I thought."

"What is?"

"You. You're trying to make up your mind about some-thing, aren't you?"

"Yes, I guess I am."

"Something important?"

"Like life is more important than death."

She was serious now. "Can I help?"

"No."

"I would like to, really I would." Her voice was almost a whisper this time, and she was sliding gently across the seat to him. "If I can't help any other way, maybe I can help take your mind off it."

One soft breast was already against his arm and her lips were reaching up for his when he stopped her. "Aren't you forgetting your boyfriend?"

With the heaviness that had grown in her breathing, she whispered, "Maybe I want to forget him. Right this minute and until it is time for you to go I think I would like to forget him very much."

Their lips were together then, gently, and then less gentle as each began to respond to the other. For a few minutes the night moved in closer and the lights of a city below dissolved into nothing. Beneath his hands a slight tremble shook the girl's body as their lips parted, only to be drawn together again, almost a fierceness in them now.

When finally he pushed her away her breasts were heaving slightly with her breathing. She looked at him. "Why?"

"I'm not some high school kid, kitten. I don't make love in parked cars."

She denied it with a shake of her head. "I don't think that's it, not all of it. I think you feel the closeness between us, a closeness that has nothing to do with our bodies or the fact that we've only known each other a short time. I feel it and so do you, and for some reason you don't want that."

Maybe she was right. She was a girl with a problem without really knowing it, and maybe it would be too easy for him to get involved. It was the last thing in the world he needed. He had troubles of his own.

"I'm right," she said. "I know I am."

He twisted the key in the ignition and listened to the engine catch, then backed the car onto the highway.

"What's your address?" he asked her.

She gave it to him and then kept going in a voice filled with soft tones of disbelief and disappointment. "You're taking me home, Sand—just like that?"

"Why not?"

She shook her head slightly. "If you don't know the answer to that, I guess I was wrong a moment ago when I kissed you—in which case I should feel a little foolish."

She hadn't been wrong. He didn't know what it was, but she hadn't been wrong. He told her so.

She smiled real big for him. "I think this is going to be one of those special nights, Sand, one of those night's that is a beginning and a middle and an end all in itself with no physical connection to the lifetime surrounding it."

He managed a grin himself. "You never stop dreaming, do you, kitten?"

"Maybe. The world is prettier that way."

Her apartment was on the third floor of a modern brick building where the rent would be more than the salary a girl trying to get a start in show business could make. Sand was a little surprised at the sudden flare of anger inside him at the thought of Toilet Waters paying for this. He didn't mention it to the girl. Hell, it was none of his business. He had met the girl tonight and tomorrow he would forget her. Tomorrow he would be on a plane to Chicago. He would have sunk another foot deeper in the slime, added a little more of the stink; he would have climbed another step up the ladder.

They had a drink before they made love. One drink, and then they were again wrapped in each other's arms, no holding back, no games to play but their game of passion.

They played it well.

Her breasts were against him, responding to the rising tempo of their blood. At first there was the restricting confinement of the bra, then it was gone and there was the hot resilient flesh of her breasts and tiny rock-hard nipples rough against the palms of his hands.

Their lips made promises they couldn't keep as their bodies sought and found and continued to seek. Near the end she cried out his name, over and over, until her voice faded away.

Afterward, she lay naked in his arms, the fullness of her

thighs and the swell of her hips against him, one firm breast forever pleasantly against his chest.

They drank and they talked, and they did not think about the coming of morning. There are times when a man will talk, even a silent man, and there are times when a lovely woman will listen, cradled naked in his arms, her hair mussed from the love they have made.

This was such a time.

The girl had been right; it was a small piece of time cut out of infinity, a whole in itself, meaning everything here, if only a memory when it was gone.

Maybe he didn't really talk to the girl. Maybe he talked to himself—for the first time in a long, long time.

When he was ready to leave, she said, "You've made some kind of decision tonight, haven't you, Sand?"

He nodded. "Yes, I've made a decision."

"Did I help?"

"You helped, kitten."

She smiled. "I'm glad. I'm glad about everything."

He pulled her against him and kissed her gently, a good-bye kiss. "Some advice for you, Delia—go home. You're a good kid, and I like you a lot. This isn't the place for you."

For a moment she was sad. "I'm not sure there is a place for me."

She reached up and kissed him again. Neither of them said anything more.

The following afternoon as he waited for the plane that would take him away he wrote a note to her, advising her again to turn loose Toilet Waters and his crowd. He didn't tell her about the decision she had helped him make. At the end of the note he had written:

If you ever need a friend, remember the slice out of time we shared. Sand.

~ ~ ~ ~ ~

He closed the diary and stared up at the ceiling. The cigarette on the ashtray had burned itself out, so he lit another one. He had read every page, written in a small, neat feminine scrawl. The book in his hand wasn't real. The girl had lived life the way it came, but she had recorded it the way she wished it to be. It was a fairy tale, not a history. As a map it would be hard to follow because he would have to interpret it as he went along. But the names were there, a long string of names stretched over a short span of years.

Somewhere in there he would find a killer.

FIVE

THE VOICE WAS A GROWL when it came on the line. "Yeah? . . . Mohannah."

"Max."

"Sand?" There was a note of incredulity mixed in with the nastiness.

"See, now we're acquainted," Sand said into the phone at his end. "Who says a man never meets his neighbor in the city?"

"Who did you kill?" the detective captain wanted to know. "You must have killed somebody or else you wouldn't be calling me. No, I take that back you—that has never prompted a call before."

"I got the feeling at the airport you hadn't grown any fonder of me in my absence."

"Perceptive. Very perceptive. I'm busy."

"Yeah. I didn't really expect to find you in, but I thought I would give it a try. Can never tell when somebody important might get bumped off, in which case an enterprising civil servant would want to be around to pose for the news-hounds."

At the other end of the line the police captain's only response was a low curse growled into the phone.

"I'm surprised you don't already know what I've been up to." Sand said. "No tail?"

"I put a tail on you once and he kept your hide from roasting in a four-story blaze with a couple other deserving citizens. I don't intend to make a mistake like that again."

"I want a favor, Max."

"Favors I owe to no ex-hood, including you."

"This one is so small it won't strain you any. You've got a girl in the morgue whose name was Delia Shannon. I want to see her."

At the other end there was a silence that lasted too long. Then: "What's your interest in the girl, Sand?"

"Personal. We were friends a long time ago. I want to see she gets a proper burial."

The cop made a sound. "She's not in the morgue any more."

"Where is she?"

"Moved to a funeral home tonight."

"Details, Max."

"Another friend showed up. Or rather a friend of the family."

"The name of this friend?"

"J. Addison Rutledge." Even as he said the name his voice held a little of the awe that went with it.

"The billionaire politician?"

"That perception again."

"I read the papers. Something sounds screwy though. The girl didn't travel in his league. As far as I know, she came here a few years ago from a middle class family in some small town. She never got to mix with quite that much money, and she certainly didn't endorse his puritanical views."

"He knew her before five years ago, and I guess a man like that will try to do what he considers the Christian thing, no matter how far a person has strayed from his strict moral code. Seems she was the daughter of a deceased family servant. He hadn't seen or heard from her in years but saw her name in the papers and took the responsibility on himself of seeing that she was buried right. Her mother was her only relative, and she died several years ago. I thought it was right decent of him."

"He handle it through you?"

"J. Addison Rutledge does his handling at the top. Hell, why shouldn't he? If you want to see her it will have to be at the funeral home. There is a viewing scheduled for tonight. The funeral is tomorrow. And before you ask why I'm such a fountain of information, I'll remind you this was a homicide.

It's standard operating procedure for us to have somebody blend in and keep his eyes open at these things. Killers often have some kind of sick compulsion to put in an appearance."

"I'll want to be there, Max. How about reading off times and places to me."

The cop took a moment to find the information on his desk and gave it to him.

"Thanks, Max."

"For nothing. Just don't try to tell me this girl has anything to do with the reason you came back."

"I had no intention of telling you anything like that, Max."

Then he hung up.

~ ~ ~ ~ ~

He didn't know what he had expected to find at the funeral home; maybe he expected nothing. He didn't expect what he found, even though as soon as he walked through the door he knew it could have been no other way.

The man standing alone, close to but not at the side of the open casket, wore a face frequently seen featured in the media and sponsored for political prominence.

J. Addison Rutledge nodded slightly in recognition of Sand's presence as he entered the dimly lit room. He had the stance and features of a politician from another era, an Abe Lincoln as opposed to the glad-handing smile-meister currently in vogue.

Standing huddled close to one wall and not talking at all in the hushed atmosphere were four well-dressed young men, doubtless members of the politician's staff. They were making an obvious effort to appear attentive to the occasion.

Mopsie Steiner was there with two of her girls and her kid, Joey. Mopsie and the girls stood in the center of the room talking in murmurs among themselves.

The kid stood slightly apart from them gawking around the room with a disappointed frown.

Sitting inconspicuously in folding chairs against the wall were two plainclothes cops trying to observe without being observed.

The only other person in the room was a stubble-faced man with light colored hair and bloodshot eyes and the strong smell of booze sweating out his pours. He stood alone, well away from the casket, but unable to stop himself from walking up and glancing down at the girl inside every few minutes. One quick look and he would scurry back to his previous position and wait until he had the courage to or could not resist the urge to do it again.

Sand went first to Mopsie and the girls. Mopsie hugged him and the two girls nodded. There was really nothing to say. After a short, awkward silence Sand asked Mopsie about the light-haired man.

"I don't know his name, and I'm not sure I have ever seen him before," she said. "I suspect he might be one of the names in Delia's diary. I'm afraid to approach him because he looks like he's on the verge of freaking out."

Sand gave the man another glance and nodded his agreement. If his name was in the book they would see each other again.

He introduced himself to J. Addison Rutledge.

"My name is Sand," he said. "I was a friend."

They shook hands.

"Hello, Mr. Sand. I wasn't sure she still had any friends . . . that place where she was murdered . . ."

"Yeah. It's decent of you to do this."

"I knew Delia as she was growing up, Mr. Sand. I only wish I had known sooner where she was or the kind of life she was leading. Perhaps I could have helped."

"Yeah," Sand said again. He walked over to the expensive casket and looked down at the girl inside. It was the same face, but pale and stiff now. He tried to remember her the way she was when they parted, bright and vibrant with only a hint of sadness in her beautiful eyes. Now somebody had made her dead, and he had to do something about that.

Rutledge was watching him closely when Sand turned back to him.

"There is a look of vengeance about you, Mr. Sand. I hope

you don't intend . . ."

"You guessed it."

"There are the police."

"She deserves more than the police have to offer. She deserves somebody who cares. I care, and I know which rocks to look under. I've lived under those rocks, and I know. I know the scum that live there and they know me. They know I don't play unless it's for keeps and that I play hard. Somebody treated her badly, and somebody shoved a knife through her heart. Why I don't know; and who I don't know. But I'll find the answers, and I'll find the killer, and then it will be time for another funeral."

The man looked like he had things he would like to say but decided the time was not right, so he said simply, "Will you keep in touch, Mr. Sand?"

"I'll keep in touch," he promised. "You might be able to help by filling in some of the gaps, like before I met her. I had a sketch in the back of my mind on her background but it turned out to be all wrong."

"I can tell you everything about Delia Shannon from the day she was born up till about six years ago," he said. "Her mother and father came to work for my family years ago. Delia was born and her father died. My sister Muriel was born at about the same time and the two girls grew up like sisters. Muriel was a late child. I was already in college. When my parents passed away I took over the estate and was practically a father to both girls. Six years ago there was a terrible tragedy. Muriel burned to death in an accident. Delia's mother was the first to reach her, and the experience caused her to have a stroke from which she never recovered. It was terrible. Delia left, I suppose, because she simply couldn't bear to stay in the place where it had happened."

"I didn't mean to call up bad memories," Sand said.

"A man must go on living, Mr. Sand."

"There is one thing you might be able to tell me. Was she an extremely religious girl?"

"I am often called a religious extremist myself, Mr. Sand, but I don't believe this is true. It certainly wasn't true of

Delia. Why do you ask?"

"She kept a diary. It only stretches back over the last five years, and it's not really much of a record. All the way through it she makes references to God. The pronouns He or Him, always capitalized and usually concerning some punishment He has handed down."

Rutledge took a moment to think before he said, "Perhaps I'm wrong. A tragedy such as Delia suffered could surely have changed her in many ways."

They shook hands again.

"The funeral is tomorrow afternoon at four," he said. "On my estate there is a small family plot and only myself left to fill it. It is my intent to have Delia laid to rest there."

"Captain Mohannah gave me the address and directions," Sand told him. "Perhaps we'll have a chance to talk more."

On the steps of the funeral home he paused to light a cigarette. He had read Delia's diary and he had seen her body. Now he had work to do.

SIX

THIS WAS A NIGHT TOWN. If you knew where to find it or who to ask, there was always plenty of action. Even on a night like this when the fog ate up the people and rolled down the lonely streets like a giant monster with a damp veil for a belly. The night people who belonged to this night town didn't mind the fog. It made the night darker and closer, and on nights like this they don't expect to be bothered by outsiders.

A cellar beneath a third-rate grocery store closed for the night. From the outside you heard nothing, and if you happened to look down into the concrete hole filled with darkness and fog and broken steps you had to know about the door at the bottom.

Sand descended the steps and tapped a coin against the door.

Nothing.

It was a code. He had called in an IOU to get it. He tapped it out again.

The girl who opened the door had ratty brown hair and wise eyes. Maybe she was out of her teens, but he didn't think so. It was hard to tell what she was behind the wide slash of lipstick, sickeningly green eyelids and a wall of makeup.

"Yeah?" Her eyes were mildly interested, as she looked him over.

"Yeah, what?"

"Yeah, are you a cop?"

"Do I look like a cop?"

"Cops don't look like cops." Her mouth was as wise as her eyes.

"Let's just say I'm looking for Paddy."

As they stood there with the door half open Sand could hear music playing and voices mingling into a murmur.

"Paddy who?" the girl asked.

"How many you got?"

"Don't be vulgar."

"Paddy Clay. He around?"

She shrugged and small breasts moved against the loose sweater she wore, then she stepped aside to let him in. "Who could say?"

The door closed behind him and he saw what she meant. The night people felt safe tonight—tonight they were turning loose. The lights were so dim that faces were more like shadows. As his eyes adjusted he could make out people scattered about haphazardly, mostly sitting or lounging. There was one couple trying to dance to the recorded music and a few on their feet, most with a glass in their hand. His foot struck the leg of a coffee table and rattled glasses sitting perilously close to several lines of white powder.

A big crowd, maybe fifty people, and the night was no longer young. Close by, a guy with strange hair was trying to have sex with a girl who could have been the sister of the one who let him in. They hadn't bothered to remove their clothes, and their bed was a straight wooden chair leaning back on its hind legs and propped against the wall. The girl didn't really seem interested. While her friend struggled on, she strummed a guitar behind his back and sang a song about old soldiers.

These were the no-frills diehards of the partying crowd, no longer needing and even eschewing the conventional trappings as useless social foreplay, like the drunk who knows mixed drinks are for sissies and the uninitiated and a weak substitute for a bottle in a paper bag.

Sand began his search for Paddy Clay. Paddy wasn't a junkie, but he liked to hang with the dream crowd, maybe smoke a joint or two. Sand had bought the information on his whereabouts the same place he bought the code knock.

He nearly stumbled over another couple in the throes of passion. This pair was more enthusiastic than the other, but it mostly boiled down to the female chewing on her partner's neck like a vampire.

Suddenly the girl with the tangled hair was with him again. She glanced at the couple without interest and touched Sand's arm. "You buying, mister, or you bring your own?"

"My own what?"

"Your own whatever. This ain't no social club meeting, you know."

"Don't tell me you're the pusher who pays the overhead on this dump."

"Naw. My fellow—he makes sure the refreshments don't run short. A real entrepreneur, he is. I'm just a helper."

"Hate to cost you a sale, kid, but I'm just in the market for a fellow named Paddy Clay." He reached in his pocket and held up a bill between his fingers. "On the other hand, I could use a guide."

The bill disappeared into her palm. "Paddy Clay, you mean? *That* Paddy Clay?"

"That's the one."

"Just keep walking till you run into the back wall, then turn to your right. There's a place under the stairs—you can't see it from here. That's where he's at, him and a couple of other guys."

"Thanks." He started toward the rear of the cellar.

The girl called, "Hey, mister . . ."

He looked back to her.

"In case anybody asks,"—she held up the bill he had given her—"Paddy don't need to know about this. I ain't got a license to operate a guide service."

"Sure, kid."

The hood was where the girl said he would be, him and a half naked broad so spaced out she wasn't quite sure where she was. The other two were standard issue henchmen. Clay was a bottom feeder but he wasn't small time. He never went anywhere without a tough or two to cover his flank.

Sand said, "Hello, Paddy," and watched everybody's mood change.

The hood tried to play casual.

"Sand!" he proclaimed a little louder than he intended. "Been a long time . . . a long time."

"I was hoping it could last forever," Sand said.

"Waters said you would be around."

"I sort of figured he would."

"Didn't expect you quite this soon."

"I move fast, Paddy. You should have remembered."

"Yeah. Yeah, guess I should." He waved his hand around. "These are my boys."

"Cages must look kind of deserted down at the zoo."

Paddy Clay laughed. His bodyguards didn't.

"Your boys don't seem to have a sense of humor," Sand told him, his face deadly serious.

"Sure they do, Sand. Sure they do." He gave them a look. "Laugh."

They laughed. Only they didn't know why. All they saw was an ex-hood who had been big when he was big but who wasn't up there any more. What the hell was in a rep? Why the shakes all of a sudden from the boss?

Clay wasn't shaking, but he was grinning, and he only grinned when he was scared. Paddy Clay had been around in the early days when Sand was a growing boy in the organization and he had seen him in action. If the meeting had been on his terms it would have been better, but this was too sudden. He didn't like sudden.

Sand pulled up a chair and propped his foot on the seat. His face was hard. Nothing moved but his eyes, and there was no expression in them.

"Let's talk, Paddy."

"Sure, Sand, sure."

The dame walked a few feet away and stretched out on the floor to go to sleep. The toughs stayed by their boss, one on each side, ready to move when the word came and wondering why it hadn't come already.

"Delia Shannon, Paddy. What does the name mean to you?"

The hood's eyes became a little less uneasy. "That really all you got on your mind, Sand? Hell, I thought maybe it was something important."

"Start with how you got her from Toilet."

"I was stuck on the chick, Sand, really I was. But I don't know how I happened to get her. One minute she belonged to Waters, the next she belonged to me. I don't know. I always figured he dumped her."

"You treat her good, Paddy?"

In her diary, Paddy Clay had been a prince of a guy, only Sand happened to know he was no prince.

"Sure. Sure I did, Sand. Like I told you, I was stuck on the chick."

"Tell me about it."

"Ain't nothing to tell. We went around together for a while, that's all. She was class, you know? Guys like Waters and some of the others I come up with, they got it somehow—but me, I can't even find out what it is. The chick was nice window dressing and didn't give me no extra grief. I kinda went for her."

"How long, Paddy?" He knew how long, but he wanted to hear the creep say it. No, that wasn't what he wanted. He wanted him to lie.

"A few months. Not long. Maybe four months."

"What ended it?"

He got a funny look across his face as he reflected on it. "Now that was crazy, that was. I ain't figured it out yet."

"What haven't you figured out?"

"Well, this package comes for me one day. I open it up and my eyes nearly pop. There's this big bundle of bills in there with a note tied to it. I read the note and it's about the chick, how I should drop the girl and the dough's mine. I think at first, man, this is some joke, and then I count those bills and I know it's no joke. Nobody jokes that much money's worth. So I think, what the hell—romance over."

Yeah, a real prince.

"I thought you were stuck on her, Paddy."

"For that much dough, a bundle like out of the sky, I can get unstuck from any dame."

"You're a louse, Paddy."

"Hey, boss," the guy on his right said. "Let us take this bastard. We'll smash the juice out of this fresh son of a bitch." Real eager, this one, and pulling on his leash.

Sand grinned at all of them. "Sure, Paddy. Turn your gorillas loose."

"I don't want no trouble, Sand. Hell, we were in the same business for a lot of years. We're old friends, sort of."

"You're no friend of mine, Paddy. One more question. Who got the girl after you?"

He had to think on it. "Uh, Lobb, I think. Yeah, Al Lobb—a comer in those days. These days he ain't nothing, does a few odd jobs for the boys down at the docks and keeps his guts pickled with booze. She hung with him for a while; then he took a fall. I never did get the story on that, but one day he wasn't a comer no more. Maybe the chick didn't want to fall with him. Anyway, they split about that time. I don't know where she went after that. I didn't keep up."

Sand lifted his foot from its resting place on the chair and slide it back to where it had been.

"You've been a big help, Paddy. Maybe I'll see you around."

Then he turned his back on the three of them and started to walk away. He knew what was going to happen because he knew Paddy Clay and the way his brain worked. He had sold Delia out for money and a scribbled note. Now he was watching a fortune walking away from him with its back turned.

Sand had taken half a dozen steps when he heard the order hiss through gritted teeth. "*Now,* Jack. *Now!!!*"

Sand pivoted as he snapped the .45 out of its holster. Jack had been more than willing to shoot a man in the back. The snub-nosed revolver was already out, already aimed at where Sand's spine had been. Sand shot him in the forearm and the slug threw his whole arm back like a stick in the wind, the revolver still wrapped in his fist. The gun slammed Paddy Clay across the mouth with a wet, brittle *smack!*

The other gunsel wanted his chance but he just wasn't fast

enough. With his hand still inside his coat, his eyes latched onto the nose of the .45 Sand swung to cover him. His mouth got dry and his eyeballs started to sweat and his hand came out empty, his fingers spread so wide the skin was trying to split.

The four of them stood there while the room went crazy around them. Everybody suddenly wanted out and went scrambling for the door. The party was over.

Sand waited for Paddy Clay to shake off his confusion from the blow. It took a couple of minutes. While the seconds ticked off, nobody moved. Jack held his ruined arm and bit his tongue to keep from whimpering. His buddy kept trying to spread his fingers wider. Paddy sat there with blood spurting out his mouth until finally he was back to now and wishing to hell he wasn't.

He looked at Sand and at the .45 in his hand and opened his mouth to say something; only there was nothing to say. He kept trying until he made it.

"For Christ's sake, Sand! *For Christ's sake!*"

"Too late to pray," Sand told him.

He pulled the trigger.

Twin blasts bounced off the walls until one sound caught the other as they faded away. Then everything was deadly quiet and Paddy Clay was left staring down in shocked disbelief. Both his kneecaps had been shattered.

SEVEN

THE FOG HUNG OVER THE STREETS close to the docks like a heavy blanket, wet and close, engulfing the tenements and the people.

A good night to get drunk.

That's what Al Lobb was doing they had told him at the bar down the street.

Behind him there was a small sound of footsteps. He stopped beneath the dim hue of a street lamp and waited for the steps to catch up.

The girl was a hooker, not a particularly pretty one or a particularly wealthy one, but she could afford a light raincoat against the fog and a smile for a stranger. A girl had her rent to pay, and tonight was no holiday.

"A bad night to be outside, mister."

"It's a bad one," he admitted.

She fished a cigarette out of her purse and he lit it for her. There was no attempt to disguise the invitation in her eyes or in her voice. "My place isn't far . . ."

"Afraid I haven't got time. I'm looking for a friend."

She feigned disappointment. "A lady friend?"

"No."

That helped some. "I probably know him. I sorta get around."

"Al Lobb."

"You can't be a friend of Al Lobb, mister."

"No?"

"Even if Al Lobb had a friend, I just can't picture it being you."

"You know where I can find him?"

"That's his place right across the street. First floor in the rear."

He handed her a bill. "For the information. You were right; it's a bad night to be out. Maybe you should get out of it."

"Thanks, mister. I think I will."

Sand crossed the street and climbed the steps of the tenement. There was a smell about the place that he couldn't quite put his finger on as he moved down the dark hallway. Maybe it was a dozen smells, or a hundred, bottled up in a space that could not breathe.

He found the door he wanted and used his knuckles against it. Inside, somebody grunted something that sounded like a question. Sand knocked again.

The man who opened the door was the one from the funeral home. Nothing about him had changed, not his face, his clothes or the sour smell of booze seeping out of him. They said he was a comer who took a fall. It had been a hard landing.

Beady eyes that seemed to be floating stared at the intruder. "What you want?"

"A little talk, Al."

"Who—" he started. His eyes widened, trying to find some kind of recognition in this stranger's face. "How do you know my name?"

"Delia told me." In her diary, Al had been a real charmer, honest and funny and kind and not nearly as tough as he pretended.

"Delia Shannon?"

"That's right, Al."

"You're lying. Delia wouldn't tell you anything about me. Besides, she's dead. Do you know that, do you know she's dead?" Something changed in his bloodshot eyes. "Sure you do. I remember you. You were at that place, the place where they have Delia. Get the hell away from me!"

He made a grab for what was probably a knife.

Sand shoved him in the chest and he stumbled halfway across the room. He tripped and landed on his back, then rolled over onto his knees. Instead of getting up, his body began to heave with painful sobs that wouldn't stop. He banged his head several times on the carpeted floor to make them stop and eventually they did. This is what he had been on the edge of earlier. She had left a mark on this one; that was evident enough. There was more than booze and a casket in a silent room here. There was anger and regret and memories of other nights that were only sad when looking back.

Sand said, "Let's talk, Al."

His voice had a rare softness in it.

"I got nothing to say to you—you or anybody else about that bitch."

"Tell me how you met her. We can start there."

"I already . . ." he started and then let it tail off. "Oh, what the hell?"

He leaned his back against the foot of a bed. "Been a long time. Man shouldn't oughta have to carry a mad around this long."

Sand waited, giving him the time he needed to begin.

"I met her back when she was hanging with Paddy Clay," he said finally. "You probably know the son of a bitch, got his finger in half a dozen rackets. He dumped her and a little later me and her got together. That's all there was to it, happens a million times a year. I was in love with the broad, not at first maybe, but after a while. That little sad look she always seemed to have around the eyes, it did something to me. I wanted to protect her from everything and everybody."

There had been no sadness about her on that night five years ago. On that night her dreams had not yet begun to crumble.

"Go on, Al."

"Ain't no place else to go. Long as I was somebody everything was fine. Then I started to fall. I don't know why. Maybe somebody upstairs didn't like me. Maybe I stepped on the wrong set of toes without even knowing it. Soon as she realized it was going to be a long ride and all downhill she jumped off the wagon. She left me cold . . . and after I was willing to turn down all that dough."

Sand said, "What was that?"

"A big wad of dough. I got it one day with a note saying drop the girl and it's all mine."

"And you didn't do it?"

"No. Shows how big a fool I was about the dame, I guess."

"What did you do with the money?"

"Nothing I could do with it. No return address on it, no name. I figured I would just hang on to it a while till who-ever sent it saw I was wasn't buying and showed up for his dough."

"Did he?"

He shook his head. "No. Wasn't long after that that some-body pulled the rug out from under me. I still didn't spend a dime of the money, not even when Delia cut out on me—not until a year or more later when I finally gave up any hope of her changing her mind and coming back. By then I figured I deserved it. Most of it went for booze and gambling. Didn't take me long to get here. If she had stuck with me maybe I could have made it back. I loved the bitch. I really did."

Sand thought about it. "Maybe she loved you too, Al. She probably figured she was the cause of your troubles and that the best thing she could do for you would be to step out of the picture. You ever think of it that way?"

He hadn't, but he thought of it now—and his eyes began to change. He thought more, and the more he thought the less he shook and the straighter his body became. It was visible if you knew what you were seeing. It was a broken man begin-ning to regain a little of his manhood.

He wasn't going to need quite as much booze as he had before.

EIGHT

T HE DESK CLERK informed him a lady was waiting. It wasn't really necessary. Already the lady was cross- ing the lobby to meet him. The tall blonde with the large breasts and nice body was no longer wearing glasses. Nothing else about her had changed. She still made him wonder why he wasn't making love to her.

"Hello, blondie."

A piece of a smile. "My name is Dorothea, Mr. Sand. I hate it, but I'm stuck with it."

"The rest of you makes up for it, Dorothea. What kind of problem do you have this time of morning?"

She smiled again, more of a smile this time. "You are the one with the problems, Mr. Sand. But that isn't why I'm here."

"No?"

"Would it surprise you so much if I told you I'm here simply because I wanted to see you again?"

"It would shake my sense of perception. You didn't strike me as a fan."

"Strong silent types with big muscles don't impress me, Mr. Sand. It was something else."

"Keep going."

"My brother told me why you came. He doesn't believe it is the real reason, and I'm not sure I do either, but I would like to know."

"Why?"

"Because I knew Delia Shannon."

"When?"

"Five years ago, when she was engaged to my brother. I don't know what he told you, but he really was serious about her for a while. I liked her."

"So did I. She's dead."

She nodded. "I heard. My brother didn't do it. He hasn't even seen her in years."

"It's a shame. I would have enjoyed killing him."

"I believe you would."

"I would."

The tall blonde glanced around her as though suddenly conscious of the fact that they were standing in an open lobby. "Why don't you invite me up to your suite for a drink, Mr. Sand?"

"You want reasons or an invitation?"

"You're going to make me ask. I knew you would. Your kind can do that. Okay, I'm asking."

The elevator took them to his floor and a carpeted hallway led them to his suite of rooms. There was a bar, and he offered her a drink.

"Yes. Thank you."

She sipped at it when he handed it to her, watching him over the rim of the glass.

Sand studied the girl too. He tried to determine if her brother had sent her here for some reason or if she had been telling the truth. He couldn't. Beautiful women usually lie well, and this one was a beautiful woman.

She finished her drink and stood there, saying nothing. When Sand finished his he set the glass down, and they both stood in silence until the silence became strained.

Then he reached out and gently drew her toward him.

A tremor shook her luscious body as their lips met.

He said, "I hope this was part of the reason?"

Her lips refused to say, but her whole body gave the answer. It was in the pounding of her pulse, the sudden harshness of her breathing, in the movement of her body against his.

And finally it spilled off her full red lips. "Yes, damn you! This is why I came!"

While their lips waged a hungry war his hand went behind her back to find the zipper that would open her gown down to the base of her spine. She made a sound as he began to pull it down, a sound that urged him on.

Then she was saying it.

"Hurry . . ."

He didn't hurry. He took his time. It was a hard thing to do, but it was better that way.

Their lovemaking held in it a note of wildness—mixed in with the urgency and the testing of passion. They were strangers becoming lovers, and everything felt right.

She fought him at the last—or herself. Maybe the thing that had brought her here. Too late. Too late to stop this thing that had them in its grip. At the very end she made a sound that could have been a scream, and it was impossible to tell if the sound was ecstasy or anguish.

When it was over there was no calmness. Not in the man because in him there was always the tenseness. In the girl there was anger.

Sand lay on the bed propped on a pillow. He smoked and watched the girl.

Dorothea Waters picked up a lamp and slammed it against the wall. Then an ashtray because it was handy and light. The noises that came from her pretty throat were of utter frustration; the breaking didn't help.

There was the fire of rage in her eyes as suddenly she turned back to him. "I hate you," she said, "you know that?"

He almost grinned at her. "You should never wear clothes," he said. "Most women should, but you shouldn't. A magnificent body. You exercise regularly, Dorothea?"

"I dance," she said before she really had time to think about it. "But that has nothing to do with why I hate you. I do. I do."

"Tell me why you hate me."

"Because I made love with you. I didn't want that. I didn't come here for that."

"Yes, you did."

"No. I wanted to go to bed with you, that's all. I wanted to go to bed with the man who can scare my brother. I told you I have seen plenty of strong men, and that's true, only until tonight my brother was the strongest of them all. Then I found out it was about Delia, and if it was true it meant . . . Oh, I really don't know what it meant. But suddenly I wanted to go to bed with you, and that doesn't make sense either, but that's the way it was. I wanted to go to bed with you, to feel you against me and maybe learn what makes a man like you tick. I wanted sex with you. I didn't want to make love with you."

She didn't seem quite as angry now that she had explained it.

"The line of distinction is very fine," he said.

"But it exists. That's the important thing—and that I crossed it."

"Tell me what it means."

"It means it isn't a game any more, no longer the spoiled sister of a big-time gangster deciding she wants a man and setting gaily about the task of crawling in bed with him. It means all of a sudden out of the clear blue sky I think I'm in love with you, you bastard!"

He had to laugh at the look of her, the scrappy rebuke in her voice and the sincere intensity in her beautiful face. It was a good laugh.

For a moment she continued to stand there, a healthy, naked she-animal adrift in the intoxicating female aroma hanging about her incredible body while the shock of his laughter washed over her face. The fire of anger again flared in her eyes and a small scream of rage escaped her throat.

She came after him like the tigress she was, nails bared and flashing.

"You bastard!" she screamed. "You bastard!"

Sand tossed the cigarette quickly aside, realizing that it was probably going to burn a hole in the carpet. The sharp nails on one of her hands reached his face before he caught both her wrists and pulled her down on top of him. Every inch of her struggled against him as she fought to get at his eyes.

When one struggle became another it was hard to say, or when one kind of fierceness became another. It happened.

Neither of them had really known it would, but it happened. Their lips were together, hard, tongues darting with a furious abandonment in their seeking, the nipples of her full breasts rough, electric against his chest. He released her wrists and her nails raked at his skin, but it was in response to the tightening ecstasy of desire and not the anger it had supplanted.

This time it was better. It had been good before, but this time it was better. When it was over there was no more anger.

They lay together, the girl with her blonde head on his shoulder, her lips close enough to his skin so that he could feel the movement of them when the words came.

"Treat me good, Sand," she said softly. "That's all I ask. As long as you keep me treat me good."

NINE

THEY SLEPT LATE. When they woke they made love. Then they went downstairs and had breakfast in a nice restaurant with a lot of other people who were having lunch.

Dorothea didn't ask him what Delia had meant to him or why her death was important enough to bring him back. She didn't ask him not to kill her brother if he turned out to be mixed up in it or not to break his arms and legs just for the hell of it. She had asked only one thing of him, and it had been asked the night before.

When there was nothing left of the breakfast but empty dishes scattered on the table he picked up the car he'd had the hotel rent for him and drove the girl to her own apartment.

When he dropped her out she asked if he would be back. Not when. She asked it very simply, trying to keep her face as impassive as possible because she didn't know what the answer would be. Then she stood there waiting for the answer. Would he be back, or was this the end of something too short, or too long, depending on how you looked at it?

He made her happy.

"I've never been in love with a girl named Dorothea before," he said.

She smiled. A fleeting thing, but it lit up her face with a glow that showed him how lovely she was when she was happy.

"I'll pack some things. Is that all right?"

"I like you fine the other way, but it would be a little unorthodox for street wear."

For that he got another smile.

"I don't think I'm sorry any more that I fell in love with you," she admitted.

What could he say to that?

"This . . . Us . . . It doesn't change the other thing, does it?"

He shook his head. "No."

"I didn't think so. You don't throw away the old when you take on the new, do you, Sand? Most men would I think—probably because they're narrow, or weak, or maybe its human nature—but you aren't like other men. I think I knew that. I think that's why I fell in love with you so quickly."

After he left her, he drove until he found a public phone with its local directory still attached. He didn't make a call, but he used the book. The names in Delia's diary kept getting smaller, and most of them from here on were new to him. He needed addresses.

Eight more names.

Add them to the first three.

Eleven men in five years.

All of them steps, if looked at objectively. Eleven steps from the girl he had known that one night etched in his memory to the whorehouse where some lousy bastard had shoved a knife through her heart. Every step down, further into the darkness of despair.

He stood there gathering his addresses and ignored the impatient guy behind him tapping his foot. When he had what he wanted he left and let the guy behind him make his call.

He took them the way they came on the list. That's the way it had to be, one step at a time.

They weren't easy to find. These were types who worked hard at not being easy to find. The first one wasn't home, but he was at somebody else's home sleeping off a hard night with a big redhead who didn't seem to know his name. The second, he located in a cross between a pool hall and a leaky sewer; the third, in a cheap bar a couple of blocks from the address listed for him in the phone book. The fourth and fifth hadn't been listed, so he had to ask around. One of them stayed at a boarding house but wasn't home. It took an hour to find him. He didn't have time to go after the fifth name on the list because he had a funeral to attend.

As he drove back to the hotel he felt a little better. Not much, but a little. He had broken an arm and smashed a collarbone and kicked one face in today, all for very deserving bastards. Delia wouldn't rest any easier because of it, but he would.

The rest of them would get their turn, but it would be routine from here on, territory to cover only because he was thorough by nature. He knew what each story would be. They had all been the same so far.

The money.

Always the money, stuffed inside a plain envelope with the anonymous note explaining what it was for. All the way down the line. Not always the same amount. For the first few it had been the same, but it shrunk as the men shrunk until for the one he just left it sounded like an insult.

The money proved he had been right in the beginning. The girl hadn't made the trip by herself—somebody had been pushing. Two things might make a man pay through the nose to destroy a woman like Delia Shannon. Love or hate, maybe some strange combination of the two. Who? An answer he didn't have. Waters maybe—his was the only story without the money. His sister said he had really cared for her and Waters himself had said she walked out on him. The most likely possibility, but something about it just didn't ring right.

He had stopped by the hotel for a quick shower and change of clothes when the call came.

He lifted the instrument from the hook to stop it from ringing and grunted something to let whoever it was know he was there.

"Sand? Sand, is that you?" The feminine voice belonged to Mopsie Steiner.

"Yeah, Mopsie, it's me."

"I been trying to get you for an hour or more," she said. "I guess you been out."

"Yeah, I've been out."

Her voice picked up a slight note of excitement now. "I've got something I thought you would want to know. One of my girls has been out of town for a week or two. She just got back. She was sort of Delia's best friend since she came here, but she didn't even know about her being killed until she got back a little while ago."

Sand began to feel the excitement himself. "Let's have it, Mopsie."

"I don't think it's such a good idea talking it out on the phone. Besides, I'm not sure I got all the details straight: I thought maybe you would want to come out and talk to the girl."

He checked his watch. "Keep her there, Mopsie. I'm on my way."

It didn't take any longer today than it had the night before when there was the fog to fight instead of the traffic. Still, it ate enough time off the face of his watch to convince him he would never make it to the estate of J. Addison Rutledge by four o'clock.

He parked in front of Mopsie Steiner's place in about the same spot the cab had been sitting when a couple of hoods started shooting up the windows.

Inside the parlor of the big house he saw the edge of one of the heavy drapes move slightly and knew somebody had watched him until he climbed out of the car. He was on his way up the walk now. Just as he reached the door it opened for him.

He walked inside and the door closed behind him.

Mopsie Steiner locked it while he watched. At night her door was open to anybody with cash and without a badge, but this time of day you couldn't buy your way in. She was jumpy and it showed.

"Where is she?" he asked.

"My office."

They crossed the parlor and entered the office. The girl had been pretty once and a hint of what had been still lingered, but the prettiness itself was gone. Her hair was black, cut short and combed back along the sides of her head in something of a Mannish style. Her eyes were frightened as she looked at Sand. She had been around long enough to know talking about things that were part of somebody else's business could get you in trouble. Right now she was wishing she had kept her mouth shut.

"This is Tina," Mopsie said, aiming a finger at the girl. "Tina, tell Mr. Sand what you told me about Delia's regular guy."

The girl's lower lip began to tremble. She bit it, and when she turned it loose there were tooth marks.

"I . . . I only saw him three times," she said. "I don't know his name or nothing. I . . . I'm not even sure. Delia didn't tell me he was her regular or her boyfriend or nothing. All I know is the first time he saw her his mouth dropped wide open like she was a queen or something. He was with some other fellows that time, all of them wearing sweaters with letters on them like college kids—only they looked older. The other times I seen him he came by himself and waited around till Delia was free before going up. I guess he was here more than those times, but I didn't see him. I keep kinda busy sort of."

"You never heard his name?"

She shook her head.

"You said he wore a letter sweater the first time. Do you know what college?"

"Uh huh. Because I seen one like it before. This kid once, he had one just like it. He said he went to State."

"Did you talk to Delia about this guy?"

"I asked her about him . . . when I saw her being so happy looking. It was the first time I ever seen her happy and I figured it must be because of this guy. She didn't say either way, just acted kinda evasive sort of. So I knew it was him. I've seen it happen before. There's always some guy comes along who wants to take you away from all this."

"You think maybe he killed her, Tina? Could be he changed his mind about taking her home to mama."

The fear in her eyes grew and her lip started to tremble again. "I don't think nothing about things like that, mister, nothing at all. What I told you, that's everything I know."

Sand turned to Mopsie. "Has he been back since the murder?"

"I called some of the girls. A couple of them remembered him. They can't remember seeing him since Delia was killed."

"Was he here that night?"

She shrugged. "Nobody can say for sure. With the town flush with conventioneers things have been pretty hectic around here. You saw how it when you were here. That's the way it's been every night for a while."

"And nobody knows his name?"

"If they did, it would probably be different from the one he wears outside."

Sand nodded. Was this important or just a coincidence caught up in the puzzle?

He checked the time on his watch.

"If you think of anything else that might help, Tina, tell Mopsie so she can get in touch with me. Will you do that?"

She hesitated for only a second before she nodded.

Mopsie was standing closest to the door. She opened it and stepped into the parlor to show Sand out.

The abruptness of the move caught the boy by surprise. He barely managed to get his back to the door and a few feet away before he was visible to the others. It was evident to Sand that he had been eavesdropping. Either it wasn't to his mother, or she preferred to ignore it.

"Joey," she said, "did you get rid of that gasoline like I told you?"

He turned back to them, his face a mask of surprise to learn he wasn't alone. "Sure I did. I put it in the tank of my car. No sense letting it go to waste by just pouring it out. It was nearly a whole gallon." Then he kept on going like he had been going somewhere to begin with.

"Found it upstairs," Mopsie explained to Sand as they walked across the parlor to the front door. "No telling what

people are liable to leave laying around." She unlocked the
door and opened it for him. "I hope you'll excuse Joey,
Sand. He's a kid, young and curious."

He couldn't tell if she was referring to the eavesdropping
just now or the likelihood it had been curious Joey who
tipped Toilet Waters he was here that first night and nearly
got him shot.

TEN

IF THERE HAD BEEN ANYONE ELSE, they were gone.

J. Addison Rutledge stood alone by the graveside, a man of great dignity, his sorrow really for a different, younger girl than the one whose body lay under the ground.

He turned as Sand approached.

"Sorry I couldn't make it sooner," Sand told him. "Got held up."

"Something to do with Delia's death, Mr. Sand?"

"Yeah."

That's all there was to say at the moment. They stood there together and looked down at the girl's grave. There was no headstone yet, just the grave. It was like any other grave, and the realization played in Sand's brain. It seemed that the grave should be different because the girl had been different.

When the time came to leave, the two men left together. The private plot was located on a shaded rise landscaped unobtrusively within a natural setting. The new grave was set slightly apart from the others. They walked from the gravesite across an estate that seemed to have taken on a sad melancholy of its own.

When they reached the mansion the politician invited him in for a drink.

"I'm afraid we will have to fend for ourselves," he said. "There is no one but me now and I spend most of my time in the capital, so this place is shut down except for the rare occasions when I find time to spend here."

He opened the door with a key and led Sand into a massive den filled with a large desk and other furnishings crafted from dark woods and leather. There was a bar, and bookcases filled with books and various awards. One wall was almost completely covered with framed honorary certificates awarded for distinguished services and achievements. The room contained no stuffed trophies that he could see, but across from the desk was mounted a large gun rack displaying an impressive array of hunting rifles and shotguns.

"I see you're a hunter," Sand said.

He glanced at the gun rack. "Not so much these days. A little quail shooting during season if I'm able to find the time. A drink?"

Rutledge poured a drink for each of them at the bar and they took seats across from each other in comfortable stuffed chairs with armrests.

He asked if Sand had learned anything new since they talked and Sand gave him a brief rundown on events so far. He told him about talking with people she had been involved with, but pretty much left it at that. He didn't mention the money or the notes or the malicious pattern they seemed to represent. It would serve no purpose to add that to the man's grief.

"You work faster than the police," he said. "I talked with the commissioner this morning and he, in turn, with the detective in charge of the investigation. They seem to have made no progress at all. Do you think it was the man who was seeing her at this place where she worked?" He couldn't quite bring himself to give the place a name.

"No," Sand said. "Just a hunch, but I don't think so."

"And I would suspect you are a man who trusts his hunches, Mr. Sand."

"I've found it pays."

"With some men it does. I must follow the route of calculated reason myself, but I have always admired men whose instinct tends to guide them true. Will you continue to keep me posted?"

"Sure," Sand said. "And if you think of anything that might help, let me know."

"Perhaps you should tell me where you're staying so I will know where to reach you."

Sand told him and got up to leave.

"And if I can help in any way . . ." The wise politician let it hang there.

"I'll be in touch."

The drive back into the city took the better part of an hour, the first part of the trip through some of the loveliest countryside he had ever seen and the rest on the cold and impartial thoroughfare, crowded with other speeding cars and decorated with billboards.

He stopped at a filling station for gas and put a call through to Mohannah.

The detective captain answered with his usual growl. Public servants so seldom consider themselves servants of the public.

"Good afternoon, Captain. You probably remember me. Sand. S-a-n—"

"What the hell do you want now, Sand? To come down to the morgue and look at another body?"

"You're getting good, Max. You got it right on the first try."

That stopped the conversation. It wasn't exactly the pause that refreshes, but it was definitely a pause. The cop was quickly running down a checklist he kept inside his head. Nothing cried out to him, so he said, "Spill it, Sand."

"You hear from the commissioner today?"

"I heard from the commissioner today," he admitted, "because he heard from a very influential citizen by the name of J. Addison Rutledge. Seems Rutledge would like to know who killed a certain prostitute in a certain business establishment with a certain knife. Only we don't know who used the knife or why, and if we close this one it's going to be the biggest surprise I've had since I joined the department. Now tell me whatever it was you called to say because I got better things to do than hang around talking to ex-hoods running around trying to fulfill a death wish."

"You hear about Paddy Clay."

"I heard the vice boys finally got him on some small rap because somebody busted his knees and left him as a lingering guest at some kind of doper party. A rumor I picked up.

Don't mean a damn thing to me. Paddy has his vices, but he doesn't go around killing people. Spill."

"Just thought I would check and see if you had any unidentified bodies lying around, preferably one with the time of death shortly before or after Delia Shannon was killed."

Sand waited out a substantial pause on the other end of the line. When the fat cop got around to speaking again he couldn't cover up the sudden interest in his voice.

"Don't play games with me, Sand. Games I play with kids and people I like."

"Delia had a boyfriend."

"She had a hundred."

"A special one."

"Name?"

"He didn't wear one around the house. Young, but not too young. Probably not a bad looking guy. You got anybody like that?"

"We got him," the cop said. "Fished him out of the river this morning. I don't know how pretty he was. If he was pretty before, he's not any longer. How the hell did you—"

"Any identification on him?"

"No. We wired his prints to Washington. If he was ever in the service or in jail we should have a make on him soon. Now tell me how—"

"Just a guess. How did he get it?"

"A knife between the shoulder blades. But we hadn't gotten around to connecting it with this other thing. What else do you know?"

"Time to trade."

"I don't trade."

"You trade, Max. Cops always trade. Besides, you'll be feeding it to the reporters as soon as you get it anyway."

"I'm not promising anything," the fat cop said into the phone, and that meant he had decided to trade. With the commissioner breathing down his neck on the girl's murder, he was damned interested in anything that might be connected with it.

"He was connected with State College," Sand said,

"probably an athlete, not necessarily part of the current roster."

"And for that you want favors?"

"Just that I get the word on his identity as soon as you do."

"Maybe."

"I'll call you later."

"Yeah." A short pause now. "You know, Sand, damned if I'm not beginning to believe this thing actually is what brought you back here."

Sand grinned into the phone. "Now you're getting it—that perception we were talking about."

~ ~ ~ ~ ~

The doorman was a wrinkled old guy named Gus. Sand didn't know the kid. They both wore uniforms that made them a part of the hotel, and they were both there on the sidewalk when he drove up.

He left the car running because the kid was already coming around to park it. He was smiling, the kid, like it was his job to smile and like maybe he felt like it anyway. Old Gus never smiled; he didn't consider it part of his job, and he probably figured it would detract from the dignity of his elegant uniform. Sand had known old Gus a long time and he had never seen his face lose that staid poise the old man felt went with his position.

That's why the surprise tugged at the base of Sand's brain as he was entering the door being held for him and, through the corner of his eye, saw the carved stiffness of the doorman's face begin to crack. The expression started like a smile and grew into a grimace, and Sand's surprise grew right along with it. It wasn't until the old man started to fall that Sand realized something was wrong.

Not until then that he saw the dark spot of blood blooming into an ugly circle on the breast of his uniform.

Reflexes took over then, the reflexes that kept a man alive long after the odds called him out. He let the old man continue to fall while he yelled something at the kid about duck-ing. Then he made a dive for the concrete—backward. He heard the *spat* of the second bullet as it flattened against the stone of the building. People always dive in the direction they're facing; it was almost a rule. If he had followed the rule the slug would have made a nice round hole in the back of his head.

Even as Sand's back touched the concrete, the sniper was already trying to correct his aim. A window crumbled above him somewhere and rained glass down on him. On each side of the entrance to the hotel there was a tropical plant of some kind in a large concrete base. He couldn't see it now, but he knew it was there because he was a man who paid particular attention to details, even such small and common ones. He did a quick roll as soon as he landed and an instant before a new slug ricocheted off the spot where be had been.

The heavy .45 that had lived with him every day for years was automatically in his hand. A trained response. It required no thought. But it might as well have stayed in its harness. The opposite side of the street was lined with a row of office buildings. The guy with the rifle could be anywhere.

Sand glanced over at Gus. The old man was still and pale, the blood forming a puddle under him. The puddle was still growing, so he wasn't dead yet.

He cursed and the hand wrapped around the butt of the .45 itched. It wanted a target that bad, wanted to get the son of a bitch in its sights while the finger squeezed and squeezed and squeezed.

A noise was building around him now, shouting voices demanding to know what the hell was going on.

The rifle hidden somewhere across the street had made no sound because it had a silencer.

A crowd came.

No more shots.

The rifle would be clearing out fast—probably was al-ready gone.

Sand holstered the .45. The boney man with the scythe had missed him again. But it had been close.

Somebody had called an ambulance. It would need to hurry. Sand looked down at Gus and judged it a tossup. He wasn't dead yet, but he was dying fast. A high-powered rifle can do a lot of damage.

Sand lit a cigarette and waited for the ambulance and the cops, ignoring the questions fired at him in an unbroken stream by the growing crowd.

The beat cop made it first and managed to keep the mob from stomping the old doorman until the ambulance arrived. The plainclothes boys got there just as the ambulance was leaving. They got a brief rundown from the uniform cop and then divided up to cover both Sand and the kid who parked cars at the same time.

Sand told the story the way it happened and didn't bother to add that the sniper had actually been after him and the old man just happened to be standing in the wrong spot.

The plainclothes dick took it down the way Sand told it and then frowned at the notes he had made.

"You're not by any chance the same Sand who used to be around five or six years ago, are you?" he asked.

"Yeah."

A funny look out of the cop, but no more questions.

His buddy got the same story from the kid. They compared notes and took off. Most of the crowd had already disappeared. The excitement was over.

Sand picked up his key at the desk, and a shaken desk clerk apologized for his nearly being killed on hotel property. Sand accepted his apology.

With his key, the clerk handed him a sealed envelope.

"A message for you," he explained. "It came while you were out."

Sand took the envelope and the key and crossed the lobby to an elevator. Inside his suite, he dropped the key and envelope on a convenient dresser, went into the bathroom and splashed cold water on his face from the lavatory. Back in the bedroom, he opened the envelope and read the words scribbled out in long hand.

Sand:

You're dead. Really dead. For a while you were quiet and everything was all right. You're not quiet any longer, and we can't afford to let you go around muscling our boys. We're sure you will understand as I explain that we have found it advisable to raise the price on your head. This is now an open contract. Come one, come all. Our advice would be that you make funeral arrangements as quickly as possible.

The Council

The Council was made up of a select group of mob bosses; collectively they and their organizations controlled practically every racket in the country. He grinned without humor. Smart of the big boys to up the ante and open the contract to anyone desperate enough to take a chance. They had sent their paid assassins after him before and got them back in pieces. Now they were sicking every hood in the country on him, from their top shooters right down to any two-bit punk with enough nerve to stake out an ambush.

He dropped the message back on the dresser and lit a fresh cigarette. There was just one thing that didn't make sense. When the big boys write a note they intend for it to be read. Since he just got it, that meant the word wouldn't be on the street yet.

Yet somebody with a rifle had wanted him bad enough to make his play in broad daylight on a busy street . . .

ELEVEN

S HE WAS STANDING THERE on the curb waiting for him, her hair being tossed about slightly by the wind that had grown in the late afternoon. A big blonde female animal standing there unconscious of the wind tugging at her dress as she waited for her man. She saw him and a smile reached her lips, not a big smile but soft and subtle and filled with meaning.

He braked to a stop at the curb, reached across the seat and opened the door for her. "Hop in, blondie."

She did, giving him a kiss, then twisting around in the seat to deposit her overnight bag in the back. It was a pleasant sight.

"Are you going back to the hotel, Sand?"

"First I thought we would have something to eat. It's been a busy day."

"I'm game."

"Good." He reached out for her and she came against him again for another kiss, a real kiss this time. It surprised him to realize he had missed her. "You're a beautiful hunk of woman, Dorothea. You know that?"

This time it was a big smile. "Just for you, mister, just for you."

He took her to a little place he had known five years ago. The old Greek couple who had owned it then was dead, but their son and daughter-in-law had taken it over. The atmosphere and the food were still the same. The girl liked it; her eyes told him she did.

They talked.

They talked like friends and lovers.

About many things.

But not about the thing that had brought him back and not about what he had to do.

Afterwards, they drove to the hotel. While the girl was unpacking her overnight case Sand got Max Mohannah on the phone.

"Max, this is Sand. The lead pay off yet?"

A grunt at the other end. "Yeah. I guess this is once you did the department a favor. The Washington deal didn't come off. They didn't have his prints on file. We contacted the college though and finally managed to tie a tag on his toe."

"Graduate student?"

"Alumnus. You were right about the sports angle. He was a gridiron hero from a few years back, rich, handsome and well liked by everybody. He attended an alumni get-together on campus a couple of weeks ago."

That would explain why he had been wearing the sweater. "Who was he, Max?"

"Another wheel, or the son of a wheel, anyhow. This case is beginning to be full of them. William Tarrence, son of you-know-who."

Sand whistled. He did know. Stephen Tarrence was in the same league as J. Addison Rutledge, both leading lights within their party.

"I suppose his father has been told?"

"The family has been notified, and they've made positive identification of the remains. All they know right now though is that he's dead, not that he might be involved in this other mess. If it turns out that he is and the story hits the papers, which it will, Tarrence might as well throw his political career in the waste basket."

"You talk with any of his friends yet? Been able to tie him in with the girl?"

"We talked, but we haven't tied. If it's true, he kept it to himself. If you belong to that class, or any class for that matter, you don't go around bragging to your friends that you're planning to marry a prostitute as soon as you can convince her to switch addresses."

The fat cop was right on that score. He said, "Let me know if anything breaks, will you, Max?"

"I'm not making any promises," the voice in the phone said.

That meant yes; otherwise, his answer would have been a flat no. Max might not be lovable, but he wasn't shy either.

"Thanks, Max."

"For nothing."

The phone went dead in his hand and he hung it up.

While he was talking Dorothea had decided to take a shower. She hadn't bothered to close the bathroom door and a foggy mist from the hot water was billowing out into the room where he stood. He lit a cigarette as he stood there listening to the mellow sound of her humming.

After a while the humming stopped, and then the sound of the shower, and a moment later she stepped out of a wall of steam into the bedroom.

A blonde goddess!

She hadn't bothered to wrap herself in the towel.

Invisible hands cupped the rich fullness of her breasts, holding them out for him. She stood there for his inspection, enjoying the feel of his eyes as they drank in the loveliness of satin skin sliding ecstatically over sensuous peaks and dipping down into shadowy valleys of temptation. She raised the towel to touch the damp edges of her hair and the movement pulled her luscious breasts even higher.

There was something shining in her eyes as she said, "Thank you, Sand."

"What do you have to thank me for, kitten?"

"For treating me like a woman—for making me feel like a woman. You know you don't have to, and that makes it special."

Without taking his eyes off her he crushed the cigarette out in an ashtray.

She came to him, slowly, without modesty or hesitation. She was beauty in motion. She was a woman claiming her man and wanting it no other way.

He opened his arms for her, and she filled them, her lips

stretching up for his, suddenly hungry and filled with a growing urgency.

There was a violence in the way he took her, because there was a violence in their passion. Their bodies became one in a sexual hunger that cried out for satisfaction.

There was the bed, the room, the night, and for a while nothing else existed in this shrunken world but the two of them. Nothing else existed until it was over.

Sand found a fresh cigarette and lit it while the girl lay with her blonde head on his outstretched arm. They said nothing, for there was nothing to say. Everything had been said without words and the shaded meaning of words.

They were still that way when the phone began to ring.

"Don't answer it, Sand." Her hand tightened on his arm and there was a sudden strangeness in her voice.

He turned to her, letting his eyes ask the question.

She shrugged, or maybe it was a slight shudder. "I don't know . . . a feeling . . . I don't know."

He swung his feet off the side of the bed and lifted the phone.

He didn't recognize the voice, but the name was familiar. "Mr. Sand? Is that you? This is Jessey Jollie. I think I got something maybe you want . . ."

TWELVE

S AND GOT NOTHING OUT OF HIM over the phone except that the information he had was about Delia Shannon and an address where he could be found. The voice sounded drunk; maybe that was what had loosened his tongue, or maybe he knew Sand would be getting to him pretty soon and wanted to make it easy on himself.

The thing that mattered was that he was ready to talk.

"Stay where you are, Jollie," he said into the receiver. "I'll be there in half an hour."

"What is it, Sand?" the girl asked as he hung up. "Something about . . ."

"Yeah. I have to go out for a while."

"Who was it?"

He told her.

"But how do you know it's not just a trick? It might not have been him at all."

A good point he decided.

He lifted the phone again and dialed a number. The voice that picked up sounded familiar. The brunette from the other night. He asked for Mopsie Steiner and a couple of minutes later he had her.

"Mopsie, this is Sand."

She said something appropriate, a question built into it.

"You know Jessey Jollie pretty well?"

"I'm on a first name basis with every louse in this town, Sand, you know that. Why?"

"I want you to tell me if he talks with a slight lisp." The man on the phone had talked with a lisp.

"Sure, that's him."

"Thanks, Mopsie."

"Something to do with Delia?" she asked before he could hang up.

"Yeah. The picture is still kind of murky but there's a chance it might be starting to clear up. I'll let you know when it's finished."

He could almost see her smile on her end. "Don't bother. When it's finished, I'll know."

He thanked her again and hung up.

Dorothea watched him dress. She didn't say anything about what she was thinking, but he could read it in her eyes. She still had that feeling she had told him about. Maybe she was right but, then again, maybe she was just a woman afraid for her man. It had been Jollie on the phone, so chances were good that the deal was on the up-and-up. He couldn't afford to take a chance on it not being that way.

Because he had a feeling of his own—a feeling that something was getting ready to break.

When he was dressed, he slipped into the shoulder rig, pulled the .45 loose to check it, then tucked it back in its holster. Just in case.

She went as far as the door with him, the message still in her eyes. It was in the kiss too, the way she clung to him and didn't want to let go.

"Take it easy, blondie. I'll be back."

"Please . . ." That was all she said. Not begging him to stay, but begging him to come back.

He didn't wait for them to bring his car around. He got it from the garage himself. The less time he wasted the better his chances were of finding a drunken punk named Jessey Jollie where he was supposed to be and still in a talkative mood.

Fog had begun to crowd in on the night as he began to move in the brisk early evening traffic. Overhead there were no stars and no moon because of the overcast. The fog wasn't really too thick right now, but it seemed to be getting that way, already making weird patterns in the glare of his headlights.

The address Jollie had given him belonged to a small bar

and grill in a neighborhood he was familiar with.

It took him the full half hour to get there. He did a slow drive-by to check the place out and parked the car a block away.

Between the car and the bar he passed a huddle of gang-bangers showing off for a cute young thing dressed out like the latest singing sensation and lapping up the attention. She gave him the eye as he passed, and her friends gave him a dirty look.

The bar had an old neon sign that hummed and sputtered and threatened to go out every couple of minutes. About half the stools inside were filled with various sized, shaped and gender buttocks, and that made it a good night. The fog. The fog always drove them in. A jukebox tucked in a corner was playing a tear-in-your-beer ballad low enough to creep into your brain but not loud enough to distract from any serious drinking.

Sand didn't see anything that looked like it might be Jessey Jollie. He should have asked Mopsie to describe the bastard to him.

The bartender saw him and began inching half-heartedly in his direction while keeping his attention on a television behind the bar.

Sand placed a bill on the bar and asked in a low voice the guy two stools away wouldn't be able to interpret over the competition of jukebox and TV: "Jessey Jollie?"

He looked at Sand and down at the bill in his hand like he was thinking about giving it back.

"Nobody pays to find that clown, mister. He ain't worth the trouble."

"He was here thirty minutes ago."

"No."

"He was here."

"Not here. Upstairs. A lousy room up there the boss rents for peanuts. It's where Jollie hangs his hat when he's got enough chips to afford one."

"He got a phone up there?"

"Yeah. Big operator."

"He up there now?"

The bartender shrugged. "Could be. He's got sort of a private entrance, a stairway off the alley outside."

Sand had wanted to ask him if Jollie was alone, but if he got upstairs from outside the question was useless. He walked out of the bar and into the alley. It was short and dark with a dead end. Battered garbage cans were filled with dead liquor bottles.

Climbing up the brick wall of the bar was a shaky set of metal stairs that had probably originally been called a fire escape. He took them two at a time, wishing there was some way to keep them from squealing under his weight, but the only way was to build a new set and he didn't have the time.

There was only one door at the top. He filled his hand with the butt of the .45, standing to the side of the door as he used his knuckles against it.

Nothing from inside.

He waited a minute in case Jollie was having trouble making up his mind, then rapped his knuckles against the door again.

Still no movement and no sound.

He twisted the knob. Open. He gave the door a shove, then counted off two seconds before he moved.

Somebody had been considerate enough to leave a nightlight burning, one of those deals that plug directly into the socket. The plastic lens over the bulb was yellowed with age.

But it was enough to help him find Jollie.

The little guy had looked kind of funny in life, the kind of funny nobody laughs at. He still looked a little funny, the way he had his head cocked to one side and his eyes wide open. He looked almost alive. At first Sand thought he was, until he saw the shiny thing sticking out of his throat in the eerie glow of the nightlight—the point of a knife somebody had shoved through the back of his neck.

There was only one room and a bath, plus another door that would open onto some stairs down to the bar. If the killer had taken that way out he was already long gone. He tried the door anyway. It opened into a narrow dark hall with a strong smell of dust and mildew. With it open he could hear the jukebox faintly.

Sand looked at the little man propped up on the bed. Too bad, too damn bad. Not because he had died, but because he had died before he had a chance to talk.

Cautious not to leave any prints he methodically began to go over the room. Jollie could no longer talk, but there was a small chance he had left something behind that would do his talking for him. The search didn't take long. The dead man had owned little more than the clothes he was wearing.

Nothing.

Not a damn thing.

Go over this room with a microscope and there was nothing to indicate Jollie had ever known a girl named Delia Shannon.

He was standing in the middle of the room when he heard the metal stairs begin to squeal.

Company.

An outside possibility the killer had decided to return for something.

Sand pulled the .45 from its nest and stepped into a corner not penetrated by the small nightlight.

The guy didn't knock. He opened the door and stepped inside casually, like he paid the rent on the place. He was big. Not really tall, but wide. If his shoulders had been a couple of inches broader he wouldn't have cleared the doorway.

He must have sensed something wasn't right the way he suddenly stopped dead still. Or maybe it was the sight of Jollie on the bed.

"Come on in," Sand said softly, "and shut the door behind you."

"Who . . . who the hell are you?" He was straining his eyes in the semidarkness.

"Why don't we turn that question around?"

He was too big to be scared, too slow to run. "Sumpter is my name. House Sumpter. But I'm still asking."

Sand stepped out of the shadow and let him see the gun. House had liked it better the other way.

"Let's talk, House. What are you doing here?"

"Suppose I don't want to talk?" His voice said he didn't intend to put up with this shit.

"Suppose I blow half your guts outside into the alley?"

Okay, maybe a little shit wouldn't hurt. "I . . . I come up here to see Jollie."

"Why did you come up here to see Jollie?"

"Because me and him are good friends, that's why. Why else?"

"My question."

He shrugged. "Ain't no answer except the one I gave you. Me and Jollie, we pal around. Sometimes I drop by and we go out and have ourselves a few."

"Jollie's dead."

"I got eyes and I been using them."

"The way you came in, maybe you already knew he was dead."

"If I knew he was dead, mister, I wouldn't of come in the first place."

Sand was standing there thinking about how reasonable that sounded when he realized the sound coming from the jukebox below had suddenly grown louder.

The door!

Damn it, the door behind him!

He started to spin, but be didn't make it before the roof came crashing down on him.

THIRTEEN

T HE DOOR WAS STILL OPEN and the jukebox was playing. He couldn't make out the lyrics of the song, but
it had a sad sound.

Only he shouldn't be hearing it. He should be dead. That's
the way the game went.

Underneath his face he could feel the grit of a floor that
hadn't been swept. Above him somebody was breathing. He
hadn't been out long. Instinctively he knew that. He sensed
the .45 had just been plucked from his fingers by the heavy
breather standing over him.

Downstairs the record ended and then started up again, the
same song.

Somebody shut the door and most of the sound went
away.

"I think you put him down too hard, Louie," House told
his buddy. "That was some swing you took."

"A big bastard like him—I wanted to make sure he would
stay down." It was Louie doing the heavy breathing. He
sounded like he probably had a sinus condition.

"We gonna take him?" Louie asked. "Or we gonna wait
for him to come around?"

"Wait."

"I don't much like being in a room with no dead man."

House gave a short laugh that was more of a snort. "Many
as you killed, you scared of a dead man?"

"That's different."

"If you say so, Louie."

They were in no hurry, but there was no advantage in de-
laying things. Nobody was rushing to his rescue. He let them
know he was awake.

Louie stepped away from him with a jerk. "He moved,

House. I seen him move."

"Okay, Sand—get on your feet," House said. Apparently he was the decision maker for the pair.

Sand raised himself as far as one knee, experiencing a slight dizziness and the pain he had expected. No blood met his touch as he reached up with one hand to explore the damage done to the back of his head. He was lucky Louie was a pro. A blackjack isn't nearly as messy as the barrel of a gun.

They waited until he was already on his feet. He reached out for a chair as though he needed it for support. The weaker they thought he was, the more relaxed they were likely to be. That was the one advantage he could hope for after falling for their play the way he had. They had been lucky. The steps from inside the building could have been as noisy as the others. The door could have squeaked. Anything. They had been lucky, but he should have been ready.

"Let's go," House ordered, waving a gun of his own.

"Where?"

House grinned. "Away from here. Louie, he don't like being around dead people."

"I take it I won't be coming back."

"Smart. I always heard you were smart, Sand. But, then, I always heard you were tough too—and look how easy Louie and me took you."

Louie laughed a little. "Easiest pile of money I ever made."

Sand pointed a finger at the body of Jessey Jollie, whose wide-open dead eyes couldn't seem to understand why a knife was sticking out his throat.

"You boys do that job too?"

"Naw. A punk. Me and Louie don't bump off punks except maybe it's for fun. Who would pay to get rid of a bum like him?"

"Somebody put him out of the way."

"Probably some dame. Dames are funny that way."

"It sounds more reasonable that you boys bumped him off to cut him out of his share of the reward. After all, he was the one who arranged the setup. He got me here so you could make your play."

The broad hood called House was looking at him with a funny expression. "You must be crazy. That ain't the way it was at all, is it, Louie? Me and Louie, we don't work with a creep like that."

"How else could you know I was here?"

"We got ourselves one of them anonymous phone calls. You know, like they always show on TV. This guy has heard that when it comes to pulling a rub out me and Louie are about as good as they come. I don't say we are and I don't say we ain't, not on no stinking phone to some guy I don't even know. Then he asks us if we heard the word about the great Sand's head being worth a king's ransom. Those are the words he used. Sure we heard, like everybody else. Don't take long for news like that to spread. Then he asks how we would like to collect that dough, and I say ain't much chance of that. Sure there is, he says, because he knows where Sand is going to be in thirty minutes, a sitting duck."

It sounded too damn reasonable not to be true, and yet it didn't jell at all. Jollie had been killed by somebody who overheard the little man's conversation with him earlier and knew he would be coming here. The same somebody had then called these two. Why not stick around and collect the dough himself? And why kill Jollie?

House waved the gun again. "Come on, Sand. Get going. We done wasted enough time."

"One more question," Sand said as he got to his feet. "Since you plan to bump me off, why not here? Why take the party wherever you're planning on taking it?"

That snort of his again, trying to pass for a laugh. "You in a hurry to get it or something?"

"I figure you've got your reasons. I'm just curious."

"Go on, House," Louie urged. "Tell him. Show him how smart we are."

"Yeah, House—show me how smart you are."

"Okay, if you gotta know to die happy. See that dead guy over there in the bed. Me and Louie didn't do that job; so somebody else did, see? If we bump you here, what's to keep this other somebody from claiming he made both hits and trying to cut us out of our king's ransom. That's kinda the way we got it figured. The guy on the phone wants us to take all the chances while he wriggles around and gets the dough."

"And you're going to see that doesn't happen."

"Damn right. Me and Louie got it figured perfect, ain't we, Louie? Ain't nobody else going to be able to claim they took out the famous Sand, because ain't nobody else going to know where your body is hid. Now get going—out the door and down to the alley. At the street turn right and don't make any funny moves like trying to make a run for it because you won't get two feet. Louie, you go ahead of him to make double sure he don't try nothing. I'll be right behind him with my rod in my pocket."

Louie had been holding Sand's .45 in his hand. As he walked out of the room he made sure the safety was on and shoved it under his belt. Not the wisest thing to do, but maybe he didn't intend to get close enough for Sand to make a grab for it—or maybe he just didn't think about it one way or the other.

With the three of them on the stairs the thing made sounds like it might come off the wall. It would have been just the break Sand needed at this point, but it didn't happen.

The fog had grown thicker and begun to roll, obscuring anything more than ten or fifteen feet away. Nobody on the sidewalk. That's the kind of night it was.

House and Louie belonged to a beat-up green Chevy parked down the block from the alley. The three of them walked the distance single file.

It was hard for Sand to tell how professional these two were. So far they had done everything right, but there was an outside chance it was more luck than skill. They had done a lot of talking, and pros in this game usually do very little.

Time would tell.

But time was running out fast.

Louie walked around the car and climbed in under the

wheel. House told Sand to sit in the front, waited until he was in and climbed in the back seat, pulling the gun out of his pocket as he did.

"Okay, Louie," House said, "let's go. Take it slow and easy. Remember we're hauling cash money here."

Louie thought about it and got happy all over. "Jeez, House, just think of that. All that dough, without a dime of tax out of it." He whistled to himself at the thought. "I think I'll buy every dame in this town, especially the ones who wouldn't talk to me before I was rich."

House gave them the benefit of his snort-laugh. "With that kind of dough you don't have to buy 'em. You just let 'em smell it."

That made Louie even happier. He believed in thrift. He thought about his money for a while and then remembered how he had come to be rich.

"You keeping him covered good, House? We don't want the bastard to get away."

"Just keep your eyes on the road and drive. He's covered plenty. And watch those lights. The last thing we want is a cop down on us."

They weren't pros, Sand decided. Just pretenders in over their heads. But lucky.

Of course, that wouldn't make him any less dead unless their luck changed.

They knew where they were going. Either they had worked it out in advance or had made a quick decision after finding Jollie dead. The car crept along in the fog until it found the thoroughfare Sand had taken this afternoon to get to a funeral.

"I don't suppose anybody would like to tell me where we're going?" Sand asked.

House said, "I don't guess it would hurt nothing. Do you, Louie?" he asked, and without waiting for an answer he went on. "It's like this, there's this place me and Louie happen to know about out in the country a ways. Sort of a country church that used to be a church but ain't any more on account of it burned down three or four years ago and they built the new one someplace else. Behind this church is a pretty big graveyard with an old brick fence all the way around it. Kind of private you might say. Now what better place could you put a corpse than in a graveyard."

Not bad. Not bad at all. They would claim the reward for the kill and would be able to produce the evidence at any time.

Louie was grinning at the windshield. "That's really pretty good, House, you know that? Rubbing a guy out in a grave-yard. We oughta go down in history or something."

"I think it has been done before," Sand told him.

That dampened his mellow mood somewhat, but he didn't let it get him down. "Still a good idea," he mumbled.

Now it was House's turn. From the back seat he said, "Too bad we only got one shovel, Sand—otherwise me or Louie could help you dig. Save you from dying all worn out."

"Well, it's the thought that counts."

"Yeah, ain't that the truth." He chuckled, without the snort this time.

They left the thoroughfare and traveled down a twisting asphalt road for about five miles. There was a river some-where close by with a stink rising from it. That could explain why so few people lived along this stretch. There were houses, but they were spread pretty thin.

Sand watched for an opening, but the two hoods were making no mistakes tonight. The .45 tucked under Louie's belt was the only chance he saw for getting out of this, even that not a good one. It would have to be smooth and fast or House would blow him apart before he finished his play.

The car slowed as Louie strained his eyes against the fog searching for the place where they were taking him. He gave a pleased grunt when he saw it.

Standing somewhat askew in the hovering fog was part of the chimney that had belonged to the church. A narrow un-paved road lead around where the building had been to the crumbling brick wall of the cemetery. Louie parked the car parallel to the wall and cut the engine.

"Climb out and get the shovel from the trunk, Louie, while I keep him covered," House said from the back seat.

Louie came up with a flashlight and climbed out. When he came back he had the shovel.

House waved his gun at Sand. "Okay, out."

He had a chance at the one in the back seat as they climbed out of the car, but the other one was in a position to blast him before he could make it good. They were still living lucky.

House kept running the show. "You lead the way, Louie. I'll follow right behind our friend."

Louie followed a footpath through the scattered gravestones. Sand followed him, and House brought up the rear, the gun in his fist leveled on his spine.

"How far we going, House?" Louie asked over his shoulder, his voice low, as though to show respect for the sleeping.

"Keep going till you find a good spot for another grave. Toward the back of the place will be best. We don't want nobody to stumble on him by accident."

"This place is kinda spooky with all the fog and stuff," Louie said. It sounded like a little more than a casual offhand observation.

"Just keep going and shut up. The quicker we get this over with the quicker we get our money."

Let one of them stumble, Sand thought. A small thing like that, anything, would be the break he needed. So far all the luck had been on their side. Unless it changed soon it would be too late.

Louie found the spot he wanted and they left the footpath. He turned around and handed the shovel to Sand. "This place is all right. Start digging."

Sand took the shovel. Louie stepped away from him a few feet and held the beam of the flashlight on the ground where the digging was to be done. Sand began digging, weighing the possibilities of the old dirt-in-the-face trick and discarding it. House was too ready.

After ten minutes the hole began taking on a semblance of

what it was intended to be. Sand could feel his time running out.

"You don't have to dig much more, Sand. Two or three feet will do it. That way, it won't be as much work when me and Louie have to uncover you and get our money. I think that's about—"

Clink!

The sound was that of the shovel blade striking a rock.

Think fast, Sand! The bastard is getting ready to pull the trigger. It's now or never.

"I think you chose the wrong spot for my remains, Louie. There's already a grave here."

Without any hesitation Louie did the most common thing in the world in such a situation, the very thing Sand wanted him to do, the mistake he had been waiting for. Louie stepped up to the hole to get a better look, close enough for Sand to reach the gun under his belt.

For the second it lasted, everything was motion. Sand grabbed the arm holding the flashlight and pulled as he pulled his gun from under the man's belt, thumbing off the safety as it came free. Louie gave a sharp cry as he felt himself jerked off balance. He fired the gun in his other hand, but he was shooting at the moon. On the heels of that first shot came two more, in unison this time, twin roars that hurt the ears.

House wasn't slow, but his luck had run out. Sand fired even as he saw the flash from the other man's gun, the magnified sound rolling over him. It was that close. Sand knew it would be close. That's why he had pulled Louie off balance, to put Louie between him and his pal. His body was now lying in the shallow grave Sand had dug.

Louie took the slug right between the shoulder blades that had been meant for Sand—just as the bullet from Sand's .45 split House's wide face apart.

When the pressure of the heavy sound was gone the night was quieter than any night should be, even in a graveyard smothered in fog. No sound. Nothing. Not even the chirping of a cricket. Just the sharp, acrid smell of burned gunpowder and the bodies of two street-toughs who had come close to grabbing the gold ring—as close as the grave.

He reached down and picked up the flashlight a moment before the stream of thick blood flowing from Louie began to soak into the soft dirt under it.

Sand left the two hoods the way they were. He owed them nothing.

Flashing the beam of light ahead of him, he found his way back to the footpath and started back toward the car.

Maybe it was an accident that the spread of the light's beam touched on the tombstone, a coincidence that he noticed the name. How it happened wasn't important. The important thing was that suddenly he found himself frozen into a cold stiffness as his eyes stared and began to understand. He read the name carved into the granite—a familiar name, so familiar that it did strange things to his insides.

He read the date and counted off the years. Five. Nearly six now.

He didn't have to force the answers, for suddenly they came flooding in on him. All the questions that had been there before were suddenly gone, because this grave was the key, and now he knew who had lied and why, and he had the name he wanted.

Before he twisted the beam of the flashlight he knew the other grave would be there, the second grave . . .

FOURTEEN

NO QUESTIONS LEFT. Substantiating a truth, that was all that remained now. No real hurry. There was time.

From a phone booth he placed a call to a famous man named Stephen Tarrence, and a few choice words got the famous man on the phone even though he had been notified only a few hours ago of the death of his son. Sand asked the questions, and he knew what the answers would be before they came.

So simple.

Unbelievable and incredible; but so very simple.

He drove the car that had belonged to Louie back to where it had been parked down the street from the bar. With a handkerchief he wiped clean every part of the car he had touched. Then he walked to the short dead-end alley and climbed the squealing metal stairs to the room where Jessey Jollie still stared out a nothing from the bed. Here he used the handkerchief again. The cops would be around in the morning, and he intended to leave nothing behind that would show he had been here.

When the job was finished he walked through the foggy street back to his own car and drove to the hotel.

Dorothea opened the door, and for a moment there was relief on her lovely face. It faded into concern as she saw in his eyes that this thing wasn't over.

"Sand . . ."

"Soon," he told her. "It will be over soon."

He walked past her and into the bedroom. In the top drawer of a dresser he had left the diary. He took it out. He wanted it with him when the end came because it would help him hate. She had written a fairy tale because the real story had been too ugly. A good girl who fought until there was no fight left.

A good girl who finished dead.

He took the diary and slipped it in the pocket of his coat. Then he checked the .45 and slipped it back in its rig.

The tall blonde was standing in the doorway behind him, as beautiful as a woman can be.

"You know, don't you, Sand? You know who killed her."

He nodded. "I know who did it all. The murder was only the final act. It began a long time before."

Her voice was sad. "And you came here for revenge."

"For a man like me revenge is law, Dorothea. An eye for an eye. It's the only workable philosophy. It's animal, but it's accurate—and in the end Justice gets her due."

It was hard for her to understand, but she tried. Maybe she made it and maybe she didn't, but she didn't try to stop him. She didn't even ask if it was her brother.

He told her anyway. "It's not your brother, Dorothea. He's a louse, but he's just a louse. The world is full of them. It's evil I'm going to meet tonight."

"I'm glad, Sand, about Torbert. I asked myself if I would hate you if you hurt my brother. I couldn't find an answer. I just didn't know."

"You're a lot of woman, Dorothea."

"I'm your woman."

He walked past her into the other room. He wanted to kiss her, but he didn't for fear she would taste some of the hate bottled up in him.

"Get on the phone as soon as I'm gone," he told her. "Call the airlines. I want a reservation out of here tonight. To any-where. Mexico City, maybe."

She nodded, but the big sadness was back. She stood there in the light robe she had slipped about her to meet him at the door, the thing not really hiding the lushness of her body.

He said, "Make that two reservations, kitten. Mexico City might be lonely this time of year." She deserved better than what she was getting, but he supposed she had a right to find it out for herself.

Downstairs the car and the fog and the night were waiting

for him. He climbed in the car and began to drive. There was no tenseness in him, not even with all the hate. He thought about the girl and the killer, and he knew revenge was going to be sweet.

The drive didn't seem as long this time, maybe because of the things going on inside him. The lights told him the killer was home.

When he pressed the bell J. Addison Rutledge answered it himself. There were no servants because there was no family and he seldom returned here.

"Hello, Mr. Sand. This is a pleasant surprise. Won't you come in?" The look of honesty was still in the man's eyes, the look of sincerity. "I hope you have further word for me on your progress. Come. We can talk in the den." He led the way without waiting for a reply.

The wealthy politician walked behind his desk and indicated the chair opposite it to Sand.

"Now, tell me, Mr. Sand. What brings you all the way out here this time of night? Have you learned something new?"

Sand was amazed at the calmness of the man. This was a man you would want to trust, a man you would want to believe, a man you *would* trust and believe because the man you saw did not exist. He probably had never existed.

"You might say I learned something old," he said.

"Oh? What was that, Mr. Sand?"

"I learned that sometimes you can chase a lie without knowing it, or even suspecting it. Of course, when you chase a lie the things you learn tend to point in a false direction."

"I can see how it would," he agreed.

"Only suddenly you learn a truth, the basic truth, and everything changes direction."

"And?"

"And you find a killer."

The man actually smiled. "I suspected you had learned the truth, Mr. Sand. As soon as I saw you at the door when you were supposed to be dead, I knew you had found out. How, I haven't the slightest idea, but I knew. That's why I brought you in here."

Sand cursed and started to reach for the .45, ready to blow the son of a bitch to hell, but the even calm of the voice stopped him.

"Please don't, Mr. Sand. You will only die sooner than necessary. Please look behind you."

Behind him was the gun case he had noticed this afternoon. Only this afternoon the glass doors had been closed. Now one of them was open and a shotgun had dropped down the way it had been rigged to do when tripped by some hidden control. The barrel of the gun was aimed directly at the back of the chair where Sand sat.

J. Addison Rutledge was still smiling. "Rather ingenious, don't you think, Mr. Sand? I conceived the idea myself. My finger is resting on a button that will cause it to discharge, in which case you will be very quickly and completely dead. I've never used it before but I'm pretty sure it will work."

Probably he was right. There was a chance he wasn't if the man in the chair did exactly the right thing at the right time. The chair was heavy and leather covered with a padded back, not enough to stop a load of shot but maybe enough to take some of the bite out of it, especially birdshot. He had said his hunting was limited to quail these days, so there was a good chance that was what the gun was loaded for. If he could get his head and shoulders down before the blast . . . but it wouldn't work right now. The man on the other side of the desk was too ready.

"You see how it will be, don't you, Mr. Sand?"

"I see it."

"I probably should push this button right now, but I'm not a man to hurry things. And I must admit that I'm quite curious. I would appreciate it if you would be good enough to tell me how you came to find the truth, Mr. Sand—thereby buying yourself a few more minutes of life."

"You know the story, Rutledge."

He smiled again. "I would still like to hear it from you."

"Okay. I won't tell it the way I learned it, because I picked it up in pieces and the pieces were out of order. Instead, I'll tell it the way it happened, the way it looks when all those pieces are tied together in the right sequence. It's not a pretty picture, but you shouldn't mind that because you are what makes it ugly."

"Please don't make me angry, Mr. Sand. It won't be to your advantage."

Sand told him how it had been. "Let's say it began about six years ago. It took root a lot further back, but that's when you committed your first murder. Nobody ever called it murder, but if it hadn't been the rest of the story wouldn't have happened. That little story you gave me about your sister and Delia Shannon, it was true. Maybe you treated both girls like a father at first, but little girls have a habit of growing up—and I figure you fell in love with Delia Shannon, insanely in love, if my guess is right. The one unfilled gap is why you killed her."

He watched the man's face change.

"Sure, I know, Rutledge. She didn't set herself on fire; you did it. And it was Delia Shannon who burned to death six years ago. I could have found that out by simply checking the records, but why should anybody check the records when they have received the details of the tragic incident from the great J. Addison Rutledge himself. What did the girl do that was so bad she deserved to burn to death, Rutledge, refuse to go to bed with you?"

The politician's face lost its mask of calm so quickly his shout was a real surprise. "She was a tramp! An immoral tramp! A *harlot*! She sinned, and she paid the price of sin. The price of sin is fire." His voice was now filled with the insanity that must have been in him the night he made a human torch of her.

"What was her sin, Rutledge?"

"She was with child! A baby—put there by some stud tramp with no more decency than she. He wouldn't have married her, not even if he had known. I know that kind. *Her* kind. *His* kind. Evil sinners without shame. I held out my hand to her. I offered to marry her, to protect her. I told her I would forgive her. She laughed. She laughed at me. The evil was that strong in her. I offered her redemption and she chose damnation. She deserved the fire!"

The pitiful thing was that he believed it. To this day. He had no idea how sick he was.

"So Delia Shannon died six years ago," Sand said. "Probably the part about her mother is true the way you gave it to me—either that or you killed her because she knew or suspected the truth. Muriel must have known too, but she couldn't turn you in. After all, you were her brother, more like a father. Besides, unless she was actually a witness, it would be her word against yours; and you are one of the wealthiest and most respected men in the country. So she left you and this place. That was the one thing she could do, get away.

"Maybe she took the name of the girl you had killed because she felt it was the last name you would expect her to assume. Whatever the reason, she became Delia Shannon."

"She took the name of that heathen to spite me," J. Addison Rutledge declared. "She took her name and her ways, and she had to be punished. She deserved to be punished, more even than her sister in sin, for she would have flaunted her vulgarity in my face."

"You're lying, Rutledge. I guess you're so sick you're actually lying to yourself. All she wanted to do was get away from you. On the way she searched for something she was still young enough to think she could find. She probably wouldn't have made it, but once you found her you made sure of it. Part of her punishment I guess you called it. The money-filled envelopes, that was you right down the line. That was the first phase of her punishment. Anything she wanted you took away." It cost plenty, but I'll bet you thought it was worth every dime. Waters was the first. He claimed she walked out on him, but that was a lie, wasn't it, Rutledge? I figure he got the first payoff, the first and the largest. The payments got smaller as the men got smaller, but the object was always the same—to push the girl down, make her suffer, make her pay."

"She deserved no leniency!" he cried, and almost raised his hand to emphasize his words in his agitation before remembering its purpose on the button. "Damnation is what she deserved, to wallow in the torment of her sins and scream in the fires of hell."

Sand held himself in check with an effort. If he made his move now he would never finish it alive. He couldn't beat the blast of the shotgun behind him. As for his body, J. Addison Rutledge would simply call the police and become a hero. Any story he decided to tell would be fine with the cops. Politician kills famous mobster in self-defense. The publicity would push him right into the White House.

"Five years," Sand continued. "That's how long it took to push her all the way, to break her spirit completely, until there was nothing left of the girl of five years earlier. All it cost you was money—with the exception of Al Lobb. With Al it took more than money, with him you had to go a step farther and become more directly involved. What did you do, make a payoff higher up? Or maybe you just went to one of the big boys. They would break a hundred Al Lobbs to have J. Addison Rutledge owe them a favor. You couldn't force him to give up the girl, but the end result was the same. The girl knew what was happening and cared enough to let him go.

"Five years of hell you put her through before she finally reached bottom, whoring herself to any bum with a few bucks in his pocket. How much further were you planning to push, Rutledge? You weren't through. That's the kind of sick shit you are. You would never be through until she was in the flames—in the flames with the real Delia.

"But just when you were fully savoring the punishment and pain you had brought to bear on her you detected an anomaly. It was nothing really, just a ripple in the flow of misery. Mopsie Steiner reached out to her. Not a big thing, you knew that, but an annoyance, something you hadn't planned. Still, you would want to keep a close eye on her. I figure you reached inside and found Joey, Mopsie's kid, to do the job.

"That's how you learned the ripple had turned the flow and it was coming back for you. Something happened, something that would let the whole world see the twisted little man buried in your belly, the real J. Addison Rutledge. You wouldn't be pretty and popular any more. No one would vote for you. No one would like you and give you accolades to hang on your wall."

The man was calm now, dead calm. "What happened, Mr. Sand?"

"A young fellow named William Tarrence, the son of your political rival. He knew the girl. And he knew her as Muriel Rutledge, not as Delia Shannon. They had gone steady as kids back in high school, and apparently he was still stuck on her despite everything. He saw and talked to her one night, and he continued to come back. When Joey told you about it you got scared. If it became public knowledge that the great J. Addison Rutledge's sister was a common prostitute your career was ended.

"You had to kill them both. You got into Mopsie's place okay, but the killing didn't go as smooth as planned. You had to settle for shoving a knife in her when it had been your intention to watch her burn the way you had the real Delia Shannon."

"You couldn't—"

"I told you I had it figured, Rutledge. Once I got the picture in focus it was all there. This afternoon I saw the kid removing a can of gasoline that had been found upstairs. It didn't mean anything at the time but I didn't really know you then.

"You killed the girl, and then you took care of her boyfriend. There was only one more thing you had to do and it should have all been over, with you winning right down the line. A calculated risk on your part, but it still must have made you nervous. You aren't used to taking risks at all. The dead girl had to remain Delia Shannon, and if the cops checked far enough back they were going to find that the real Delia Shannon had been dead six years. That's the thing you couldn't let happen. So you waited until her name appeared in the papers and promptly went down to give them all the information they needed and take the body off their hands.

They ate it up just like I did and just like anyone else would. Who would stop to doubt anything told them by J. Addison Rutledge himself?

"Everything was going smooth, everything just like you wanted it. Then I showed up. It must have surprised the crap out of you when you found out I was looking for Delia's killer. You didn't know about my relationship with the her, but ten to one you knew my reputation as a tough bastard with not a damn thing against cracking heads and breaking bones. If I looked long enough and hard enough I just might find something. The cops didn't really worry you, but I did. With me it was personal. So you fed me the same story you had given the cops and I ate it up. The diary must have worried you too. You hadn't known about that."

Rutledge nodded his head on the other side of the desk. "Yes. I am very interested in the diary, Mr. Sand. I will want you to tell me where it is. I'm sure you will agree that it must be destroyed if I am to be perfectly safe. You don't, by any chance, have it with you?"

"Yeah, I've got it."

He smiled.

An idea began to form in Sand's mind. A long shot, but maybe it would work when the time was right.

"I started looking," he said, "and I began to pick up the pieces. Only the pieces didn't fit. If I had known the truth about the her I would have known that the He she kept referring to in her diary wasn't God at all, but the man who thought he was a god, the man who had persecuted her for five years. I gathered all the pieces, Rutledge, but they didn't fit.

"If you had left everything alone I might have ended up butting my head against a stone wall. But you got scared—I moved too fast, found bits and pieces of information I shouldn't be able to find. This afternoon when I was here I scared you plenty when I told you about the guy who had been seeing her at the house. You wanted that phase of the thing to remain completely in the dark, and here I was dragging it into the open. The play you made after I left proves how scared you were. The sniper waiting for me at the hotel had to be you. You left here right after I did and beat me back to town."

"It was unfortunate that I missed, Mr. Sand. I wouldn't have if it hadn't been for a—"

"But you did miss. So you contrived another plan. You knew I would be going after Jessey Jollie sooner or later; he was my last link to the girl before she moved into the house. You went to him and bribed him to call me. You must have been standing right beside him when I talked with him on the phone. As soon as he hung up you paid off the bribe with a knife through the back of the neck. You knew about the open contract on my head. You've got your connections. Jollie would have already told you how to contact the two hoods. You got in touch with them and told them where I would be and when I would be there. That should have finished it, and it damn near did. From that point on I guess fate played a hand. The little party ended up in a graveyard, and on the way back I nearly stumbled over the key to the whole puzzle."

The man on the other side of the desk knew before he asked. The word graveyard had told him. But he asked the question anyway. "And what was that, Mr. Sand?"

"A grave. Two graves actually. Delia Shannon and her mother."

He thought about it. "An accident. It wouldn't happen again, not in a hundred years."

"It only had to happen once."

He nodded. "Yes. And now, Mr. Sand, it has come time for you to die. But first, the diary . . ."

He held out his right hand for it, his left still on the button that would set off the shotgun.

Sand took the book out slow and easy. This was his plan, and the time was now or never. To pass the diary to the man behind the desk he had to lean over, and leaning brought his head and shoulders lower until they were no longer above the covered back of the chair. Now to buy the fraction of a second it would take to reach the .45.

He dropped the diary almost by accident.

Rutledge reached for it before he caught himself.

Then he pushed the button!

Sand was toppling forward as his hand found his gun and squeezed off three rounds through the back of the desk.

For an excruciating moment the whole room was filled with sound and pain. Sand had a sense of Rutledge's body dancing in his chair as the .45 slugs ripped through him even as he felt pellets from the shotgun rip into the flesh of his back and kick him from the chair to the floor.

For a while he was paralyzed. He didn't know how long, probably for just the moment it took the sound to evaporate and leave behind its aftermath of ear-ringing silence.

He got slowly to his feet, the pain in his penetrated muscles leaving his whole body in a cold sweat. It hurt like hell but he could tell the angle of entry kept most of the damage close to the surface.

Two of the slugs had caught Rutledge low in the belly, ripping through the fleshy part of his body. He was still sitting in the chair.

Sand fought back his own pain and moved around the desk to stand over him, the gun still in his hand.

He wasn't dead. He didn't move, but his eyes were wide open and staring at the gun. His lips parted. "Don't . . . Don't . . ."

Sand eased the .45 back into its holster. "That would be too easy, Rutledge. This doesn't end easy. Remember what you said? Evil must burn in hell."

He saw comprehension creep into the man's eyes.

"If you can still crawl, it's time to start crawling, because hell is coming . . ."

Sand did not look back as he drove slowly away from the mass of dark smoke and twisting flames filling his rearview mirror. In the raging fire consuming the mansion burning timbers split and screamed at the night. It was impossible to hear anything above the sounds it made.

ENNIS WILLIE GETS THE THIRD DEGREE

Interview by Stephen Mertz

In the early to mid-1960's, Camerarts Publishing, Inc. of Chicago, Illinois published what were sometimes called "men's magazines" or "girlie magazines"—*Men's Digest*, *Rascal* and *Best for Men*—and two lines of paperback originals, Novel Books and Merit Books.

Novel and Merit were direct descendents of the Spicy line of pulp magazines of the 1930's and '40's and, like the Spicy pulps, were not available at every bookstore or newsstand. Thus, these paperbacks are extremely rare today.

Novel Books, on each copyright page, claimed to publish "high quality books, written by knowledgeable, mature, professional writers and intended for mature, adult readers." The books were priced at more than double the average paperback of the day, with "For Adults" or "Adult Reading" gracing the covers of books with titles like *Nympho Lodge*, *Swamp Lust* and *Dammit, Don't Touch My Broad!* As for sexual content, in a time when *Tropic of Cancer* and *Fanny Hill* were fighting in state and federal courts for the very right to exist, the Camerarts product (again like the earlier *Spicy* lines) were not only *not* pornographic, but were mild to the point of seeming downright innocent when compared to contemporary mainstream standards. There were no four-letter words, no clinical descriptions of the sex act; in fact, there was no graphic sex whatsoever.

These books were, for the most part, short, ultra-hardboiled adventure and detective fiction aimed at male readers who could not get enough of the racy, tough guy prose purveyed by writers like Mickey Spillane and Richard S. Prather. The roster of Camerarts authors included John Jakes, "Big Bob" Tralins, George H. Smith, Con Sellers and Duane Rimel (Rex Weldon), among others.

Novel Book's most long-running series was a Shell Scott knock-off starring Tokey Wedge, "the shocking stud", written by Jack Lynn (Max van der Veer). Here's the back cover copy for *Passion Pit*: *Guys—if you go for cigarettes, whiskey and wild, wild women (and don't care too much about the cigarettes and the whiskey), you'll go for this newest Tokey Wedge original!*

Merit Books, on the other hand, were relatively more sophisticated. In fact, the spine of most Merit Books carried their motto: "Uncensored, offbeat novels for sophisticated adults." The covers were generally head-and-bare-shoulder shots of female models rather than the lurid, garish cover illustrations of the Novel books. The Merit titles, though, were hot enough: *Luscious, Teasing Body, Carnal Love Nest*, etc.

And that brings us to Ennis Willie, star writer of the Merit Books line.

There's something special about Willie. Everything about his work places him not only head-and-shoulders above anything else Camerarts ever published, but puts him squarely in the first rank of the '50's/early-'60's hardboiled masters. Willie's fiction represents a largely unknown treasure trove of 40,000-45,000-word, sexed-up tough guy melodrama at its best; bare-knuckled, .45-toting heroes, gorgeous babes and violence that roars off the page.

His heroes are matchless specimens of male chauvinism with names like Birch Sunday, Cruss Ballard, Trace Bronson and Gard Hogan. These are tall tales told at a breakneck pace, drenched in palpitating purple prose, with opening lines like "The big naked bitch standing up on the bed was screaming to high hell," or "It occurred to Tripp Fortune suddenly as he entered the bar that he didn't know who he was."

Willie published between 1961 and 1965. All but one of his books appeared under the Merit Books imprint, all of them yet-to-be-discovered nuggets of gold with *Luscious, Teasing Body* (reprinted as *The Sensualites*) and *Carnal Madness* (reprinted as *To Live Dangerously*) among the best, and that's saying something since every Ennis Willie novel has its moments.

And then there's Sand, "The Man Nobody Walks On". Willie's one series character appeared in nine novels (starting with the *tour de force, Scarlet Goddess,* in 1963) and three short stories.

The front cover copy for *Warped Desires* presented him this way:

Sand is a man's name. It's his only name—now. He was once a top member of the crime syndicate, but he quit. Because he couldn't stand the daily diet of vice and corruption. The mob wants him dead. Bought and paid-for police won't help him. So he's running—with a loaded .45 that answers any questions.

How tough is Sand? Here's a sample:

Sand got a grip on the banister and pulled himself to his feet. He didn't bother to examine his side. He had been shot enough times to know that, even though it hurt like holy hell, it was more a burn than anything else. The slug had hardly broken the skin.

Sand's adventures involve the people he encounters along the way while he stays on the move, solving murders, dallying with beautiful babes and periodically dispatching mob hit squads. We're told that he saw combat in WWII and Korea, but beyond that all the back-story we need is provided in the debut novel:

The great Sand. The man who had taken every rotten dollar the organization had to offer, then bucked it when he got fed-up with the daily corruption. And he had gotten away with it. Others had tried and failed. But they weren't Sand, the fair-haired boy of the underworld, tough and smart and going places in the organization until he decided he had enough dough to retire. He had known they would come after him, and he was ready for them.

In San Francisco a planted bomb had turned his car in-

side out, and the next morning the hood who planted it was floating face-down in the bay. In Detroit he had hit the pavement a couple of inches under a barrage of lead from a burp gun, pulling his .45 as he went down. The guy issuing bullets by the pound was in the rear seat of a speeding Caddy. Sand shot him between the eyes, knocking him back- ward with his finger locked on the trigger. For a moment the Tommy gun had gone wild inside the car. The two hoods in the front seat didn't have time to spit before they were turned into chopped liver. The car piled into a brick wall and caught fire, and blood ran out of the fire onto the street.

And the women this guy encounters? Here's more of Wil- lie at his best:

Golden hair in a pageboy that melted lovingly against her shoulders. Her face, the soft, narcotic beauty you dream about in the middle of a war when there has been no woman for a long time and you have had time to forget that nothing is without flaw. At a time like that a man can build a perfect woman in his mind, piece by piece. The hair; the eyes; the lips so soft and red, with the sparkle of moisture over lip- stick; breasts like twin mountains, full and high and proud; a flat belly flowing down and flaring into the hips of a woman made for love; full thighs and long, tapering legs that would respond to passion.

The sex in these books is steamy but not graphic:

She came across the room at him in a naked run, hard- nippled breasts jutting out at him.

The little bitch planned to rape him! he decided half a second before she was all over him, all tight, warm flesh and sharp nails raking at his clothes like a tigress.

Maybe he was a fool for not just standing there and taking it as it came to him. This blonde sex-cat was probably more woman than he had ever been with. But he didn't, and it wasn't because of any damn scruples, for Sand had come up in a world where every scruple, every moral constituted a weakness. But it went against his grain to be raped, even by a nympho with a luscious body she couldn't control.

Only this cutie had no intention of being stopped.

Unfortunately for the nympho, Sand and the reader, the cutie *is* stopped when her parents return home unexpectedly, leaving Sand to wonder "what you were supposed to say to a man when he walks in and finds his daughter naked in your arms."

Each Sand novel packs a wallop, though the debut, along with *Aura of Sensuality* and *Warped Ambitions*, deserve honorable mention. My personal favorite is *And Some Were Evil.*

Allow me to interject some autobiography here.

I discovered these books when I was a high school kid in Milwaukee. In those days, my meat was hardboiled tough guys and I read 'em by the truckload: Spillane was king, but there were plenty of others: Prather, Carter Brown, Frank Kane, Brett Halliday, William Ard, Mike Avallone and countless more. But those books were widely read, published by top-line paperback houses. Most of my complete collection of Ennis Willie was purchased new, off the spin rack at Ben-Mor Liquors on Wisconsin Avenue in downtown Milwaukee. Either I appeared (if not acted) mature for my age, or the cigar-chomper behind the counter didn't give a damn. I dropped in to check that spin rack every two weeks for new releases. My parents would have killed me had they caught me reading this stuff (heck, they didn't even approve of Mickey and Prather!), and I didn't know anyone else who was aware of Ennis Willie despite the rave reviews that were printed on the back covers of some of these books:

"Unquestionably one of the top three popular fiction writers on the stands today! His women are voluptuous, earthy creatures whose unrestrained passions make them worthy of his 100% virile heroes. I, personally, read every Ennis Willie book I can get my hands on." —Editor, *Rascal Magazine.*

It wasn't until much later that I came to know that *Rascal* was edited by Tony Licata . . . who just happened to be Willie's editor at Merit Books!

But who *is* Ennis Willie?

As the years rolled on, even fans who fondly remembered his books could uncover nothing about the man. Some of those fans went on to become writers. I was one, and so was my friend, Max Allan Collins who inscribed one of his early novels to me, *From one Ennis Willie fan to another.* Ed Gorman is a fan who kept the legend alive. "Miniature masterpieces," he wrote of Willie's work, "with an ambiance all their own. Part Spillane, part spaghetti western—all Ennis Willie."

And yet, because the books' distribution had been so sparse and spotty all those years ago, few modern readers have had a chance to read the man who, with Mickey Spillane, was hands-down the toughest of his generation of hard guy writers. A legend and a mystery grew up around the author of those long-ago "sex books." The discovery of a black poet named Willie Ennis led to conjecture that Ennis Willie was a pseudonym used by a black man. I went so far as to suggest in print that Ennis Willie was a pen name for Spillane himself.

Then, one day in 2004 on Gorman's blog, *Ed's Place*, the mystery was solved with the morning mail. This e-mail was posted:

> I know who wrote the Ennis Willie books. It was Ennis Willie. I know because that's me and I remember all the chain smoking and coffee consumption that went into them. I'm sure Mickey Spillane will be thrilled to learn he's not the guilty party . . . I was born in Wrens, Georgia on April 30, 1939. I grew up in another small town fifteen miles away called Louisville, Georgia and moved to Atlanta in the early sixties, where I still live. Oh, and I'm not black. That's about all I know about myself, but if anyone would like to ask about any specifics I will be happy to respond.

I followed through on Ennis Willie's invitation and found a friendly, generous man willing to share at length his insights and experiences.

The following interview was conducted via e-mail, September-October, 2004:

First off, how does it feel to be "rediscovered" and inter-viewed about books you wrote some forty years ago?

Painless. I was a little reluctant to be rediscovered and put myself in the spotlight, but it has its compensations. I've picked up some great new writer friends. That's a definite plus. Like my character Sand, I can use every friend I can get.

Your first novel, THE WORK OF THE DEVIL, was pub-lished in 1961 when you were 21 years old. Could you tell us something about your background, and how this book came to be written?

My background . . . I grew up in a small town called Lou-isville, Georgia on the same street as the shirt factory where my parents worked. I attended the local school and the local pool hall and the high spots in my life were sports and mov-ies.

When I was around twelve of thirteen I began changing the marquee of my hometown movie theater the night before each new feature started. The job didn't pay any money but I got to see all the movies free.

I also began to spend time in the projection booth every chance I got, which is to say every time the manager was gone. He had standing orders that I was to be kept out.

Then the night came when the projectionist and the man-ager had a real falling out right in the middle of a double fea-ture and the projectionist announced he was quitting and he was walking.

The manager said, "You can't just walk out. Nobody else knows how to run the film."

But there was someone . . . and I was sitting downstairs that very minute watching the first half of the double feature.

The short version of the story is, the manager was shocked, then furious, then relieved. I got the job, and this one did pay money. I was fifteen at the time.

A couple of years after that I was showing a matinee when I realized the theater was filling up with smoke. Right after that I got a frantic call from the lobby to shut everything down quick and make sure everyone was out of the balcony. A fire had broken out in one of the supply rooms behind the screen. A lot happened in the next couple of hours, including the theater being gutted and me watching the screen ignite like flash paper. That was the end of my movie career.

On a brighter note, I did get to meet Lash Larue. He really could take a cigarette out of a girl's mouth with his bullwhip. You wouldn't have wanted to see him miss his target. He pulled the whip back at one point and hit the pegboard wall leading up to the stage and it cut a one inch groove in the wall that would still be there if the fire hadn't come along.

I had, a few years earlier, discovered the thrill of reading in the paperback bookrack at the Rexall drug store. There was a wider world there, an education beyond the bounders of the classroom, with alleys and avenues to explore and mean streets to travel.

I started with the essentials.

From Mickey Spillane I learned about dumdum bullets and paraffin tests; that vengeance is a better motivator than all the rest, and how you gotta let her have it if she has it coming, even if maybe you love her and you have to spend weeks in the bottle to forget the pain.

Richard S. Prather introduced me to *BODIES IN BED-LAM* and *THE WAILING FRAIL*, and how you can make up your own words that didn't mean anything until *you* said so.

David Goodis taught me that on the *STREET OF THE LOST* you can find a hero even among the lowest of the low, because there can come a time when any step up, no matter how small, is a triumph.

Peter Rabe showed me an underworld where they would *MURDER ME FOR NICKELS.*

The list goes on. It's long and it's star-studded, and I reveled in the adventures flowing out of an ever-changing rack of titles. "Complete and Unabridged" was my anthem.

That's when the Writing Monster got a grip on me.

As for my first novel, *THE WORK OF THE DEVIL*, it came to be written like all those that followed—because I couldn't stop it.

Wanting to write isn't enough. Having to write, not being able to get on with your life until you do, hoping it's good, thinking it's crap, and plowing on into the unknown, that's writing.

I might add that if you work hard enough and long enough you may be able to shake this monster. But don't count on it.

At the time *THE WORK OF THE DEVIL* was written I was living in Augusta, Georgia—trying to get an education during the day and working as a chase man for a small loan company at dawn and dusk, a job where you seldom see a friendly face and one that occasionally includes some turbulence.

A woman once casually opened a dresser drawer, pulled out a gun about the size of a cannon, held it a foot from my face and said, "If you didn't have the police with you I would shoot you dead."

I had two deputies with me at the time.

She then put the gun back in the drawer and closed it. It all happened so fast nobody had time to blink.

"Yes, ma'am," I said. A certain amount of respect seemed in order.

This has nothing to do with the book itself, except that I can't seem to look at one without thinking about the other.

Who were you reading in those days?

It's a strange thing, but I'm so single minded I've never been able to concentrate on writing and reading at the same time. Of all my flaws, that's the one I like the least.

It's also the reason I felt something of a sense of relief when I realized that after five years of one and not enough of the other I was about ready to flameout.

I could practically count the keystrokes.

It would be impossible to discuss your work in depth

without mentioning Mickey Spillane. While Mickey's success in the 1950's spawned countless first-person tough-guy private eye writers, you were the most successful at emulating his style of larger than life heroes, vivid scenes of violence, frequent italicized passages and powerful last-page surprise endings. Yet you never wrote a traditional private eye novel and you wrote in third person. What's interesting is that your first novel is written pretty much "straight", and the Spillane influence becomes more noticeable with each book. Was this an editorial suggestion, or a natural progression on your part?

I guess you would have to call it a natural progression. Nobody ever suggested it, or even mentioned it.

I may have been more aware if I were reading my novels instead of writing them, but the first time it was brought to my attention was when I read it in a magazine. It was a compliment and I was complimented. My style was being compared to one of the greats.

You wrote 21 novels in five years. How long would it take to write one of those books? What were your work habits?

It's hard to think of my erratic behavior in a term like 'habits' but I guess it's close enough. Between books I would take a break and relax. In short order the next one would show up and demand its turn. I could hurry things along if I were broke or had made overly optimistic commitments concerning deadlines, but with so many books trying to get out slowing down was a bigger chore than speeding up.

I didn't tend to write anything down between books. No plot twists or outlines or catchy snippets of dialog. I would just think about the new book. I drove and thought. I walked and thought. I thought looking off into space. I thought watching TV, often having to explain to my wife that I *was* working. When the thinking was done I had the book pretty much in my head.

I then sat down at my typewriter and commenced to beat

on it. There was no set amount of time it took to get the job done. Sometimes it came easy and sometimes it came hard. Usually it took about three or four weeks at the typewriter.

The fastest I ever produced a finished manuscript was five days, when I was staring a deadline in the face. A lot of cigarettes, coffee and NoDoz.

The longest was six months when I was convinced the words on the paper were stilted, stiff and embarrassing and would never be any other way. With that book there were days when I would hit a hot streak and everything would be gold, and other days when the gold turned to grime and eventually I would have to push on with a promise to come back and fix it later.

When the book was done and I went back to polish the grimy spots I couldn't find them. There was no difference between the gold and the grime.

I'm sure there is a moral in there somewhere.

I heard that Georges Simenon would write a book straight through, then go out whoring as a reward. The faster he did one, the quicker he got to the other. That idea has always appealed to me in principle, but I've never finished a manuscript that didn't leave me too tired for anything but sleep.

Your novels are sexy tough guy melodramas, but with no graphic sex whatsoever. Yet the titles are outrageously titillating. Were these your titles, or foisted upon you by the publisher?

The publisher did it. Maybe you and I could get together and go find somebody to beat up.

Paperback collectors have long been fascinated by Camerarts Publishing of Chicago, which published the Merit and Novel Books lines as well as some magazines. Rumors have even circulated that Camerarts was a mob-fronted business. Tell us what you know about them, and any interesting experiences you may recall about writing for them.

I think you can forget the mob thing. They didn't have that much money.

My only contact with the company was through my editors, Tony Licata and Frank Sorren by phone and mail, and not much of that.

After somebody badly edited a key paragraph in my first novel, we decided there would be no editing unless I did it, including the punctuation. (You would never know it today I'm so laid back, but in those days I was tight as a bowstring.)

Starting with the second book, each one went to press exactly as it came out of the typewriter, and that greatly eased the burden on my psyche.

PASSION HAS NO RULE BOOK is the only book I recall reaching the newsstand with an error in it. Worse than that, there was nobody to blame. It came out of my typewriter that way, the finished manuscript was that way, and the printed book was that way. It was a minor error as errors go, but it still rankles.

Sand confronts three goons blocking his way. He breaks one guy's nose and explains to the others, "The game is called Freeze. You play it by standing very still. The first one who moves becomes a stiff."

Then he crossed the floor and knocked on the office door . . .

And there it was for all to see. Nobody did see, except me, but this is no time for splitting hairs.

What kind of pantywaist shuts down a bunch of goons and then knocks *on* the boss's door? This is Sand we're talking about here.

DOWN!

He knocked *Down* the door.

Down, dammit!

Ahhh . . . that feels better. I've needed to get that off my chest for a long time.

Now about the publisher-foisted titles.

I probably should have complained about those god-awful titles. Still, I can't help but notice that used copies of *CAR-*

NAL MADNESS always seem to have a higher price tag than *TO LIVE DANGEROUSLY*, even though they are the same book.

Did you have any contact with other Camerarts authors?

No. A few Atlanta writers were the extent of my social circle. Writing can be a lonely business. It was for me and I was content with that. To this day the words "cocktail party" send a shiver down my spine.

Did you write under any pen names during this period? If so, which ones and for what publishers? Inquiring collectors want to know!

Most writers have at least one pen name. Magazines are very averse to publishing more than one story in the same issue by the same author. I had one in reserve for that purpose. It was never used on a book. I don't think I'm prepared to confess what it was. Maybe after the torture . . .

How do you feel today about the books you wrote during that time? Do you have a favorite among them?

I loved them then and I love them now. That's the truth. I don't hold them up in comparison to other stories or other writers. That was never my concern. My judgment is based on how well they produce on paper what I saw in my mind's eye.

There is maybe one I would re-read carefully before sending it out into the world again. There is one that I would probably revise.

Of your novels published during that period, all but one appeared under the Merit Book imprint. The exception is VICE TOWN, published by Vega Books. Could you tell us the story behind that and anything you may recall about Vega?

VICE TOWN . . . I love that book. I actually wrote *VICE TOWN* twice. I set the first draft aside for a long time, then came back and re-wrote it from scratch. Only two paragraphs and the underlying plot of the first version survived.

In the second version the main character is a disillusioned soldier of fortune returning to a small town where he had briefly lived ten years earlier. In this version he only has one leg. In the next version he will just have a cast on that leg. (The leg thing is very important to the plot.)

The title, even though it's not my working title, actually fits the book very well. At the time it was written I was living across the river from Phenix City, Alabama, which was still trying to live down the title "Sin City U.S.A." and served as a very loose setting for the story.

I don't know much about Vega Books except that the imprint belonged to a publishing house known for its racy titles. It was trying to break that mold by adding a Science Fiction Library, a Western Library, and a Suspense Library. *VICE TOWN* was number V17 in the Suspense Library.

Merit Books had published my first novel, *THE WORK OF THE DEVIL*, but they were scared of *VICE TOWN*. They felt a hero with a missing leg wouldn't match the image they were shooting for. (Did I mention the leg would just be broken in the rewrite?)

. . . On the other hand, *are we going to put up with that kind of crap?*

No!

Forget the rewrite.

During the 1970's and '80's, Pinnacle Books had a long-running series, written by a variety of house name authors, called The Butcher, about an ex-mob boss who walks away from his life of crime. The premise of that series is that there are scores of hit men tracking him at every turn, and his adventures grow from the people he encounters while on the run. This is, of course, the premise of your one series character, Sand. Did you have anything to do with the Pinnacle se-

ries?

Now *that's* a zinger! I guess the answer is both "Yes" and "No".

When Pinnacle Books was just starting up an editor I knew well called to tell me he had mailed me the first two or three books they were planning to release. (They were the first books in *THE EXECUTIONER* series.) He was very excited about the whole thing and wanted me to consider coming on board.

I said I would read the books when they arrived and give it some serious consideration. Which I did, even though I was currently working sixteen to eighteen hours a day on the startup of a non-writing project. I think I mentioned the way I work, the thinking and the total concentration and all that. Well that goes for everything I do, not just writing.

Anyway, what they really wanted was a spy series. Spies were very big at the time. We discussed the situation in depth over a period of a few weeks. The upshot of the whole thing was:

I didn't want to do spies. Probably because I didn't think of it myself.

I would be interested in continuing the Sand series.

No problem—Sand can be a spy.

Yes, problem. Sand is a mean son of a bitch and he likes things the way they were meant to be. And I guess I do too . . .

The end result was no Sand and no Sand spy, and everybody was happy.

Not the end of story.

A couple of months later I spotted a Pinnacle book in the rack with a character whose description was virtually identical to Sand. On closer examination I saw that the first chapter was basically a paraphrasing of my Sand novel *CODE OF VENGEANCE*, even though more than a few passages still existed exactly as I had written them. I would have begun to get irritated about then except for two things.

One, the book quickly veered off in its own direction.

Two, I recognized the direction. The plot was one a friend and fellow writer had discussed with me once. Of course, it was just a spy plot at the time and there was no imitation Sand involved. He was also a friend of the editor mentioned earlier.

So "what the hell . . ." I thought. Maybe I had already begun to mellow out. Or maybe, other than the fake Sand, it was nothing like the Sand spy series I would have written . . . Or the fact that one line of dialog apparently proved impossible to paraphrase: "Go find your own pig."

So the next time you're in town, Doc, come see me. All is forgiven.

Care to bring us up to date on what Ennis Willie has been up to for the last 40 years?

I've already mentioned tackling a non-writing project. One day I was reading something that was particularly well printed and I thought, "I'll do that." I don't know why. No such thought had ever crossed my mind before. I knew absolutely nothing about printing or the business of printing. I had never been inside the production area of a printing plant, didn't even know a printer.

But, to make this one of my short stories, I just grabbed on to the idea and didn't let go, and thus became the founder of what has evolved into a print production and management company. My current title is CEO.

What do you read these days for pleasure?

Actually, I read everything. And I do mean everything. But the mystery genre in all its shapes, forms and subgenres is where my heart is.

Can we look forward to any new Ennis Willie books in the near future?

Until recently I would have said not a chance, but lately I

have become aware of a strange tingling in my fingertips. I do have an awful lot of plots I've been trying to ignore.

Thank you for the interview, and for all those great books!

Don't mention it. You probably saved me a trip to the shrink.

AN ENNIS WILLIE
BIBLIOGRAPHY

SAND BOOKS:

SCARLET GODDESS, Merit 683 (1963)
AURA OF SENSUALITY, Merit 6101 (1963)
HAVEN FOR THE DAMNED, Merit 6M422 (1963)
GAME OF PASSION, Merit 6M434 (1964)
AND SOME WERE EVIL, Merit 6M461 (1964)
WARPED AMBITIONS, Merit 6M480 (1964)
THE CASE OF THE LOADED GARTER HOLSTER, Merit 6M484
    (1964)
PASSION HAS NO RULE BOOK, Merit 6M487 (1964)
CODE OF VENGEANCE, Merit 6M492 (1965)

SAND SHORT FICTION

"Flesh House" (SAND), *BEST FOR MEN* (August, 1965)
"Con's Wife" (SAND), *RASCAL* (May, 1965)
"Unsubtle Sensualite" (SAND), *BEST FOR MEN* (December, 1965)

NON-SERIES BOOKS:

THE WORK OF THE DEVIL, Merit 519 (1961)
(Reprinted as *MODERN LOVE*, Merit 678 (1963)
MODERN GIGOLO, Merit 668 (1962)
(Reprinted as *EROTIC SEARCH*, Merit 6M489 (1965)
LUSCIOUS, TEASING BODY, Merit 661 (1963)
(Reprinted as *THE SENSUALITES*, Merit 6M478 (1964)
VICE TOWN, Vega Books V-17 (1962)
CARNAL LOVE NEST, Merit 675 (1963)
(Reprinted as *THAT KIND OF WOMAN*, Merit 6M491 (1965)
CARNAL MADNESS, Merit 682 (1963)
(Reprinted as *TO LIVE DANGEROUSLY*, Merit 6M493 (1965)
THE TWISTED MISTRESS, Merit 694 (1963)
POLITICIAN'S PLAYGIRL, Merit 6M403 (1963)
SO NAKED! SO DEAD! Merit 6M415 (1963)
A NEW KIND OF LOVE, Merit 6M441 (1964)
INCREDIBLY SEDUCTIVE, Merit 6M456 (1964)
SENSUAL GAME, Merit 6M451 (1964)

About the Editors

Max Allan Collins is best known as the author of the graphic novel, *Road to Perdition*, source of the Academy Award-winning film. He received a Lifetime Achievement Award from the Private Eye Writers of America for his Nathan Heller historical novels. He collaborated with Mickey Spillane on the *Mike Danger* comic book of the '90s as well as numerous anthologies, and was chosen by Spillane to complete the Mike Hammer novel, *The Goliath Bone*, and other projects in progress at the time of Spillane's death in 2006. He is also an independent filmmaker in his native Iowa, his most current film *Eliot Ness: An Untouchable Life* (2007, VCI Home Video). He sometimes writes in collaboration with his wife, Barbara Collins (as "Barbara Allan") and is a leading author of TV and movie tie-in novels, including the USA Today-bestselling *CSI* series and the New York Times bestselling *Saving Private Ryan* and *American Gangster*.

Lynn Myers has been collecting suspense and private eye novels since 1977. A researcher for author Max Allan Collins, he has contributed historical information for 16 books. He has also contributed to four collections of short stories by Mickey Spillane and shares a byline with Max Collins on *Primal Spillane* (Gryphon, 2003) and *Byline: Mickey Spillane* (Crippen and Landru, 2004). He is also co-editor (with Max Allan Collins) on the forthcoming *14 Slayers* (the collected works of Paul Cain), and formerly was a columnist for *Mystery Scene*. He is also a short story writer and a literary agent.

Steve Mertz has written novels under a variety of pseudonyms that have been widely translated and sold millions of copies worldwide. He lives in Arizona and is always at work on a new book.

About the Contributors

Bill Crider has published more than 50 mystery, horror, and western novels. He collects old paperback books, mainly those from the era that inspired Ennis Willie.

A professional author for nearly thirty years, James Reasoner has written over 170 novels in a variety of genres. He is best known in the mystery field for his cult classic private eye novel *TEXAS WIND*, which was recently reprinted by PointBlank Press. His most recent project is a contemporary crime novel, *DUST DEVILS*, which will also be published by PointBlank Press.

Gary Lovisi is a MWA Edgar nominated author for Best Short Story of 2005, who has written numerous crime novels and stories as well as non-fiction about the genre and collectable paperbacks. He is the publisher of *Paperback Parade* and *Hardboiled* magazines and the founder of Gryphon Books. You can reach him at his website:
www.gryphonbooks.com

Bill Pronzini has published more than 60 novels, nearly half of them in his long-running "Nameless Detective" series. Among the many anthologies he has edited is *HARDBOILED* (Oxford U. Press, 1995), a comprehensive compilation and history of hard-boiled crime fiction.

Wayne Dundee lives in the once-notorious old cowtown of Ogallala, on the hinge of Nebraska's panhandle. He relocated there after spending the first fifty years of his life in the state line area of northern Illinois/southern Wisconsin.
A widower, retired from a managerial position in the magnetics industry, Dundee now devotes full time to his writing.
To date, Dundee has had six novels and over twenty short

stories published. All of the novels and most of the short stories have featured his PI protagonist, Joe Hannibal. (Like the author, Hannibal, too, has recently relocated to west central Nebraska.)

Dundee's work has been nominated for an Edgar, an Anthony, and six Shamus Awards. He is the founder and original editor of *Hardboiled Magazine*.

RAMBLE HOUSE's

HARRY STEPHEN KEELER WEBWORK MYSTERIES

(RH) indicates the title is available ONLY in the RAMBLE HOUSE edition

The Ace of Spades Murder
The Affair of the Bottled Deuce (RH)
The Amazing Web
The Barking Clock
Behind That Mask
The Book with the Orange Leaves
The Bottle with the Green Wax Seal
The Box from Japan
The Case of the Canny Killer
The Case of the Crazy Corpse (RH)
The Case of the Flying Hands (RH)
The Case of the Ivory Arrow
The Case of the Jeweled Ragpicker
The Case of the Lavender Gripsack
The Case of the Mysterious Moll
The Case of the 16 Beans
The Case of the Transparent Nude (RH)
The Case of the Transposed Legs
The Case of the Two-Headed Idiot (RH)
The Case of the Two Strange Ladies
The Circus Stealers (RH)
Cleopatra's Tears
A Copy of Beowulf (RH)
The Crimson Cube (RH)
The Face of the Man From Saturn
Find the Clock
The Five Silver Buddhas
The 4th King
The Gallows Waits, My Lord! (RH)
The Green Jade Hand
Finger! Finger!
Hangman's Nights (RH)
I, Chameleon (RH)
I Killed Lincoln at 10:13! (RH)
The Iron Ring
The Man Who Changed His Skin (RH)
The Man with the Crimson Box
The Man with the Magic Eardrums
The Man with the Wooden Spectacles
The Marceau Case
The Matilda Hunter Murder
The Monocled Monster

The Murder of London Lew
The Murdered Mathematician
The Mysterious Card (RH)
The Mysterious Ivory Ball of Wong Shing Li (RH)
The Mystery of the Fiddling Cracksman
The Peacock Fan
The Photo of Lady X (RH)
The Portrait of Jirjohn Cobb
Report on Vanessa Hewstone (RH)
Riddle of the Travelling Skull
Riddle of the Wooden Parrakeet (RH)
The Scarlet Mummy (RH)
The Search for X-Y-Z
The Sharkskin Book
Sing Sing Nights
The Six From Nowhere (RH)
The Skull of the Waltzing Clown
The Spectacles of Mr. Cagliostro
Stand By—London Calling!
The Steeltown Strangler
The Stolen Gravestone (RH)
Strange Journey (RH)
The Strange Will
The Straw Hat Murders (RH)
The Street of 1000 Eyes (RH)
Thieves' Nights
Three Novellos (RH)
The Tiger Snake
The Trap (RH)
Vagabond Nights (Defrauded Yeggman)
Vagabond Nights 2 (10 Hours)
The Vanishing Gold Truck
The Voice of the Seven Sparrows
The Washington Square Enigma
When Thief Meets Thief
The White Circle (RH)
The Wonderful Scheme of Mr. Christopher Thorne
X. Jones—of Scotland Yard
Y. Cheung, Business Detective

Keeler Related Works

A To Izzard: A Harry Stephen Keeler Companion by Fender Tucker — Articles and stories about Harry, by Harry, and in his style. Included is a compleat bibliography.

Wild About Harry: Reviews of Keeler Novels — Edited by Richard Polt & Fender Tucker — 22 reviews of works by Harry Stephen Keeler from *Keeler News*. A perfect introduction to the author.

The Keeler Keyhole Collection: Annotated newsletter rants from Harry Stephen Keeler, edited by Francis M. Nevins. Over 400 pages of incredibly personal Keeleriana.

Fakealoo — Pastiches of the style of Harry Stephen Keeler by selected demented members of the HSK Society. Updated every year with the new winner.

RAMBLE HOUSE's OTHER AUTHORS

The End of It All and Other Stories — Ed Gorman's latest short story collection

Four Dancing Tuatara Press Books — *Beast or Man?* By Sean M'Guire; *The Whistling Ancestors* by Richard E. Goddard; *The Shadow on the House* and *Sorcerer's Chessmen* by Mark Hansom. With introductions by John Pelan

The Dumpling — Political murder from 1907 by Coulson Kernahan

Victims & Villains — Intriguing Sherlockiana from Derham Groves

Evidence in Blue — 1938 mystery by E. Charles Vivian

The Case of the Little Green Men — Mack Reynolds wrote this love song to sci-fi fans back in 1951 and it's now back in print.

Hell Fire — A new hard-boiled novel by Jack Moskovitz about an arsonist, an arson cop and a Nazi hooker. It isn't pretty.

Researching American-Made Toy Soldiers — A 276-page collection of a lifetime of articles by toy soldier expert Richard O'Brien

Strands of the Web: Short Stories of Harry Stephen Keeler — Edited and Introduced by Fred Cleaver

The Sam McCain Novels — Ed Gorman's terrific series includes *The Day the Music Died, Wake Up Little Susie* and *Will You Still Love Me Tomorrow?*

A Shot Rang Out — Three decades of reviews from Jon Breen

Mysterious Martin, the Master of Murder — Two versions of a strange 1912 novel by Tod Robbins about a man who writes books that can kill.

Dago Red — 22 tales of dark suspense by Bill Pronzini

The Night Remembers — A 1991 Jack Walsh mystery from Ed Gorman

Rough Cut & New, Improved Murder — Ed Gorman's first two novels

Hollywood Dreams — A novel of the Depression by Richard O'Brien

Seven Gelett Burgess Novels — *The Master of Mysteries, The White Cat, Two O'Clock Courage, Ladies in Boxes, Find the Woman, The Heart Line, The Picaroons*

The Organ Reader — A huge compilation of just about everything published in the 1971-1972 radical bay-area newspaper, *THE ORGAN.*

A Clear Path to Cross — Sharon Knowles short mystery stories by Ed Lynskey

Old Times' Sake — Short stories by James Reasoner from Mike Shayne Magazine

Freaks and Fantasies — Eerie tales by Tod Robbins, collaborator of Tod Browning on the film FREAKS.

Seven Jim Harmon Double Novels — *Vixen Hollow/Celluloid Scandal, The Man Who Made Maniacs/Silent Siren, Ape Rape/Wanton Witch, Sex Burns Like Fire/Twist Session, Sudden Lust/Passion Strip, Sin Unlimited/Harlot Master, Twilight Girls/Sex Institution.* Written in the early 60s.

Marblehead: A Novel of H.P. Lovecraft — A long-lost masterpiece from Richard A. Lupoff. Published for the first time!

The Compleat Ova Hamlet — Parodies of SF authors by Richard A. Lupoff – A brand new edition with more stories and more illustrations by Trina Robbins.

The Secret Adventures of Sherlock Holmes — Three Sherlockian pastiches by the Brooklyn author/publisher, Gary Lovisi.

The Universal Holmes — Richard A. Lupoff's 2007 collection of five Holmesian pastiches and a recipe for giant rat stew.

Four Joel Townsley Rogers Novels — By the author of *The Red Right Hand: Once In a Red Moon, Lady With the Dice, The Stopped Clock, Never Leave My Bed*

Two Joel Townsley Rogers Story Collections — Night of Horror and Killing Time

Twenty Norman Berrow Novels — *The Bishop's Sword, Ghost House, Don't Go Out After Dark, Claws of the Cougar, The Smokers of Hashish, The Secret Dancer, Don't Jump Mr. Boland!, The Footprints of Satan, Fingers for Ransom, The Three Tiers of Fantasy, The Spaniard's Thumb, The Eleventh Plague, Words Have Wings, One Thrilling Night, The Lady's in Danger, It Howls at Night, The Terror in the Fog, Oil Under the Window, Murder in the Melody, The Singing Room*

The N. R. De Mexico Novels — Robert Bragg presents *Marijuana Girl, Madman on a Drum, Private Chauffeur* in one volume.

Four Chelsea Quinn Yarbro Novels featuring Charlie Moon — *Ogilvie, Tallant and Moon, Music When the Sweet Voice Dies, Poisonous Fruit* and *Dead Mice*

Five Walter S. Masterman Mysteries — *The Green Toad, The Flying Beast, The Yellow Mistletoe, The Wrong Verdict* and *The Perjured Alibi.* Fantastic impossible plots.

Two Hake Talbot Novels — *Rim of the Pit, The Hangman's Handyman.* Classic locked room mysteries.

Two Alexander Laing Novels — *The Motives of Nicholas Holtz* and *Dr. Scarlett*, stories of medical mayhem and intrigue from the 30s.

Four David Hume Novels — *Corpses Never Argue, Cemetery First Stop, Make Way for the Mourners, Eternity Here I Come,* and more to come.

Three Wade Wright Novels — *Echo of Fear, Death At Nostalgia Street* and *It Leads to Murder,* with more to come!

Eight Rupert Penny Novels — *Policeman's Holiday, Policeman's Evidence, Lucky Policeman, Policeman in Armour, Sealed Room Murder, Sweet Poison, The Talkative Policeman, She had to Have Gas* and *Cut and Run* (by Martin Tanner.)

Five Jack Mann Novels — Strange murder in the English countryside. *Gees' First Case, Nightmare Farm, Grey Shapes, The Ninth Life, The Glass Too Many.*

Seven Max Afford Novels — *Owl of Darkness, Death's Mannikins, Blood on His Hands, The Dead Are Blind, The Sheep and the Wolves, Sinners in Paradise* and *Two Locked Room Mysteries and a Ripping Yarn* by one of Australia's finest novelists.

Five Joseph Shallit Novels — *The Case of the Billion Dollar Body, Lady Don't Die on My Doorstep, Kiss the Killer, Yell Bloody Murder, Take Your Last Look.* One of America's best 50's authors.

Two Crimson Clown Novels — By Johnston McCulley, author of the Zorro novels, *The Crimson Clown* and *The Crimson Clown Again.*

The Best of 10-Story Book — edited by Chris Mikul, over 35 stories from the literary magazine Harry Stephen Keeler edited.

A Young Man's Heart — A forgotten early classic by Cornell Woolrich

The Anthony Boucher Chronicles — edited by Francis M. Nevins
Book reviews by Anthony Boucher written for the *San Francisco Chronicle,* 1942 – 1947. Essential and fascinating reading.

Muddled Mind: Complete Works of Ed Wood, Jr. — David Hayes and Hayden Davis deconstruct the life and works of a mad genius.

Gadsby — A lipogram (a novel without the letter E). Ernest Vincent Wright's last work, published in 1939 right before his death.

My First Time: The One Experience You Never Forget — Michael Birchwood — 64 true first-person narratives of how they lost it.

A Roland Daniel Double: The Signal and The Return of Wu Fang — Classic thrillers from the 30s

Murder in Shawnee — Two novels of the Alleghenies by John Douglas: *Shawnee Alley Fire* and *Haunts.*

Deep Space and other Stories — A collection of SF gems by Richard A. Lupoff

Blood Moon — The first of the Robert Payne series by Ed Gorman

The Time Armada — Fox B. Holden's 1953 SF gem.

Black River Falls — Suspense from the master, Ed Gorman

Sideslip — 1968 SF masterpiece by Ted White and Dave Van Arnam

The Triune Man — Mindscrambling science fiction from Richard A. Lupoff

Detective Duff Unravels It — Episodic mysteries by Harvey O'Higgins

Automaton — Brilliant treatise on robotics: 1928-style! By H. Stafford Hatfield

The Incredible Adventures of Rowland Hern — Rousing 1928 impossible crimes by Nicholas Olde.

Slammer Days — Two full-length prison memoirs: *Men into Beasts* (1952) by George Sylvester Viereck and *Home Away From Home* (1962) by Jack Woodford

Murder in Black and White — 1931 classic tennis whodunit by Evelyn Elder

Killer's Caress — Cary Moran's 1936 hardboiled thriller

The Golden Dagger — 1951 Scotland Yard yarn by E. R. Punshon

A Smell of Smoke — 1951 English countryside thriller by Miles Burton

Ruled By Radio — 1925 futuristic novel by Robert L. Hadfield & Frank E. Farncombe

Murder in Silk — A 1937 Yellow Peril novel of the silk trade by Ralph Trevor

The Case of the Withered Hand — 1936 potboiler by John G. Brandon

Finger-prints Never Lie — A 1939 classic detective novel by John G. Brandon

Inclination to Murder — 1966 thriller by New Zealand's Harriet Hunter

Invaders from the Dark — Classic werewolf tale from Greye La Spina

Fatal Accident — Murder by automobile, a 1936 mystery by Cecil M. Wills

The Devil Drives — A prison and lost treasure novel by Virgil Markham

Dr. Odin — Douglas Newton's 1933 potboiler comes back to life.

The Chinese Jar Mystery — Murder in the manor by John Stephen Strange, 1934

The Julius Caesar Murder Case — A classic 1935 re-telling of the assassination by Wallace Irwin that's much more fun than the Shakespeare version

West Texas War and Other Western Stories — by Gary Lovisi

The Contested Earth and Other SF Stories — A never-before published space opera and seven short stories by Jim Harmon.

Tales of the Macabre and Ordinary — Modern twisted horror by Chris Mikul, author of the *Bizarrism* series.

The Gold Star Line — Seaboard adventure from L.T. Reade and Robert Eustace.

The Werewolf vs the Vampire Woman — Hard to believe ultraviolence by either Arthur M. Scarm or Arthur M. Scram.

Black Hogan Strikes Again — Australia's Peter Renwick pens a tale of the outback.

Don Diablo: Book of a Lost Film — Two-volume treatment of a western by Paul Landres, with diagrams. Intro by Francis M. Nevins.

The Charlie Chaplin Murder Mystery — Movie hijinks by Wes D. Gehring

The Koky Comics — A collection of all of the 1978-1981 Sunday and daily comic strips by Richard O'Brien and Mort Gerberg, in two volumes.

Suzy — Another collection of comic strips from Richard O'Brien and Bob Vojtko

Dime Novels: Ramble House's 10-Cent Books — *Knife in the Dark* by Robert Leslie Bellem, *Hot Lead* and *Song of Death* by Ed Earl Repp, *A Hashish House in New York* by H.H. Kane, and five more.

Blood in a Snap — The *Finnegan's Wake* of the 21st century, by Jim Weiler

Stakeout on Millennium Drive — Award-winning Indianapolis Noir — Ian Woollen.

Dope Tales #1 — Two dope-riddled classics; *Dope Runners* by Gerald Grantham and *Death Takes the Joystick* by Phillip Condé.

Dope Tales #2 — Two more narco-classics; *The Invisible Hand* by Rex Dark and *The Smokers of Hashish* by Norman Berrow.

Dope Tales #3 — Two enchanting novels of opium by the master, Sax Rohmer. *Dope* and *The Yellow Claw*.

Tenebrae — Ernest G. Henham's 1898 horror tale brought back.

The Singular Problem of the Stygian House-Boat — Two classic tales by John Kendrick Bangs about the denizens of Hades.

Tiresias — Psychotic modern horror novel by Jonathan M. Sweet.

The One After Snelling — Kickass modern noir from Richard O'Brien.

The Sign of the Scorpion — 1935 Edmund Snell tale of oriental evil.

The House of the Vampire — 1907 poetic thriller by George S. Viereck.

An Angel in the Street — Modern hardboiled noir by Peter Genovese.

The Devil's Mistress — Scottish gothic tale by J. W. Brodie-Innes.

The Lord of Terror — 1925 mystery with master-criminal, Fantômas.

The Lady of the Terraces — 1925 adventure by E. Charles Vivian.

My Deadly Angel — 1955 Cold War drama by John Chelton

Prose Bowl — Futuristic satire — Bill Pronzini & Barry N. Malzberg .

Satan's Den Exposed — True crime in Truth or Consequences New Mexico — Award-winning journalism by the *Desert Journal*.

The Amorous Intrigues & Adventures of Aaron Burr — by Anonymous — Hot historical action.

I Stole $16,000,000 — A true story by cracksman Herbert E. Wilson.

The Black Dark Murders — Vintage 50s college murder yarn by Milt Ozaki, writing as Robert O. Saber.

Sex Slave — Potboiler of lust in the days of Cleopatra — Dion Leclerq.

You'll Die Laughing — Bruce Elliott's 1945 novel of murder at a practical joker's English countryside manor.

The Private Journal & Diary of John H. Surratt — The memoirs of the man who conspired to assassinate President Lincoln.

Dead Man Talks Too Much — Hollywood boozer by Weed Dickenson

Red Light — History of legal prostitution in Shreveport Louisiana by Eric Brock. Includes wonderful photos of the houses and the ladies.

A Snark Selection — Lewis Carroll's *The Hunting of the Snark* with two Snarkian chapters by Harry Stephen Keeler — Illustrated by Gavin L. O'Keefe.

Ripped from the Headlines! — The Jack the Ripper story as told in the newspaper articles in the *New York* and *London Times*.

Geronimo — S. M. Barrett's 1905 autobiography of a noble American.

The White Peril in the Far East — Sidney Lewis Gulick's 1905 indictment of the West and assurance Japan would never attack the U.S.

The Compleat Calhoon — All of Fender Tucker's works: Includes *Totah Six-Pack, Weed, Women and Song* and *Tales from the Tower,* plus a CD of all of his songs.

Totah Six-Pack — Just Fender Tucker's six tales about Farmington in one sleek volume.

RAMBLE HOUSE

Fender Tucker, Prop.

www.ramblehouse.com   fender@ramblehouse.com

228-826-1783   10329 Sheephead Drive, Vancleave MS 39565

www.ingramcontent.com/pod-product-compliance
Lightning Source LLC
Chambersburg PA
CBHW022006010726
47494CB00003B/908